THE RELUCTANT WARRIOR

THE RELUCTANT WARRIOR

The Journey Begins

Charley Green

Cover Art by Jerry Yarnell
Yarnell Studio & School of Fine Art
PO Box 1120, Skiatook, OK 74070

Interior Illustrations & Drawings
by the late Jack J Wells, Western Artist
Oklahoma City, OK 73127

Cover layouts by Jonathan Hurst
- J & L Collective -
- Urban Fox Productions -

www.charleygreen.com

Printed in the United States of America

ISBN: Softcover   978-1-63871-637-2
             eBook   978-1-63871-638-9

Republished by: PageTurner Press and Media LLC
Publication Date: 10/19/2021

To order copies of this book, contact:

PageTurner Press and Media
Phone: 1-888-447-9651
info@pageturner.us
www.pageturner.us

Foreword

This is a fictionalized story of one man's journey westward from a civil war that tore this country apart and destroyed families. The timelines are close, and the events portrayed may not be exactly as it was, but in my opinion, it could've been under the right circumstances. The objective is to tell a great story, not necessarily to be historically correct but rather historically close.

There's a warrior of varying degrees in all of us. Joel Richards embodies the same ideals as the biblical character Gideon who would rather go to great lengths to avoid a fight but would always step up when called. I believe everyone's life identifies with or is a representation of a certain biblical or historical character that is really a part of our persona whether or not it's acknowledged.

I've always had an affinity for the quiet heroes; those who step up when called and refuse to back down when cornered, regardless of the consequences. There comes a time in all our lives when confrontation is inevitable, leaving us no other option but to stand tall and give it our best. Joel Richards as "The Reluctant Warrior!" does just that.

Contents

PART I
The Beginning

Nothing to Lose

Joel Richards, astride his Morgan horse, leads a pack animal, a sturdy, versatile Kentucky Mountain Horse named Bluebonnet. Slowly he rides into the town of Linwood on an overcast fall day in Wyoming in 1881. The horse and rider look like they've been on a few too many roundups and cattle drives.

Richards keeps his head hung low. His face hasn't been creased with a smile much in the last few years, not since his wife, Rosalie, died in the town of Gideon back in the fall of '78.

Weather beaten, Richards looks older than he really is. His long, scraggly hair falls from beneath his hat and blends into his beard. He sits slouched over from having ridden countless miles out of Gideon. This cowboy's in need of a drink, breakfast, and a bath.

He reins up in front of the Black Dog Saloon, figuring after his drink he'll put his horses up at the stable down the street and then find a place to get a bath and a good sit-down meal. Glancing down, he sees an ol' mongrel sitting on the top step leading into the saloon. "Dog, you look hungry!" Reaching into his saddlebag, Joel fetches a strip of jerky. "Here, maybe this'll help." He tosses it to the dog, who catches it in midair and gobbles it down.

Dismounting, he ties the horses to a hitch rail, thinking, *I'd better leave my guns in the saddlebags 'cause I'm here for a drink, not looking for trouble.* A little voice in his head reminds him of similar places he's been, warning him to be cautious in this unfamiliar town.

The cur with a hangdog look stares up at Joel after finishing his tasty tidbit of jerky. Joel grins. "Well, partner, it looks like you haven't gotten any attention lately, so I guess you need a friend." Bending down, he gives the cur a pat on the head and a scratch behind the ears.

In the dimly lit saloon, the musty odor of cigar smoke mixes with the tang of spilled beer as Joel slowly walks up to the bar with one eye on the crowd, ever watchful of what's going on about him. Near the back, he notices a boisterous, young ruffian with a tie-down gun rig on his hip bullying an older man into a brawl. He figures the young buck wants to have a gun fight. Trying to mind his own business, he chooses a spot at the bar as far away from the conflict as possible and orders a beer.

The bartender brings his beer and then heads for a back room under the pretense of getting some supplies. Joel senses the bartender must have incurred the wrath of this bully sometime in the past and isn't about to get involved.

This bully pushes his victim, a man twice his age and half his size. Knowing he doesn't stand a chance against this loudmouth punk, the older man begins pleading and tries to head toward the door. "Please, mister, I got a wife and kids to take care of. I ain't no match for you."

"Bullshit. You're the one who was lookin' down his nose at me earlier, and if you're goin' to do that, then you got to back it up. I'm callin' you," says the bully.

The old man begins crying. "No, mister, I wasn't, and I apologize if you thought so. Please let me go."

"Well, you cryin' old son of a bitch, since you ain't gonna fight me, if you want out that door, you're goin' have to crawl like a dog on your hands and knees." The bully begins to laugh as the old man gets down on his hands and knees. "Look at that yellow coward crawlin' like an old coon dog with his tail between his legs."

Richards thinks, *This isn't my town, and since none of the other men in the saloon who appear to be the old man's friends are willing to step in, I won't get involved, as it isn't my place or fight.* Sensing the bully will soon pick out someone else to harass, Richards quickly finishes his beer, sets the empty glass down on the bar, and starts to leave.

The bully moves in front of Richards, blocking his path. "Where do you think you're going?"

Richards, wanting to find a peaceful way out of the situation, says,

"Partner, I just stopped by for a beer before I get on my way. Now I'm willin' to have another and buy you one if you'll join me so we can do some visiting. I haven't had anyone to talk to for days except my horses; they're good listeners, but they don't say much."

The bully believes he's got an easy mark and gets right in Richards's face, speaking loudly enough for the whole saloon to hear. "You know who I am?"

"I'm sorry, but I don't," Richards replies.

"I'm Bad Ass Eddie, the fastest gun in this territory! And you, you old, scraggly bastard, can't buy your way out of this at any price, 'cause I want the satisfaction of making you crawl or draw."

Backed into a corner, he looks Bad Ass Eddie in the eyes and calmly says, "Mister, if it's really a fight you want and a shooting or killing is what you aim to do, then can I at least be wearing my own gun? It's a hell of a way for an old cowboy to die if he can't try to defend himself against a younger, stronger, and faster man."

Sneering, Bad Ass Eddie says, "Git your gun. I'll be waitin' at the bar where it looks like I'll have to pour my own drink, as that chicken shit bartender is hidin' someplace."

Richards walks out to his horse, knowing he can't ride away fast enough before Eddie shoots him in the back. Speaking under his breath to himself, he says, "Why is it every two-bit town I ride into there's always someone wanting to make a name or add a notch to his gun?"

He ponders the situation while buckling on his worn gun belt that holds an old Colt .45 Peacemaker. He leans over to secure the holster tie-down to his leg, and something on the ground catches his eye. Without hesitating, he reaches down and picks up a freshly dropped apple from his Morgan.

Walking back into the saloon, Richards hollers out, "Bad Ass!" Ol' Eddie gloatingly turns to confront him, and in that split second, Richards throws the horse apple at him, catching him off guard. Bad Ass instinctively throws his gun hand up to block the horse dropping. In that moment, Richards draws his gun and fires, hitting the bully dead center in the chest. The impact from the .45 slams Eddie backward, causing both of his outstretched arms to land palms-up on the bar. His head lies on the bar top looking skyward, eyes and mouth wide open in utter surprise, with a horse turd stuck on his forehead.

Richards looks around and says, "Anybody else want a little horseshit in their day?" The customers are stunned at what just happened. He backs out the door and says, "Never underestimate an ol' cowboy who's got nothing to lose but his horse!"

He mounts his Morgan and decides it's best to be riding on. "Damn it! I hate these kinds of situations where some horse's ass causes a senseless killin' to happen!" Maybe in the next town I'll have a little luck finding some friendly folks, a peaceful meal, and a bath."

From under the porch where he hid during the shooting, the cur comes out and starts following Joel. Looking down, Richards says, "Dog, if you're going to tag along with Morgan, Bluebonnet, and myself, I just hope you've chosen your friends wisely. Probably no one will miss a rascal like you anyway. Now, you need a name besides dog, so I guess Rascal is good a handle as any, and that's what you'll be called. Well, Rascal, you're welcome to join this band of wanderers if you've got a mind to."

As Joel and his entourage pass the city limits sign, his thoughts drift back to other places he's been where similar situations have unfolded. Later, after settling down from the shooting, Richards shifts into a reflective moment. "I wonder if this is going to be my place in life 'cause it ain't at all what Pa had in mind for me when I returned home from the war."

Looking back to the Civil War years, Richards strives to make sense of where he's been, where he's at, and where he's going. He replays in his mind various situations that guided him on this path, with possibly the Civil War having the greatest influence of all.

The Last Battle

hortly after midnight, Sunday, April 9, 1865, thirty miles south of the Union lines, a light, cold rain drips off the ponchos of forty shivering Third Cavalry Rangers under the command of Union Army Captain Lawrence Sullivan. It's raining just enough to soften the ground, muffling the sound of horse's hooves stepping cautiously between the trees. The troopers take up positions just inside the tree line—ready, poised, spread out in attack mode about a hundred paces away from the military objective, a supply depot. The best guess of Union intelligence is that it contains grain and ammunition and is defended by fifty or more Rebel soldiers.

Above the distant rumble of cannon fire and the rustling of wet leaves, the rangers can just make out the chatter of the Rebels around their campfire. Captain Sullivan has taken the point position with his first sergeant, Joel Richards, to his immediate right and Corporal Clayton on Richard's right side. They intend to destroy the depot along with any and all supplies stored there and then capture, disperse, or eliminate any enemy soldiers who fire on them. After that, the plan is to retreat before a reaction force can be organized to retaliate. Their mission has always been to hit and run, extracting as much damage and causing as much confusion as possible before retreating.

Captain Sullivan whispers to Richards, "Sergeant, I make out about twenty soldiers around that fire trying to keep warm and dry. But there don't appear to be any perimeter guards or pickets out."

"Pretty unusual strategy," Richards says. "Either they feel real safe this far from Union lines …"

"Or their commander's incompetent," Sullivan says. "Look, Sergeant, we've got time here. You and Corporal Clayton dismount and take a look. Work your way around the camp, making sure there aren't any soldiers or cavalry units hiding back there in the woods."

Clayton says, "Lead the way, Sergeant. I've got you covered."

When the two return almost an hour later, the sergeant reports, "Sir, it's mighty strange, those southern boys around the fire are a ragtag lookin' bunch, and they don't seem to care much what's in that depot. There's not a guard posted anywhere."

"Good work, Sergeant. You boys get mounted. We'll surprise them and get this over quickly without any casualties. Everybody knows what to do, so stand by."

Captain Sullivan throws his poncho back over his shoulders and draws his saber, which is the signal to prepare to advance. Moments later, he yells, "Charge!"

The rangers burst out of the trees, spurring their horses into a full gallop toward the Confederate depot. The water-laden leaves on the trees begin shedding water droplets as the earth shudders under the vibration of all those hooves pounding the ground. The rangers are yelling and firing their weapons into the air, creating a thunderous effect of gunshots echoing throughout the woods, with the intent of giving the impression of a much larger unit of Union soldiers attacking. The Confederate soldiers scatter, scrambling for their lives. Several dash for the woods as the rest seek cover in the depot.

Only one, a sergeant, stands his ground and faces the oncoming rangers, drawing his Colt 1851 Navy revolver, but Joel quickly takes aim with his Colt Dragoon and fires, hitting the sergeant dead center in his chest. The Rebel's legs give way at the knees, but as he's falling to the ground, summoning the last ounce of life and energy remaining in his body, he takes aim at Captain Sullivan, fires, and hits him. Having fulfilled his duty to defend his troops and the cause they are fighting for with his life, this honorable and courageous southern soldier collapses silently into a heap beside the campfire.

Sergeant Richards reins up beside Sullivan's horse and quickly dismounts, just in time to catch the captain falling off his mount. Joel senses the Confederate noncom inflicted a mortal wound, as blood is oozing from deep within the captain's chest, and he appears to be dying. Quickly Joel applies pressure to the wound, trying to stop the bleeding as Sullivan coughs and says to Richards, "Report, Sergeant!"

By now the rangers have surrounded the depot. Corporal Clayton shouts out to the men inside, "You Rebs got thirty seconds to come out with your hands over your heads or we're going to set fire to the building, and you'll burn in hell!" The Rebels begin filing out of the depot with hands held high.

Joel hollers for Corporal Clayton to give the captain the captured and wounded report. "Sir, fifteen of the enemy were captured, four escaped, and one was killed. The ones captured are all young boys, probably not one of 'em over sixteen years of age. The only shot fired from these Johnny Rebs was the one that hit you, sir."

Richards, with a tear running down his cheek, says, "Captain, you were the only casualty on our side. I regret I wasn't able to get him sooner."

"Sergeant, I saw him but not in time. It wasn't your fault. I got overconfident seeing those soldiers run. Now, find out why there was little resistance and take the information back to headquarters." The captain coughs blood up into Joel's bandanna. Then, looking up into Joel's eyes and remaining the commander to the end, he says, "You're the ranking noncom now. It's your job and duty to get these men back to our lines. Promise me you'll do that?"

"Yes, sir, I promise."

Coughing and trying to take in a breath, Sullivan looks up at Joel. "You're a good man, Sergeant. I'll miss serving with you."

By this time, a number of cavalry men have dismounted, joining Sergeant Richards around the captain to pay their last respects. Sullivan looks up, clinches Richards's shirt, and passes away with a gasp, exhaling his last breath. Corporal Clayton says, "Let's kill all these Rebel bastards for what they did!"

Sergeant Richards says, "Corporal! We'll have none of that. Revenge isn't part of our mission. The captain knew what the risks were. It was his time, that's all. He was a good commander, and we'll not disrespect what he stood for by killin' unarmed men, especially young boys. Is that clear?"

"Sorry, Sergeant. I just wanted to do *something.*"

"All right, Corporal, before we move out, let's get the captain wrapped up in a couple of blankets secured over his saddle … and ask for a volunteer to lead his horse back."

One of the cavalrymen says, "Excuse me, Sergeant. I'd like that honor."

"Okay, Private Cromwell, the responsibility's yours; help get him ready to go."

Sergeant Richards stands. "Corporal, take five men and inventory the supplies left in the building before you torch it. Then let's find out from these prisoners why they didn't resist. The rest of you keep an eye on the prisoners. Don't let 'em surprise us with a gun or a knife they've got hiding somewhere. Let's get about our business and get the hell out of here!"

The prisoners are searched. Under armed guard, they line up in front of Sergeant Richards, who questions the one who appears to be the oldest. "How old are you and these other boys?"

"I'm seventeen, sir. Some are fifteen, sixteen, and a couple are fourteen."

"Where's your officer? Who's in charge of this unit?"

"They all got killed, sir. Our sergeant was the only noncommissioned one here."

"Why didn't he run or surrender like the rest of you?"

"He was an old man, slightly crippled. He'd been in some hard battles.

He told us how he'd like to go out as a true soldier facing his enemy. I guess he did."

"Why did none of you take up weapons and return fire?"

"Sergeant, we would have, except we don't have any guns or ammunition. Only our sergeant had any, mainly to keep us from running for home when we found out we had nothing to fight with."

Corporal Clayton comes up to Richards. "Sergeant, you're not going to believe this, but that supply depot is nearly empty. No guns, ammunition, or explosives and barely any food! It looks like our intelligence didn't get a good look inside this depot before reporting."

"You, Reb, what's going on here?"

"Well, sir, everything of use was taken up to Appomattox, including all our ammunition and guns, except for the sergeant's. They left us here with the old man in case things changed. We got no word from anywhere. We don't know what's goin' on. We been sleeping in the depot out of the rain and was about to get on in there when you attacked, scaring the livin' hell out of us."

"Listen, soldier," Richards says, "the war is close to being over, and you boys are on the losing side. It may only be a matter of days or weeks, but it won't be long."

"We kinda figured 'cause there hasn't been any good news for months. What are you going to do with us?"

"Normally, we'd take you back to headquarters, but the way things are here, I'm going to ignore those orders, leaving you in charge to look after this place and those boys. You boys can't do any damage, and besides, our prison camps are overflowing. So bury your sergeant and be sure and tell whoever that he died like a true soldier facing his enemy and made it count.

"Then hang around here. I'm sure either some of your troops or ours will be by this way shortly with word on the war. Then you decide your own fate at that time. By the way, you might want to call out to those four who got away, telling them to come on in, 'cause we're not coming back."

Sergeant Richards calls Clayton over. "Leave them as much food as we can, pack up the captain, and let's head out."

"What about the depot? Do we torch it?"

"No! These boys will need some shelter, and this place doesn't really have any military value far as I can see. It'll make a good granary for some farmer one of these days. It just might be one of the few remaining buildings left standing in these parts. Let's get ready to move out."

The young Rebel soldier bows slightly to Sergeant Richards and then raises himself to an upright stance, shoulders back, and snaps to a military position of attention. "Sergeant, we're beholdin' to you and your men. We salute the Third Cavalry Rangers." All of the boys raise their hands in an awkward salute.

"How do you know who we are?" Sergeant Richards asks.

"Rumors spread pretty fast. Your unit is well known in these parts. Besides, your troop designation is right there on your captain's saddle blanket."

As Sergeant Richards mounts, settling into his saddle, a slow grin spreads across his face. Glancing at the ragtag bunch of young boys looking up at him, he returns their salute. "Good luck, gentlemen." He rolls his horse around to the right, moving into position to lead the rangers back to their own lines.

The Ride Back

The rangers, now led by Sergeant Richards, begin retracing their steps, heading back to the base camp. Richards is curious how his report's going to be received. His unit is bringing back no prisoners, didn't destroy anything, and lost their captain to an aging, crippled Confederate sergeant who commanded a squad of young, unarmed boys.

"Corporal Clayton, get the scouts out front and rear. We want to be far away from here as quickly as we can before daybreak. We don't want to be running into trouble if we can avoid it. I can hear a cannon over there. Might be some Rebs not too far away.

"Private Cromwell's to stay at the rear with the captain's body. Have two scouts drop back about a quarter of a mile to cover our backsides in case one of those boys gets away and alerts any cavalry in the area that might want to give chase. We're not going to be running these horses in the dark. We'll walk awhile to keep 'em fresh so if that time comes they'll be ready to run."

"Yes, Sergeant." Clayton orders two scouts to go up ahead and assigns two other cavalrymen, Privates Peterson and Allen, to drop back to cover the rear as word is passed to walk the horses.

After about an hour of walking, the men mount and, now weary to the bone, begin slumping in their saddles. It's been a long march with very little sleep and will be at least another long day before they're behind their own lines where they can rest.

Dawn is breaking above the tree line just off the road to their right. It will be another hour before daylight, which means they're getting closer to their lines.

Peterson, one of the rear guards, comes galloping up, reining to a halt next to Richards. "Sergeant, you were right. One of those boys that got away must have found a cavalry unit 'cause there's about thirty riders coming hard on our trail better than a mile behind us. I told Allen to stay back and keep an eye on that bunch, making sure they're still headed toward us."

"How long before they get here?"

"About an hour at the most, depending on their horses. They've been riding 'em awfully hard."

"You ride up ahead and warn the forward scouts, then rejoin B Squad. Corporal Clayton, take B Squad up the trail about fifty yards and back yourselves into the trees on the right side. Stay mounted at the ready. I'll keep A Squad here with me, and we'll do the same on this side of the trail. If they've been riding hard for the past two hours, they're going to be givin' those horses a break if they've got any smarts at all. Hopefully it'll be right here in front of us. If it goes that way, getting them to surrender is the first priority. I'll keep the men under cover before we ride out to meet 'em on this side in case they choose to fight it out at close quarters. If they do, we'll be standing at the ready with rifles drawn. Just as soon as you hear me tell them to surrender, you swing out from your side and advance down the road toward us to block off any escape. If they refuse and all hell breaks loose, you know what to do."

"Yes, sir."

Allen, the other rear guard, rides up. "Sergeant, they're about a half a mile away, still coming, but have slowed to a walk. It looks like they may be stopping to give their horses a break. If they do, they'll be here in thirty or forty minutes."

Both A and B squads fall into place hidden in the trees. The jaws of the trap are set, ready to be sprung, if Richards figured right.

The Confederates dismount about a hundred and fifty yards away and begin walking their exhausted horses. The man leading the Confederates, a major wearing a patch over one eye and a plumed hat on his head, can be heard from about fifty yards away. "Men, we've got to give these sorry-ass animals a rest before deciding whether to go on or turn back. When we get to those trees just ahead, get off the road out of sight and take a break. It's fast approaching daylight. Bein' this close to the Union lines, I don't want to be caught out in the open.

14

"You scouts keep walking your horses down the road for about half a mile. Keep an eye out for any signs that'll tell us how far ahead they are. When you reach what you think is a half mile, mount up, ride on back here, and tell me what's ahead. I'll decide then if those Yankee sons a bitches are within reach or we best head back to our own lines. All right, get in those trees."

As the unsuspecting Confederate cavalry prepare to leave the road and disperse into the trees, Sergeant Richards shouts out from the protection of the tree line, "This is the Third Cavalry Rangers. You're surrounded. Throw down your weapons or face certain death."

Totally surprised, the Confederate major shouts, "Like hell we will," drawing his ivory-handled Remington 1858 New Model Navy revolver, and begins firing. His men blindly follow suit even though they are in an exposed, indefensible position on the road.

Squad A unleashes a volley of deadly rifle fire from the woods, hitting, wounding, and killing cavalry men and horses. Some of the Rebel soldiers try to take cover behind the dead horses that are facing Joel's squad, but leaving themselves exposed to Squad B, which consists of twenty mounted rangers armed with Henry rifles, advancing down the road toward them and firing rapidly from horseback. The attack is over in minutes, and Richards cries out, "Cease fire!" The remaining Rebels still standing drop their guns, raising arms in surrender as the rangers close in, surrounding the Rebel position, alert for any resistance on the part of those still alive.

As Joel and his squad ride out from the tree line, he quickly surveys the number of dead and wounded. Out of the thirty Confederates standing when the ambush unfolded, fifteen are now dead, and ten are wounded, including the Rebel major along with twelve of the horses. Only five escaped unscathed, and because of the surprise attack and the protection of the trees, the rangers didn't lose a man.

Joel dismounts, approaching the wounded major lying behind his dead horse. The major makes a feeble effort to draw his saber, but Richards has drawn his own sword and places the tip against the major's throat. Expressionless, with coldness in his voice and eyes, Joel tells the Confederate, "Your move. It's up to you whether you live or die right here."

The major releases his grip on his saber, and then with fire in his eyes and contempt in his voice, the major asks, "What's your name and rank, Yankee?"

"I'm Sergeant Richards."

"Richards, I live today so I can meet you again and take my revenge."

As Joel keeps his saber on the major's throat, he unhooks the major's waist belt holding his saber and empty holster and then picks up his Remington revolver and puts it back in its holster. Richards then hangs the belt on his saddle and turns to the major. "What's your name?"

"Major Clarkson."

"Well, Major Clarkson, however it works out for you, nothing can take away the stupidity and arrogance you displayed here. You sacrificed your men and horses in an unwinnable action against overwhelming odds and firepower. That's what you'll have to live with, how you wasted your men for nothing.

"All right, men, search the Rebs for weapons. Destroy those you find, except for any souvenirs you want. Then bandage up the wounded as best you can. Those that can't walk, tie them on their horses and prepare to move out. Corporal Clayton, get your scouts in position with B Squad providing armed guard over the prisoners."

One of the prisoners asks to speak to whoever's in charge. Clayton leads him over to where Joel is preparing to mount. "Sergeant, this Reb wants to speak to the commanding officer."

Joel looks at his stripes. "I see you're also a sergeant. What's your name?"

"I'm John Leslie."

"Well, Sergeant Leslie, I'm the one in charge now 'cause one of your boys back at the depot killed our captain. Before you tell me what it is you want, I need to know how you got on our trail so fast. Was it one of the boys from the depot?"

"Yeah, one of those boys that got away came looking for help and found us about a mile from the depot. He told us what happened, and we headed to the depot as fast as we dared in the dark. The boys there told the major what you'd done and which way you headed. Knowing this part of the country, I figured you'd be taking this road.

"The major was hell bent to catch you at any cost; the horses and men meant nothing to him. I finally convinced him it would be best to rest and save our horses for the battle when we really needed them. He agreed to a walking rest break. I'm not into running these animals to death like some I know. Anyway, it looks like we're gonna see those Union lines in a way we hadn't planned.

"By the way, Sergeant Richards, I'm grateful for the treatment you displayed back at the depot to those boys. One of them was my nephew, and just maybe he'll come out of this war with some hope it hasn't been all about killing and destruction."

"Sergeant," Richards says, "the war's about over. However, we're honor bound to finish our duty, so you and what's left of your cavalry will be taken prisoners to our headquarters."

"Sergeant Richards, I understand. My men are short on rations, tired, and just by looking at them, you can tell there's not much fight left. Six months ago, most would've tried to make a run for it, but not now."

"Sergeant, my men will be on guard on the sides, front, and rear. Bear in mind, we're still at war, so if you or any of your men attempt to escape or attack any of my cavalrymen, they will be dealt with swiftly. Understood?"

"Yes, clearly."

"One last thing, Sergeant Leslie. I'd keep my eyes wide open when you're around that major 'cause he may not take kindly to your visiting with me."

Richards turns to Clayton. "Have the prisoners form up behind Sergeant Leslie on foot. In two hours, we'll take a break, providing the scouts give us an all clear."

"Gentlemen, let's head for our lines and get some hot food and rest."

News Travels Fast

It's now six thirty in the cool morning. The light mist has lifted, the sun is peeking over the treetops, and the rangers with prisoners in tow begin their northward march. The scouts are rotating back and forth, keeping Joel informed on the road ahead and behind. Allen is the first to report from the rear. "Sergeant, the road behind and on the sides is clear. The cannon fire we've been hearing all night off in the distance is getting quieter."

"Okay, Allen, fall back to your position. In two hours, we'll be stopping if the way is clear. Keep me posted. Corporal Clayton, have Sergeant Leslie come forward."

"Sergeant Richards, what's on your mind?"

Richards says, "Leslie, I'm curious. What breed of horse were you riding? It's a good-looking animal."

"It's a Morgan, bred for strength, stamina, versatility, and temperament. There's none better in my opinion."

"Maybe one day when this war's over, I'll be fortunate enough to own one of those. Where're you from and what did you do before getting into this war?"

"I was an accountant, volunteering my skills in supply, keeping track of the books, shipping and receiving. Not a bad job in wartime, but by '64, manpower was running short. Because I had my own horse, I was reassigned to the cavalry, given the rank of sergeant, a saber, revolver, no training, assigned to Major Clarkson, and told to prepare for battle against the Union Cavalry."

"How successful were you?"

"Not very. It's one thing to be a good rider, quite another to go up against cannon and battle-trained cavalrymen such as yourself. We retreated more often than we advanced, and in most cases, we were outgunned, outfought, not for lack of trying. We just weren't good enough."

"I understood your officers usually furnished their own horses. What about the enlisted men?"

"Horses are in short supply in the army. Most of the men own their horses; that's one of the reasons they wind up in the cavalry. Sergeant, I see you weren't hesitant to use your saber. Are you any good with it?"

"It's got a few nicks in it, but it's not my favorite weapon to use."

Corporal Clayton pipes up. "Don't take the sergeant lightly about his saber. I'm glad I'm by his side, not going against it, 'cause I've seen him in action. He never draws it unless he's got no other choice. Then look out."

"That's enough, Corporal. Ride up ahead. Pick a spot off the road where we can take a one-hour break."

"Yes, sir."

It's nearing nine in the morning. Corporal Clayton rides up and says, "There's a clearing ahead just off the road behind that row of trees. Looks good and out of the way."

"All right. Take your squad. Set up a guarded area to receive the prisoners and picket their horses. Signal when ready. We'll bring 'em in and join you."

Fifteen minutes later, Clayton signals they're ready. Joel leads his squad and the Confederates off the road, placing the prisoners in the center of the clearing, with guards on all sides.

"Okay, men, break out your rations. If you got any extra, share with the Rebs. From the looks of 'em, they haven't eaten in a while. We're not far from our lines where food and hot coffee's waiting on us, so no fires."

The men start eating cold rations when suddenly everyone begins looking around apprehensively, and an eerie silence descends. Clayton senses it too and speaks up. "Sergeant, what's going on?"

"I don't know, but does anyone hear any of that cannon fire we've been listening to all night and part of this morning?"

"No, we don't, Sergeant. What do you make of it?"

"I don't know other than to say it seems each side has quit firing. That's good news for the poor bastards who've been in the middle, regardless which side they're on. Sergeant Leslie, any ideas?"

"No, it's strange though, but I'm hoping it doesn't resume. When do you think we'll get to your lines?"

"It'll be late afternoon, possibly earlier if we get a move on now. Corporal, time's up. Let's get moving. Keep the prisoners walking."

Private Cromwell approaches and says, "Sergeant, I think Captain Sullivan's starting to get a little ripe. This cool weather's helping. However, his horse is getting a little nervous. What do you want me to do?"

"Why don't you get out ahead of us and get to the camp as soon as you can without burning those horses out or losing the captain. Corporal, pick three men to accompany Cromwell and, Private, when you get there, take care of the captain first. Then alert the commander we'll be bringing in some Confederate cavalrymen, both wounded and walking. We should be there by late afternoon. Now get going!"

"Yes, Sergeant, see you in camp."

By midday, one of the lead scouts heads back to Joel's unit at a gallop, whooping and hollering with another Union rider who's not a member of the Third Cavalry. Reining up, Joel abruptly says, "Calm down! Tell me why you're hollering, letting the whole country side know we're here. Is there an enemy force coming at us?"

Everyone in the group, including the prisoners, is trying to listen to what's going on with the scout.

"No, Sergeant. You're not going to believe this—the war's over."

A big shout of "Hooray!" is heard from the Third Cavalry, but Joel quickly calls them down.

"How do you know? Who's this private with you?"

"I'm Private Thomas, Sergeant, dispatch rider from headquarters, out trying to contact all our units to let 'em know to cease firing."

"Is that right? Tell me who's given the orders."

"Sir, it comes directly down from General Grant himself. Myself and several other riders have specific written orders signed by General Sheridan ordering us to ride with haste to inform as many units as we can to cease firing, and at this time, the Rebels are doing the same with their army."

"When did it happen?"

"It happened shortly after noon today. Lee surrendered to Grant at Appomattox Courthouse. Sergeant, the war's over!"

"Sergeant Leslie, tell your boys this war's over. That's all I know at this point, and we'll find out more when we get to headquarters."

"Sergeant, that's good and sad news for us, good that it's over and sad we've lost. May I ask a favor of you?"

"You can, sir. Can't say if it'll be granted until I hear it."

"Sergeant, when we head into your camp, may I order the men to mount their horses and ride in formation, not to show our arrogance, but as men who've accepted defeat, not humiliation?"

"So be it, Sergeant. However, we'll keep the guards posted around your cavalry. Inform them, but remember you are still officially prisoners until I have specific orders otherwise. Understood? You can lead the horse carrying the major, and your men can lead the horses carrying your other wounded."

"Yes, sir, I thank you."

"Inform them now and, sergeant, you will only mount on my command, taking your position directly behind me. Select one of your men to carry a white flag, who will ride beside you. I don't want any unknowing or unsuspecting soldier to misunderstand what's going on here. Agreed?"

"Agreed!" Leslie salutes Joel out of respect and returns to his men as Joel speaks to Private Thomas.

"Unless you have any other information for us, you best be on your way."

"Sergeant, headquarters said it's going to be a while before everyone gets the word. You're not to let your guard down, so don't go celebrating early. Other than that, good luck."

"Corporal, let the scouts know to maintain a sharp lookout. We're too close now to be caught by any enemy soldiers who've not gotten the word."

The War's Over

An hour later, Joel signals the Third Cavalry to halt. "Gentlemen, we'll walk our horses for thirty minutes, then prepare to mount for our final leg into camp. Sergeant, get your men and the white flag ready."

"Sergeant, we got a white cloth but nothing to hang it on."

"Corporal, did anyone pick up one of the old muskets these troopers were carrying they can use as a flagpole for the white flag?"

"No, Sergeant, nobody wanted any of those old guns, especially since we're all carrying Henry Rifles."

"We're not about to hang a white flag on a Henry. Sergeant, if I allow you to employ your saber to attach the white flag, do I have your word that is the only purpose it will be used for—and then returned upon officially surrendering at headquarters?"

"You have my word, Sergeant Richards."

Richards says, "Since you'll be bearing the flag, you will ride beside me."

One of the advanced scouts returns and says, "Sergeant, our camp is only about a half mile or so away, and it looks like a contingent of officers is headed our way."

"Corporal Clayton, join the scout. Ride out to meet our welcoming party and escort them back to us. In the meantime, we'll get mounted."

"Yes, Sergeant, let's go!"

"Third Cavalry Rangers, Confederate cavalrymen, prepare to mount ... mount! You Confederates, fall in behind your sergeant. Post your flag. Rangers, look sharp. We got official company coming. Forward at a walk … march!"

Being in the company of the rangers, the Confederates now mounted have taken on a military bearing complimenting their captors; almost like they consider it an honor to have been captured by the Third Cavalry. The way they're riding, if not for the uniforms, it'd be difficult to distinguish between the Union and the Rebel cavalrymen.

"Sergeant Leslie, I see officers from the camp approaching. Just to let you know, I'll do my best to make sure you and your men are treated fairly."

"That's all I can ask. You've been most fair with us. Sergeant, I would consider it a personal favor if you would look after my Morgan until it's known what's to become of me."

"If it's possible, I will make every effort to make sure she's taken care of."

"Thanks. I'm beholden to you."

Final Surrender

The headquarters contingency arrives, led by Corporal Clayton and commanded by Colonel Jarvis. The colonel reigns up in front of Sergeant Richards and says, "Sergeant, I've been sent to meet your troop and relieve you of the prisoners. Corporal Clayton and Private Cromwell, who brought Captain Sullivan's body in, explained a lot of what went on. I see the Confederates are mounted. Sergeant Richards, is this the customary way to handle prisoners?"

"Sir, I understand the war is over, and in my judgment, these men posed no threat. It was my decision to allow them to maintain a degree of dignity during the surrendering process. Consequently, they were allowed to ride in leading their wounded, still under guard."

"I see the Confederates are traveling under a flag of truce flying from a saber. Am I to assume, Sergeant Richards, this was your doing?"

"Yes, sir. I took the saber at the surrendering of his troop. However, to keep from being fired upon because we were riding with Rebels, I thought it best to have them show a white flag. Now we didn't have a flag pole of any kind, except to use one of our rifles, which was not an option. So I asked for and he gave me his word as a noncommissioned officer to use his saber only for the flag, returning it upon officially surrendering."

Colonel Jarvis looks at Sergeant Leslie. "Sergeant, will you surrender your saber at this time?"

Saluting the colonel, he says, "Yes, sir," then passes the saber hilt first across his forearm to the colonel, who hands it to his second in command.

"Well done, Richards. We will escort you and the Third Cavalry along with your prisoners to camp. After you get back, take care of your horses and get a hot meal for your boys. Then I want you to join me and my officers for dinner."

"Yes, sir. One more thing, Colonel. What's to become of these prisoners and their horses?"

"Sergeant, there are some options and conditions they'll have to comply with. If they agree, they could very possibly be on their way home in a week or two, once the final truce and surrender papers have been signed by President Lincoln. You may assure the prisoners, if they receive a favorable recommendation from you, they will be treated fairly along with their horses because they'll need something to ride home on. Thank God it's over. Let's move out."

Sergeant Leslie says, "As humbly as I can, Richards, my men and I thank you. Hopefully so will my Morgan."

"I'll make sure your Morgan's stabled with mine, and I'll be checking on you and your men later. Good luck."

Leslie says, "Richards, enjoy your dinner tonight. I have a feeling it's going to be very interesting."

As the Third Cavalry Rangers enter command headquarters, led by Colonel Jarvis, they notice the mood's a lot more jovial than when they left on assignment. However, the war is not totally over in all areas; there's still a high degree of seriousness and little celebrating among the headquarters staff. One of the officers comes up to Colonel Jarvis, walks alongside his horse for a moment, and then leaves. Jarvis turns in his saddle, addressing the Rangers. "Gentlemen, it's official. At 3:45pm this day, General Lee and General Grant have officially signed the terms of surrender and the General's Exchange Document.

"Sergeant Richards, turn your prisoners over to the provost marshal and see to your men and horses. I'll see you at dinner."

"Yes, sir."

The Offer

Arriving at Colonel Jarvis's bivouac exactly at 7:00 p.m. as ordered, Joel's met by an orderly who escorts him to the waiting area where the staff officers are mingling. Colonel Jarvis greets him, saying, "Sergeant Richards, we're please you could join us."

"Thank you, sir, but I'm a bit confused on why a noncommissioned officer is invited to an officer's dinner."

"In due time, Sergeant. I think it's time to eat."

Jarvis nods to the orderly, who announces, "Sirs, dinner is served. Please follow me."

"Sergeant, you will be sitting on my left at dinner. I'm sure you're going to find it a bit more appetizing than cold rations."

"Thank you, sir. I'm honored."

After a dinner of steak, yams, and greens, the servers pour cognac and pass out cigars and matches. Colonel Jarvis stands and says, "Sergeant Richards, your mission and capture of these Rebel cavalrymen is a significant accomplishment. We all felt the success of the Third Cavalry Rangers in this war effort was due to Captain Sullivan's superior planning, strategy, and tactics, which is why your troopers were so successful in attacking and destroying supply depots, disrupting small groups of enemy soldiers with maximum damage and minimum loss of troopers.

"Those were the reasons why the Third was always assigned specific tasks that would have the greatest impact on preventing the Confederates from getting supplies to the front lines. Captain Sullivan was a good leader of men. However, after rereading his previous reports, interviewing the men, and witnessing your capture of this Confederate cavalry, we realize his success was largely due to having the right man at his side. A man who was capable and willing, without reservations or hesitation, to take over when called, make wise decisions, and successfully complete the mission as if Captain Sullivan himself was in charge.

"Sergeant Richards, these are the qualities we like to see in our officers. Upon a personal recommendation from General Sheridan, of which I concur, the United States Army would like to confer upon you a battlefield promotion to the rank of Second Lieutenant. However, there are two conditions attached. Now that the war is over, you must remain in the army for three years and attend officer's school. Well?"

"Colonel, sir, I'm honored, but I don't have the education most of these officers have."

"Sergeant, what you have is the ability to grasp military strategy, implement it, manage men, and make battlefield decisions that determine the outcome of an engagement. These are qualities only few officers possess; the book learning is something that will come from officer's school and studying on your own. Now I realize you're tired and short on sleep, so would you like some time to think it over?"

"Yes, sir, I would."

"You have a week. Let me know your decision. Now if you will excuse us, I have a staff meeting with these men. Goodnight, Sergeant."

"Goodnight, sir. Gentlemen, by your leave."

To Stay or Go

Joel walks back to his tent with a lot to think over, not having a confidant or close friend to discuss it with. He's in a quandary about what the best course to follow is. He misses his family, as it has been three years since he's seen his father, mother, and sister, Elizabeth, and it's been a year since their last letter. Although he's written several letters since then, there have not been any responses. Joel doesn't even know if they're alive. Another consideration is the army itself. Having spent the last three years in constant skirmishes and battles, he's mixed up on his feelings about the army and whether or not he wants any further involvement. It seems every friend he's made has been killed in action in one battle or another, giving him a sense of aloneness.

Then again, it's a heck of an opportunity, especially not really knowing what the future holds for him back home. Joel's thinking. *I'm worn out. I'd better sleep on it and take another look at the whole situation in the morning.*

Reveille (morning wakeup) is sounded at 6:00 a.m. Joel begins stirring from a restless sleep. He makes his morning visit to the latrine, shaves, washes up, and heads back to his tent to put on a clean uniform before heading over to check the horses. He plans to curry them down and make sure they're fed and in good health before he returns after breakfast to give them some light exercise.

Joel heads on over to the noncommissioned officers' mess for breakfast, where he's offered congratulations by a couple other sergeants who've already heard about his promotion. "Gentlemen, I haven't decided whether or not to accept the commission. How about we talk about it later?"

After breakfast, Joel heads over to the stables. Upon arriving, he notices both his mount and Leslie's Morgan are in pretty good shape, having been cleaned up and given oats since he checked them in. One of the stable hands comes up and says, "Sergeant, I've made sure these two mounts of yours have been well taken care of. I cleaned 'em up and brushed 'em down good per yours and Colonel Jarvis's instructions."

"Thanks for taking good care of them. I'll be back later this morning to give 'em some light exercise."

"Sergeant, I'll be glad to do that."

"No, thanks. These horses are special to me, so I'll be doing it."

Joel walks over to headquarters, finds a desk, and begins filling out his report on the last mission. The headquarters staff is scurrying about trying to keep up with incoming news delivered by dispatch riders and telegraph as well as sending riders and telegrams to other units on the status of the surrender. From everything he hears, the battles are almost over in all the strategic and outlying areas.

After filling out his report, he turns it in to the duty officer, who briefly looks up and takes his report, filing it in a tray without looking at it. Joel figures it's time to leave. They all seem to have more important things to do than read a report. He decides to go over to the internment camp to see how Sergeant Leslie and his troopers are doing.

Joel approaches the sergeant of the guard. "I'm Sergeant Richards of the Third Cavalry Rangers. I'd like to see Sergeant Leslie."

"Yes, Sergeant, we been expecting you. Corporal of the Guard, bring Sergeant Leslie to the check-in office. He has a guest. By the way, Richards, good work on your mission and congratulations on your promotion."

"Well, Sergeant, it seems word travels pretty fast around here." Joel pauses, looking perplexed. "How did you know to expect me?"

"Captain Peters, the colonel's aide, brought the order to us this morning with instructions to give you every consideration should you wish to visit the prisoners. Richards, you've got some pretty powerful friends around here."

The corporal returns, announcing, "Sergeant of the Guard, Sergeant Leslie is in the check-in office."

"Thank you, Corporal. Sergeant. Go on in. If you need anything, just let the guard know. He has his orders."

"Thank you."

Walking into the check-in area, Joel sees Leslie sitting at the interrogation table, barely recognizable with a clean-shaven face, haircut, and clean clothes.

The guard tells Joel, "Sergeant, take your time. I'll be just outside if you need anything."

Leslie looks up at Joel with a grin. "I thought that dinner last night was going to be interesting, but I had no idea."

"John, first thing, I got an idea how they're treating you, but what about your men?"

"I didn't know prison was going to be anything like this because of all the horror stories we been hearing. I can tell you this, the men and I were expecting the worst, but, except for the fence surrounding this place, they've fed us, given us shaves, haircuts, clean beds, got us clean clothes, and treated us with respect. Are you sure you're not a general in disguise?"

Laughing, he says, "No, I'm not, but everything that's been happening around here since the dinner must be what this whole thing is about. I'll tell you later."

"How's my Morgan?"

"If you think you and your men are getting good treatment, I can assure you, your Morgan hasn't been left out. He's getting as much attention as my horse, and they're both cleaned up and well fed. Have they told you anything about being released?"

"The provost paid a special visit this morning, informing us there would be some documents to sign in the next day or two. If we agreed with the terms, including taking an Oath of Allegiance to the United States, we could be on our way home in a week or so. We've talked it over, and the men and I agree when the time comes to take the oath, there's not going to be a problem. We want to go home. It does look like Major Carlson is going to be spending a little more time here than the rest of us. I understand he assaulted one of your doctors just for being a member of the Union Army and is now under armed guard. He's a bitter man, which would make for a long ride home, although he did say one time he might head west after the war, and maybe that would be best for all of us."

"Let's hope so. There's going to be a lot of dealing with the pain of this war, and it's going to be tough for some to get back to a normal life. John,

I might be able to get you released in my custody for a couple of hours a day to take care of your Morgan. Would you be interested?"

"You bet!"

"I'll see what I can do. Guard, escort the sergeant back to his quarters. Let me know if you or your men need anything."

Oath of Allegiance

The week passes quickly. Joel still has not made up his mind. It's Thursday morning, and he's on his way over to check Leslie out of the stockade and then head to the stables to take care of their horses. Although he's been able to get him released into his custody two hours a day, no word has been received about when he and his men are going home.

Seeing Joel coming, the sergeant of the guard says, "Bring Sergeant Leslie to the gate. His keeper's here."

"Thanks, Sergeant, for the comment."

"Look, Richards, we're all getting antsy to get out of here. It's going to be a while from what we've heard, so we're trying to keep a little humor going so things don't get tense, okay?"

"I understand … it was kind of funny though."

As Leslie and Richards are leaving the compound, the sergeant of the guards says, "You boys have a nice day, you hear?"

"We hear, Sergeant, and you all, too."

"Well, Joel, have you made up your mind?"

"Lately, I've been getting a strong feeling I need to go home. There's been plenty of war to go around; lord knows you and I've had our share. I'm ready to build a life outside of the army. Plus, I want to see the folks and help my father work the farm. There has been so much destruction from this war, it's time to rebuild."

"Well, Joel, it sounds like you've made your decision. We both got a lot of life to rebuild, you in West Virginia and me in Tennessee. Let's hope we can get to it soon. I have a feeling things at our homes aren't anywhere near like they were when we left."

While they're tending their horses, the corporal of the guard enters the stables and says, "Sergeant Richards, the provost wants Sergeant Leslie back at the compound immediately. I've been sent to escort him."

"Is there a problem, Corporal?"

Showing a bit of a grin, he says, "No, sir, only if the sergeant doesn't want to go home. The provost received the documents of General Pardon and Amnesty, but they require his and his men's signatures along with taking the Oath of Allegiance. Then they'll be back in the Union."

Joel looks at Leslie with a smile. "That's good news. Get it done. The sooner you get those signed, the quicker you'll be on the road home. I'll see you later and make sure your Morgan's standing by."

Smiling, he says, "Thanks, Joel."

Late in the afternoon, Joel stops by the compound to find out how things went with the signing and oath. John is called by the guard to come to the main gate. The guard says, "Mister Leslie, will I see you back here after a while?"

"You can be assured of that."

Joel says, "John, what's that about?"

"We've signed the papers and taken the Oath of Allegiance pledging not to take up arms against the United States. It's official now. We're no longer soldiers in the Confederate Army of America and are about to become civilians. The guards have been addressing me as Mister Leslie and my men by their first names. I understand beginning tomorrow they're going to let us out of here during the day to take care of our animals. They're getting us ready to leave for home on Monday, with a new set of civilian clothes and provisions for the journey."

Joel says, "Also, you'll get one rifle apiece plus ten rounds of ammunition. I'll see you get your sidearm back. And, John, you boys be careful on your journey so you're not mistaken for an armed guerrilla unit that hasn't surrendered."

John says, "The last thing any of us want is to be shot heading home because of a misunderstanding or doing something stupid."

Joel says, "That's good because I don't want to be reading or hearing about you boys doing anything but getting your lives back in order, helping to rebuild your homes and businesses."

"Thanks, Joel, that's also our plan. To change the subject, have you told the colonel yet?"

"No, I will first thing in the morning."

"Let me know how that goes, will you? I'll see you tomorrow."

"John, things have a way of changing overnight around here, so if by some chance I don't get to see you boys leave, best of luck."

"You too, Joel. I have a feeling our paths will cross again."

The Decision

Joel has his first restful sleep in a long time, relieved to have made a clear and committed decision to leave the army. Arising at reveille this Friday morning, he cleans up, puts on his dress uniform, and joins his fellow noncoms for breakfast before his meeting with Colonel Jarvis.

After breakfast, he heads over to the colonel's office and requests an appointment with Colonel Jarvis, which is granted for 11:00 a.m. He finishes out the morning checking on his and John's horses and then visits with some of the rangers. They ask if he's made up his mind yet.

"Corporal Clayton, I have. I'm goin' home!"

"Speaking for all of us, Sergeant, we've been waiting on your decision before making ours. If you were staying, so were most of us. Now that you made yours to leave, we won't be far behind."

"I appreciate that, but you boys still got to do what you think is best for your future, 'cause that's what I'm doing. If you want to stay in the army, there's going to be plenty of opportunity. Do it because you want to, not because of me. Excuse me. I've got to get over to the colonel's office. I'll see you boys later."

As he walks into the colonel's office, his aide looks up and says, "Sergeant Richards, the colonel will see you now.

"Colonel Jarvis, Sergeant Richards to see you."

Saluting the colonel, who returns the salute, Joel removes his hat.

"Good morning, Sergeant, have a seat. I assume you have something to tell me."

"Yes, sir, I do. I've decided to leave the army and go home. I appreciate the opportunity you've offered me, but my family's calling outweighs your offer."

"I understand, Sergeant. I could grant you a leave if that'll help."

"I've made up my mind, Colonel. I'm ready to reestablish my life, helping my father build up his farm."

"I understand. So I guess bribery didn't work, did it?"

"No, sir, but I appreciate and respect you for trying, as the intent was honorable, as was your kind treatment of the prisoners. I thank you."

"Sergeant, I know your mind is made up, but if at any time you want to change it, contact me. We're going to need good soldiers to wrap up this war and protect this country's expansion westward, which I figure will happen rapidly now that this conflict is over. Speaking of that, you will be required to stay until the war is declared officially over."

"Colonel, when do you think that'll be?"

"My best guess is about thirty days or so, depending on how fast every Confederate unit in the outlying areas gets the word and surrenders their arms. It's happening slowly, day by day. If there's nothing else, I've got to get back to helping wind this war down. You need to see to your men, keeping them sharp in the event we need your assistance."

"Thank you, sir, I will." Joel gets up to leave.

"One more thing, Sergeant. General Grant will be coming down here in the next week or two. I'm assigning the Third Cavalry Rangers to be his personal honor guard. Plan accordingly, and be prepared."

"Yes, sir, and again, thank you."

On May 29, 1865, the war is declared officially and formally over. Discharge of Union soldiers begins shortly afterward. Finally the long road home for many of them begins, including former First Sergeant Joel Richards of the Third Cavalry Rangers.

Coming Home

With the end of the Civil War, Union soldiers are being discharged and are returning to homes and families with the expectations of resuming a normal life. Many of them will never be the same, winding up as drifters or vagrants, with a few living on the wrong side of the law. Joel, after serving three years in the army, is one of those receiving discharge papers.

In July of 1865, with a few dollars of mustering out pay, provisions, and a three-year-old Morgan stallion presented to him by General Ulysses S. Grant for meritorious service, Joel begins the journey home. Riding northward, he's thinking of a name to call his newly acquired horse. Deciding to keep it simple, he says, "I think Morgan would be a good name for a stud, and that's what I'll call you. Well, Morgan, let's go home!"

On the long ride back, he's reflecting on the outcome of the war, glad it's finally over, hoping the country and the soldiers and people whose lives and property were shattered or destroyed can get back to living some kind of regular life. "Morgan, I'm looking for time to rest, help dad farm the soil, and put behind me the things I saw in the war, the battles and especially ... the killing. I think returning home will help me find peace by getting back to my roots and family."

His thoughts shift to those early years before the Civil War. He was raised on a farm in the back hills of northern West Virginia. Folks there barely scratched out a living with backbreaking work, trying to plow, plant, and raise some kind of crop in the rocky soil. His pa and ma reserved

Sundays for worship, giving blessings for what they had and praying the good Lord would lead them to a better life.

They ate many a rabbit, squirrel, and whatever game Joel and his dad could trap or shoot. This scarcity of food taught him to become an expert shot with an old, single-shot rifle. He learned to make each shot count 'cause if he didn't, the family might not have anything to eat that day. There wasn't extra money to buy ammunition, so the skins of the animals were traded for bullets and powder so more game could be taken for the dinner table. His folks were trying to hold on to all they had and probably all they'd ever have.

There were happy moments though of times around the supper table with everyone sharing what had been accomplished that day and prayers of hope his mother shared of a better life for all of them. The stories his pa read from the Bible told about great adventures of various biblical heroes, such as Joshua and Gideon, how they overcame great odds and challenges in order to achieve peace and prosperity, things his father wanted for his own family.

They all looked forward to those occasional Saturday evenings on the front porch or by the fireplace when neighbors would come over, tell stories, share food, and listen to music played by various members of the community. Joel really liked ol' Gus on the fiddle, as he could get them all stomping or the old folks dancing to a waltz.

He and Elizabeth would swim in the creek, play in the woods, and climb an old oak tree down the road. They had fun playing with the animals even if they were only pigs, chickens, or an old plow horse.

"Morgan, you'll appreciate this. I used to ride that old plow horse when she wasn't being used in the fields, pretending to be Gideon conquering the Midianites with my mighty wooden sword. I hadn't realized 'til now how that fantasy and the Bible stories have played out in my life.

"When that war came along, I was nineteen. Had this notion of doing the right thing, so I left the farm against my parents' wishes and joined up with the Union Army. That was the summer of '62. Growing up shootin' all those rabbits and squirrels made me a pretty good shot, and because I could ride, the army thought I ought to be in the cavalry, so they assigned me to a unit under General Sheridan."

Joel was just a country boy and had no idea what was coming. He learned combat tactics for how a small mounted force could attack quickly with the element of surprise, inflict the greatest military damage in a short period of time, and then withdraw before any retaliation could be organized against them.

Their unit was very effective behind Confederate lines, using these tactics to disrupt supply lines and causing panic among small detachments of Confederate soldiers. In the Fall of '63, they got the latest Henry Repeating Rifles, and along with his saber, they served him well. The general let Joel keep the weapons, which he hoped he'd never have to use again.

After many days of riding, Joel begins to see familiar surroundings, such as the old oak tree off in a distance. He remembers the times he and Elizabeth, now sixteen, climbed high up on its branches so they could see the whole valley. There's a stream on the other side of the road, winding its way down to the valley below. He and Elizabeth waded in it during the summers, occasionally catching a mess of crawdads for supper.

He passes the hillside fields where his father planted crops, and the house is not far away. As his home comes into view, a chill goes up Joel's spine. He reigns up. "Something's wrong," he whispers when he sees overgrown fields that look as if they haven't been tended to in months. The chickens and pigs are missing from their pens, and the only animals visible are an underfed mule and workhorse.

The farm horse senses Morgan's presence. Her head raises high, ears pointed toward him, and she utters a soft whinny. Morgan quickly responds as Joel tightens his grip on the reins and says, "Whoa Morgan. We haven't got time for you two to get acquainted just yet. I've got to find my family first and see if they're okay."

The joy of seeing his family is slowly slipping away. Sights like this are evident all over the south after the war—run-down, destroyed farms, uprooted families, fathers and sons taken by the war, mothers and daughters doing any kind of work or service to survive. The last place he expected to see that is here.

It's late afternoon now as he reins up in front of the house and dismounts, tying Morgan to the porch railing, looking around for signs of his family. Not knowing if anyone is here, he cautiously approaches the front door, calling out; "Pa? Ma? Elizabeth? Anyone home?"

Hearing a faint sound coming from within, he opens the door cautiously. In the dimly lit cabin, he sees a man sitting in a rocking chair, covered with a blanket and looking pale and frail from various ailments. He speaks in a weakened voice. "Joel … is that you, son?"

"Yes, Pa, I'm home."

"Oh, thank God!" he exclaims as he tries to get up from the rocker, but he is too weak to do so.

Emotions begin to boil up in Joel, remembering his father standing upright and strong, never expecting to see him like this, barely able to move. Trying to control his feelings, Joel asks, "Pa, when did you last eat?"

"It was a day or two ago. A neighbor dropped by a basket of food, but I've been too weak to make any meals myself."

"Let me fix some food. Then we'll talk."

After preparing a meal along with a pot of coffee, Joel sits down beside his father. While his father is eating, he says, "Tell me about Momma and Elizabeth. What's happened since I've been gone?"

His father begins with sadness in his eyes, struggling to get the words out. "Times have been hard. The war took everything we grew, leaving just enough to get by and hang on to this place, waiting for you to come back. About a year ago, three army deserters came by. They killed most of our animals except for the mare and the mule, which were out in the pasture, and took what food we had stored."

Reliving the memories of that day, tears stream down his face. His voice quivering, he strains to continue. "They beat me and your ma half to death when we fought to keep 'em from raping your sister. Then they left us here to die. Son, I couldn't stop 'em! They took our family from us!"

Joel's face grows taut, his eyes stone cold, and he begins clenching his fist as if preparing for battle against a vile and evil enemy. His father knows the signs well, so he reaches for Joel's hand, telling him, "Don't think about revenge, son. Justice has been served. The sheriff and some Union soldiers came by shortly after it happened. They were on the trail of these deserters. They did what they could for us, then left to track down the bastards while the trail was still fresh. They caught up with 'em about five miles from here. Took 'em prisoners, bringing 'em back here for us to identify. After we did, they took those cowards down to that oak tree and hung 'em as a lesson for other deserters who might wander this way.

"Your mother never recovered from what happened, dying shortly afterwards. Elizabeth so looked forward to your return but felt shamed, thinking you or any man could never look at her again. So she took her own life, hanging herself from that same oak tree."

Joel, overcome with emotions, stands up and heads for the door to leave the house and deal with these feelings about the terrible loss of his mother, the horrible death his sister chose, and the state of his father's health. He's seen cruel and unjust situations in the war but isn't prepared to deal with these things when it comes to his own family. Emotions, suppressed in wartime, erupt from within, causing him to fall to his knees, crying in a way he's never felt.

After regaining his composure and wiping away the tears, Joel reenters the house and sits quietly beside Jeremy, not saying a word, allowing a certain calmness to settle over them.

Having finished his meal, Joel's father looks at him, speaking slowly. "Son, I've been hanging on waiting for your return so I could tell you what's gone on these past few years and to share some things you need to know."

"Pa, we can talk about those another time."

"No, I need to tell you while I still can. We can visit about other things later if I'm able. Now, all I got left to leave you is this old farm, which ain't much. Stay with me until I'm gone. Then bury me next to your mother and sister on that knoll overlooking the valley. Sell this damn old farm if you can before the sheriff and county comes to take it.

"Now there's a few dollars left in your mother's jewelry box, which you use however you want. Make a pack animal out of that work horse; she's a Kentucky Mountain Horse and will serve you well. That horse can pull a plow, buggy, or pack a load. Then take what you need and head west, maybe Texas, to a better life."

"But, Pa, this is my home! I just spent three years away in that damned war, dreaming of the day I could return to my family and help you on the farm. I never thought of leaving this place ... but you may be right, as it just isn't the same as I wanted."

"Son, you need to get away from here. Take the good memories with you and leave the rest behind. When you're ready, get some good soil under your feet, a piece of ground you can call your own. Plant something, grow something, get some animals. When you do, your wandering days will be over, and you'll leave a legacy we'll both be proud of. If you do this, no matter where it's at, your mother, Elizabeth, and I will feel we at least served a purpose for being here.

"Now I've been thinking what other words of wisdom I can send along that will help get you to wherever it is you're going. The best I can say is to make sure you ride your own horse. Don't take something for nothing, and whatever you give, make it your best. Don't forget the teachings from the Bible I believe in and the words of God, who said to Gideon, '*Go in the strength you have, o' mighty warrior, for I am with you.*' Joel, my son, I shall always be with you."

After telling Joel those things a father wants to pass along to his children, Jeremy slips into a peaceful sleep, probably for the first time in over a year, knowing his son is at his side. Watching his father sleeping, it occurs to Joel, *It looks like our roles are changing. It's like the son is becoming the father.*

The next day, Joel begins busying himself around the farmstead doing cleanup and repair work and looking after his father. Morgan's been put in the corral along with the mule and mare. Joel notices Morgan and this Kentucky Mountain Horse seem to be overly friendly with each other, and it dawns on him she's in heat. Joel softly smiles and says, "Well, Morgan, it looks like you're going to be a daddy in about eleven months." Morgan, as if understanding, nods his head.

Occasionally, when the sky is clear, the weather's warm, and he feels strong enough, Jeremy, Joel's father, sits on the front porch watching Joel work, looking out over his farm and soaking up the sun. Joel wants to spend time with his father, so anything he can do to accommodate his wishes, he does. "I pray Pa will get his health back because I ain't looking forward to that day he don't. Any farming that needs to be done, such as fall plowing and planting, can wait till he's a little stronger."

False Hope

As the months pass, Joel has almost got the farm back in the condition it was when he left for the war. He's even planted a fall crop and has begun looking forward to the spring and late summer harvest. His father seems to be regaining his strength throughout the winter months, but then as spring arrives, he begins slipping. When the doctor makes his visit, he notes Jeremy's deteriorating health.

"Doc, what's going on? I thought he was getting better as he got through the winter and was looking forward to the warm spring weather. We were even making plans for what we might do this year."

"Joel, your father did show improvement, which was to be expected with your coming home, because that gave him hope. However, his failing health returned, and he's not getting any better. Nor is he going to. Joel, we've done everything we can to keep your father alive. Son, you need to prepare yourself for this. Just try to keep him as comfortable as you can. I'll be back by in a day or two to check on him."

Two nights later, shortly after midnight, Joel is awakened by his father softly calling his name. Joel lights a lamp and goes to his side. "Pa, can I get you something?"

His dad reaches up, taking his hand and squeezing gently. "No, son, stay with me for a minute. I'm feeling it's time. I want you to remember what I told you … promise me you'll get your own place someday far away from here, and remember my words about Gideon."

"I promise. Father, you, mother, and Elizabeth will always be remembered in my heart."

"Joel, don't forget your teachings. I never told you this, son, but I love you."

"I love you too, Pa."

With that, Jeremy gives his son a tender squeeze, releases his grip, and slips into an eternal peaceful rest. Joel lays his head on his father's chest, silently crying over his father's passing, feeling a depth of loneliness deep within his soul.

Preparations

Shortly after sunrise, Joel's on his way to contact the doctor and undertaker to make arrangements for his father's funeral. He meets up with a neighbor who asks about his father. "Jim, he passed away early this morning."

"I'm sorry. Your father was a good man. Anything I can do?"

"I want to bury him tomorrow morning on the knoll over there with Mother and Elizabeth. That was his favorite spot to look out over the farm, giving thanks for what he had. And if you don't mind, could you get word to Gus and see if he could play a couple of songs on his fiddle? The folks always liked his playing."

"Joel, you bet. I'll also let the reverend and the other neighbors know. Your father liked the reverend a lot, as they had many a talks about the Bible, especially Gideon. Oh, by the way, when I came by the corral, it looked like that mare of yours dropped her colt late last night. You might want to check on her when you can."

Joel walks over to the pen next to the corral where he can see the mare standing and a colt nursing at her side. Morgan is in the corral looking over the top rail at the two of them and snorts as Joel gets closer. "Well, Morgan, it seems one life passed and another's born. It makes you wonder, don't it."

By midmorning, the word has spread, and two neighboring farmers show up to dig the grave, followed by the doctor and undertaker. By late afternoon, all arrangements have been made for the morning internment of his father.

Rest in Peace

The spring morning breaks with the sun shining brightly and a light, cool breeze coming in from the west. The neighbors begin arriving, the wives taking specially prepared food into the house for this day of sorrow as well as to memorialize the passing of a cherished friend. Gus shows up and says, "Joel, we had some good memories here playing, singing, and dancing. What songs would you like for me to play?"

"Gus, I don't know how fitting it might be, but during the war I heard this southern song a lot on both sides and wonder if you might know it. It's called 'Lorena.'"

"I do. It's a beautiful song with a haunting melody. Now I think some lively square dance music would also be fittin', as your folks loved to dance."

"Sounds okay to me, Gus. Ask the reverend where he'd like to work 'em into the service."

The men assist Joel in taking his father from his bed, where the undertaker prepared him, to the buckboard for transporting to his final resting place next to his wife and daughter. Joel and Reverend Stevens walk slowly behind the wagon, followed by a gathering of farmers and friends who have come to pay their respects. As they march up toward the grassy knoll overlooking the lush green valley below, Gus is standing next to the gravesite with his back to the sun, playing a heartfelt version of "Lorena" on his fiddle.

As everyone takes a place around the grave, Reverend Stevens begins his eulogy by saying, "Jeremy Richards was a man of great faith, strength, and courage who was willing to do what he believed God wanted him to do, regardless of his own judgment, plans, or outcomes. Like the people of Gideon, he always believed that life is sacred even though knowing firsthand many in this world refuse to live by those rules. His character was defined by his humility, faith, and obedience to a set of God's principles, which included hard work, love of family, and life.

"He lived those beliefs and was an inspiration to all of us. He will be missed, and my parting words to Jeremy is the phrase that he loved so well, the one God told Gideon when he called him to act: 'Go in the strength you have, o' mighty warrior, for I am with you.' Amen."

Gus closes with a lively version of the "Virginia Reel," reminding everyone of the great times they shared with Jeremy and his family during those Saturday gatherings. Afterward, while partaking of the dinner prepared by the ladies, Joel expresses his heartfelt thanks to each and all who attended.

Jim asks, "Joel, what are your plans? Do you intend to stay here and farm like your father?"

"No, this place has too many sad memories attached, so I'm going to keep a promise to my father and find a place of my own, perhaps in Texas or farther west. I'll only be staying long enough till the colt's weaned and the spring crop is harvested. Then I'll sell the farm and move on. Probably in about four to six months. Oh yeah, there is one other thing left to do, and that's to cut down and burn that damn old oak tree where Elizabeth died."

"Joel, I wasn't going to say anything until later, but since you brought it up, I'd be interested in your place as it joins mine on the south. I wanted to let you know so when that time comes, we could visit about it if you'd be willin'."

"Fair enough, Jim. Let's talk later after I finish up some things around here. Here's my hand on it that I won't be talking to anybody about it until we've had a chance to visit."

"Agreed! In the meantime, if you need anything, you know where we live. When you're ready to cut that tree down, I can send my boy over to give you a hand."

"Thank you kindly, but this is one job I've got to do myself."

By midafternoon, neighbors and friends have departed, leaving Joel alone to deal with the passing of the last member of his family, a passing leaving a vacuum within his soul. He looks around the house and declares, "Damn it! Why did I go off to fight a war that wound up causing the death of my family, a war I allowed to take me away and kept me from being here when they needed me most? If only it had been over sooner, I could have been here to fight off those deserters. I guess my decisions have determined my destiny."

Selling the Farm

The months pass quickly. Joel completes the harvest of grains to feed his horses and sells the rest to help pay for fixing up the family home place. Now with summer coming to an end and a hint of fall in the air, Joel begins making plans to leave the hill country before winter.

Jim pulls up in his buggy, wanting to know if Joel is still interested is selling the farm. Jim's oldest boy is getting married, and he wants to buy it to give his son as a wedding present.

Jim is not only willing to buy the farm, but also any equipment and animals Joel might want to sell, including the recently weaned colt.

Joel is taking the Kentucky Mountain Horse as a pack animal. He's named the mare Bluebonnet after a flower that's known to Texas, where he's headed. He is only taking things he can use and carry, such as personal items of his family and grain stocks for his horses. Anything else will stay with the farm. Jim and Joel agree to a sale price of $1,000.00 for the eighty acres.

"Jim, now that we've agreed, I'd appreciate it if you can get the papers ready for me to sign in the morning, as I intend to leave in a day or two."

"Then I'd better get going so I can get this done today, pick up the money, and be here first thing tomorrow. I'll bring along the judge to notarize your signature so it's all legal and proper."

Moving On

It's a gray, overcast morning as Jim and the judge drive up in a buckboard. Joel walks out to greet them. "Morning, gentlemen. Good to see you both, and, Judge, it's been a long time."

"Yes, it has, Joel. I'm sorry to hear about your father. I apologize for not being here. I was over in the next county taking care of a court issue. Didn't get the word until I got back the following week."

"That's okay. Did you bring the papers?"

"Joel, before you sign on the line, are you sure you won't stay? We've lost quite a few young men to that damn ol' war and would like for you boys returning to stick around. I think in the next year or two there's going to be some opportunity around here besides farming."

"No, sir, there's not an argument good enough to keep me here, but I appreciate what you're sayin'. Jim?"

"Joel, here's the papers, and I have the money we agreed on. If you'll take a read on it, and if it's as we talked about, then sign where marked."

Joel reads the paper and signs. The judge notarizes it and says, "Jim can take it over to the county seat, file it, and officially become the owner of record."

"Joel, here's the thousand dollars. Can you tell me what you intend to do with it?"

"I'm going to use the money for my own place someday."

"I know your father would like that. Now I've got to get the judge back to town, make the trip over to the county seat. Joel, the best to you. May your journey be safe and the Lord look favorable upon you. Blessings, son."

"Joel, that goes for me too. Take care."

"Thank you, and, Jim, tell that boy of yours he's getting a good place, a pretty fair start on life. I hope he honors his folks as I plan to do. So long."

As they depart, heading down the road toward town in the buckboard, Joel slowly walks back to the house for one last look around, feeling a sense of sadness knowing the home at one time was filled with laughter, music, and love. Reflecting for a moment on memories of his mother, father, and Elizabeth, he realizes those days are gone forever. Joel picks up the few belongings he's taking, looks around, and walks out of the house, closing the door behind him for the last time.

He finishes loading Bluebonnet, saddles up, and rides over to the knoll where his family is buried. Dismounting, he removes his hat while looking down at their graves. His voice begins quivering as emotions rise, tears flowing down his cheeks as the words of his final good-bye come from the heart. "Lord, let my mother, father, and Elizabeth hear my words. This is the toughest, gut-wrenching thing I have ever done in my life, to leave a home that was cherished and loved by us all. As God is my witness, I'm taking with me and will hold forever in my heart the love of each one of you, and I will not dwell on the bad that happened here."

Kneeling down, Joel places his right knee on the ground. Bowing his head, he puts his left elbow on his bended knee with a clenched fist resting against his forehead. "Father, my promise to you, I will never forget your parting words of wisdom and the ways of Gideon."

He closes his eyes, and in that prayerful moment, the clouds break away, and rays of sunshine appear along with a calming, reassuring voice whispering in his ear, "Go in the strength you have, o' mighty warrior, for I am with you."

A smile slowly crosses Joel's face. His body relaxes, and he exhales a sigh of relief. Rising from his kneeling position, Joel puts his hat on while looking up. In that moment, the sun highlights the bluegrass growing in the valley below with its rich blue cast reflecting the sun's rays. Smiling at the beauty to be remembered on this day, he heads back to where Morgan and Bluebonnet are standing.

Rubbing Morgan behind an ear, Joel exclaims, "Morgan, it's going to be all right!" Mounting up, Joel heads the horses down the road past the old oak tree, which is now just a burned out stump. He turns in his saddle for one last look back as a gesture of good-bye, and the journey begins.

Postscript:

Bluebonnet becomes a source of extra money for Joel when the mare mates with Morgan, producing a colt about every fifteen months on what has become a long trip to Texas. The colts are sold along the way, which Joel figures will help build his nest egg to pay for that farm or ranch when he finds the right one. For expense money, he works his way by helping out farmers for room, board, and feed for his horses. Although he could have made it to Texas quicker, he's been struggling with the loss of his family and leaving his childhood home. This journey has become a healing source for Joel as he works the land along the way, learning new farming techniques and helping to rebuild where he can.

PART II
Cattle Drive from Texas to Dodge City

Ride with the Brand

Late in the afternoon of a day in April 1873, Joel arrives in the Texas town of Comanche Junction, looking for work. Glancing around, Joel estimates the small town to be home to about two hundred people, with the usual saloon, emporium, and feed store. He continues riding down to the end of the dirt street to what looks like a combination livery stable and blacksmith shop where he will make his first stop to get his horses fed and watered.

Stopping in front of the stable, Joel dismounts and is greeted by the owner. A heavyset man sporting a beard, wearing a blacksmith's apron, with sweat rolling down his face and arms from working at the forge, says, "Howdy, from the looks of these horses, it appears you've been on the trail a spell."

"You're right. We've been traveling the past few years working our way down from the northern part of West Virginia. They could use a little extra care and rest. I'd like to put them up for a couple of days before getting back on the trail to finding me a job."

"I can do that. Far as jobs are concerned, about the only thing available around here is out at Sam Smith's place, the Single Six Ranch, where he's putting together some hands to herd a bunch of longhorns up to Kansas."

"When's he leaving?"

"I think by the end of the week. If you're interested, you'd better git out there first thing in the morning. You've got some good, strong horses; they should be okay after a good night's rest and feed. I'll check 'em over good, let you know if I see anything you need to be aware of.

Just be sure and not push 'em hard for a few days. When you stop by in the morning, I'll give you directions to Sam's place. It's only a couple of miles out of town."

Bright and early the next morning, Joel's on his way out to the Single Six. Upon arriving, one of the hands greets him. "Can I help you?"

"I'm looking for Mister Smith. I understand he might be hiring."

"Well, I don't know about that, but he's over there sittin' on the top rail of the corral."

Joel rides up to where Smith is watching a wrangler work some horses. "Pardon me, sir. Can I speak to you for a bit?"

Turning around, Smith looks at Joel for a moment, sizing him up, and then says, "Step down, son. Tell me who you are and what's on your mind."

"Mister Smith, I'm Joel Richards. I'm in need of work. The stable owner in town told me you might be hiring for a cattle drive."

"Well, I do need one more hand. Can you work cattle?"

"I'm a pretty fair rider being cavalry trained. I can handle horses and was raised on a farm, so I know a little bit about animals."

"Son, being in the cavalry, farming, and cowboying are different things, especially when it comes to working cattle and keeping them headed in the same direction. From the looks and condition of your horses, I can tell you do know these animals pretty well."

Smith hesitates for a moment. "Tell me a little more about your cavalry and war experience. I got a reason for askin'?"

"Mr. Smith, I know I'm in territory where there's a lot of southern sympathy, but for me, the war's over."

"Forget about any prejudice here; we're in the cattle business. Now tell me about your army know-how."

Joel tells Smith about his training and a few of his experiences, just laying out the facts, no bragging, and sums it up by saying, "Most of my assignments dealt with leading a small band of highly trained cavalry troops conducting raids behind the lines of the Confederates, disrupting their supply lines and troop movements."

"Well, son, were you good at it?"

"Mister Smith, best I explain it this way. The Morgan I'm riding was presented to me by General Grant himself, along with a couple of medals for my role in helping the North win."

"Richards, I like where you stand. I do need another man, especially one of your ability. You can learn cattle on the way to Kansas if you don't mind long hours, eating dust, and cussin' snakes.

"Now, we're going to be herding about 2,500 head along with about sixty-five cow ponies. Planning to cover eight or nine miles a day to get 'em to Dodge City by the middle of July. I demand hard work, loyalty, no drinking, and a hell of a lot of courage. We're going to face many challenges, including drought, death, maybe even Indians and rustlers and, heaven forbid, a stampede.

"However, I pay a good wage, a hundred dollars plus found for the trail drive and fifty cents a beef to be split among the men for every one that's sold. So it's in the best interest of all of us to git as many of these critters to market as possible.

"One more thing, since I haven't seen you in action. Out here, our word is our bond, and if your words don't match your actions, I won't hesitate to turn you loose."

"Yes, sir, fair enough. Mr. Smith. I'd like to work with you. Might even learn a few things about ranching and cattle."

"Now that's something new, a man who wants to learn! Well then, you pay attention, listen to what I say. Until you got some experience under your belt about this cattle business, you don't question my judgment or orders of the trail boss. Is that understood?"

"Yes, sir."

"With your soldier experience, you know how to work with men as a unit, and that's how we do it here in moving these cattle. Right now, there's fourteen of us. We work together, settle our own differences between ourselves like men, then shake hands and get back to work. No gunplay, except when we're called to because of raiders or Indians, for two reasons: I can't afford to lose any men, and gunshots spook cattle. If you agree, then you're hired."

Richards says, "Yes, sir, I do, and you've got my hand and my word on it."

Smith says, "Good. Now, I want to ponder a bit on what you've said and what I got in mind, so let's talk some more after supper. I want to hear your ideas on how you'd handle an attack by Indians or rustlers, so do some thinking on it. In the meantime, git to meet the men who'll be on this drive. Most of 'em are single except for Hank and me. Hank's wife and a couple of kids will be takin' care of his little spread until he gets back. He's working at building his own ranch up, and about a hundred and fifty cows of his are on this drive, so he's got a real interest in seeing it done 'cause I know his family's been having a tough time, and they're depending on him. Hank's been on drives before; he's probably one of our best all-around hands behind Jones, the trail boss.

"Speaking of Jones, here he comes now. His friends sometimes call him Jonesy. He's been up the trail a couple of times, knows how to work men and cattle and is a pretty good gun hand. On the trail, he's all business, but off the trail he's got a different side to him, which you might not see until we get to Dodge.

"Jones! I want you to meet Joel Richards who's going to be joining us on this drive. He's a little short on cattle handlin' experience, but he might come in handy for other reasons. Visit a bit and introduce him to the men when you can."

Jones says, "You bet. When you're through with him, send him by way. I'll be over by the branding fire."

Smith says, "Richards, just a little bit about the men before I git back to the house. Jones can fill you in on anything else.

"That's Ben over by the branding fire. He's an experienced cow man and will do most of the animal doctoring. It's been rumored he's a former veterinarian who came out of the South, where he lived on a plantation, enjoying the finer things in life. He's like most of these boys; they don't talk must about their past. Just to let you know, he might be our one southern sympathizer.

"The one with the branding iron is Jingles, a pretty fair hand and a good rider, but we don't know much about him either except he comes out of New Mexico. He's pretty quiet but solid. He wears those Spanish spurs, a Mexican gun rig, and rides a Mexican saddle, but seems reluctant to tell us where he got 'em. Although from the jingle of his spurs, you know where he's at most of the time.

"See those young boys out there doing the roping? That's Red, Jeff, and Davy, wet behind the ears and full of piss and vinegar. They're good riders and ropers, know a little bit about cattle, and at their age don't know any fear, willin' to try anything but not reckless. They were forced to grow up fast when their fathers and older brothers went off to war, leaving 'em to fend for their families.

Sometimes one of 'em might do or say something stupid, and it ain't long before one of the other boys is gittin' after him At least they ain't tryin' to convince everybody they got life figured out yet, which makes 'em willin' to listen. I don't hire wild cowboys no matter how good they are 'cause it seems wild cowboys got a way of making wild cows. These critters are wild enough.

"Take a look at Red's hair. You can tell how he got his name. The other two like to say their daddys named 'em after Davy Crockett and Jefferson Davis. Now Jeff doesn't like anyone calling him Jefferson 'cause even though the war's over, he's had to defend himself a few times from folks still holding a grudge about the South when they've heard his name. We'll need to keep an eye on 'em, making sure they're headed in the right direction.

"There's the cook, nicknamed Cookie."

"I've had some of his cookin' before. I can tell you this: he can do wonders with what he's got. Cookie carries the medicine bag. He'll do the cowboy doctorin' when needed. Hopefully these boys won't be gittin' any horse, snake bites, or injuries of any kind that might slow us down.

His Brown Gargle coffee is always hot, strong, and thick enough to float a horseshoe on. It may not cure what's ails you, but for a little bit, his coffee will make you forget whatever it is.

"I've seen Cookie shoot jackrabbits from his wagon. I know he can handle a gun and shoot a moving target. He carries a 12-gauge Greener scattergun by his seat, which puts the odds in his favor when it's up close. So whether he's on the wagon or the ground, he can hold his own and will back us up when the time comes.

"The boys keeping the cattle bunched up so the ropers can do their job are John, Bob, and Mike, just good ol' cowboys who work hard and take orders without question, preferrin' to mind their own business most of the time. Now these boys don't say much, but they're dependable and know cows. Sometimes in the evening around the campfire, Bob plays a little guitar, sings a bit, ol' John might break out his fiddle, and Mike might join in with his harmonica and back up Bob on his singing. They ain't bad, and it kinda gives the boys a break from just talking cows and makes them think some about girls, dancing, and home. I have a feeling they enjoy night herding 'cause they get to sing. But when they have to, they can put a horse or cow down with a single shot, but how they'll do against Indians, I don't know. Hell, I don't even know how I'll do!"

"Mister Smith, I have a feeling you'll do just fine, as anyone who's got the courage and smarts to drive 2,500 head of cattle to Kansas will be there when it counts."

"Thanks. Now, some of these fellows have a past that's none of my business so long as they do the job and get along. From what I can tell so far, they're a good and tough bunch. You'll learn the most about moving cattle from them, so pay attention to what they got to say. By the way, I'll be the drover on this drive.

"That's enough on the speech makin'. We got work to get done before we kick off the drive two days from now. One more thing. Get rid of that soldier saddle. Get yourself a western one; the kind with a saddle horn so you got something to hitch your rope to when needed. Jones might have an extra one laying around for you to use until you git your own. We'll talk about your horses after supper, so when the dinner bell rings, you and the boys come on up to the house.

"You can meet my wife, who'll be fixing our last sit-down meal before the drive begins. My kids, I got four of 'em, will be helpin' their ma out on this meal. Cookie will be taking over the cookin' chores beginning with tomorrow morning's breakfast. When we leave, my boys will be doing the chores around here, looking after things under Ma's steady eye and, when needed, a firm hand. This'll be a big part of their growin' up since I'll be gone for five months, a time for them to do those things they've learned about ranching as well as havin' to deal with the unexpected. If I've done my job, they'll do theirs, and that's about all I can ask."

The Brand

Over supper at Sam's this night, the cowboys are somewhat subdued knowing this is going to be their last sit-down meal where they'll be served a home-cooked supper for several months. Consequently, they're trying to be on their best behavior with reasonably good table manners. The talk is about many things when Joel asks, "Mister Smith, what does your brand, the Single Six, stand for?"

"When my wife and I left Tennessee before the war, we came west looking for our own place and wound up here in Texas. I guess you could say Davy Crockett was my hero. If he thought Texas was the place to be, then that was good enough for me.

"Now, you boys got to understand, we were plenty young then—thought I knew something about the ways of the world, full of spunk, thinking I could handle anything that came our way. If I had known then what the Mexicans did to Davy at the Alamo, I might have changed my mind. For protection, I only had an old breech loader and a Colt single-action, black-powder revolver that held six shots.

"Boy, we were one lucky sons-of-a-gun because not a lot of trouble came our way where I needed that single-six revolver, so when we finally settled here, I had to create a brand for our cattle, and that's where the Single Six brand came from.

"Okay, men, now you got your dessert finished, it's time to call it a night. Our day begins early, and this might be the last good night's sleep you're going to see for a while."

The cowboys begin leaving, thanking Mrs. Smith for the great food along with the kids for serving it up. Now it's time to hit the bedrolls, anticipating the great adventure lying ahead.

The Deal

As the boys are leaving, Sam asks Joel and Jones to stay. "Jonesy, as the trail boss, I want you to know everything that's going on, so I want you in on this talk. Richards, I've been thinking about how we can work your horses into this drive that'll be fair and help us both out. Here's what I got in mind. Every horse on the drive has got to pull its own weight. You've got a good pack animal there plus the rigging.

"I've talked to Cookie. He says an extra pack animal would sure come in handy, and he likes the look of yours. So if you're agreeable, we can use it to help tote stuff the chuck wagon won't have room for. Then as far as your own mount is concerned, we normally don't take along any studs, just mares and geldings. But since it's cavalry trained, I'm going to make an exception, thinking it might prove more useful to you than one of these cow ponies when we run into those marauders. Plus he's a good looking animal. Just maybe there might be a fine colt or two come out of this drive. If so, you can have the first shot at buying whichever mare or mares that might be. Hell, I might even keep one for myself and give it to my oldest son. I'll tell Wrangler the Morgan will be your main mount not to be ridden by anyone else.

"Okay, so here's my offer, I think it's more than fair. When this drive is over and the cattle are sold, I'll pay you fifty cents a day for the use of both horses. That way you still keep the horses, and we both wind up on the right side of the fence. Well, what do you say?"

"Mister Smith, it's a deal. Here's my hand on it."

"And mine. By the way, since Morgan and your pack horse are on the payroll, I'll consider the two of them my fifteenth man, rounding out our crew.

Now a real concern of mind is the possibility of havin' to fight off some Indians and rustlers on the way. Now we'll git down to the nut cuttin.' Since you're cavalry trained, look and carry yourself like a man who's been in a few battles. When we run into those Indians and rustlers, as I know we will, I'll expect you to draw that soldier sword, lead the charge, because we don't give in to threats by any damn injuns or outlaws when our property's at stake. Any problem with that?"

Richards says, "No, sir."

"That's the main reason I'm hiring you, 'cause these cowboys haven't been in any life or death battles that I know of except fistfights, and I don't want anybody panicking when it's time to shoot back. Now, tell me and Jones how you would deal with it."

"First of all, I'll need some time with the men on the trail so they'll know what I got in mind when the time comes to take a stand. Where do think it might happen?"

Smith says, "More than likely, we'll see the Indians about thirty to forty-five days from now when we cross the Red River into Oklahoma and head these cattle through the Nations. The other spot for rustlers might be when we cross the Cimarron, start bending 'em toward Kansas and Dodge City. I got a lot of responsibility to the folks here at home to take care of; I can't do it if we allow others to take something of ours that ain't theirs."

Richards says, "Mister Smith, this also brings up another point, and that's how well your men will respond when the battles happen. I know you're not wanting to create a cavalry unit, but I'm thinking you want us to have the best chance to get these cattle through to market without losing anybody, if we can."

"You're right about that, Richards. Tell me and Jones what you got in mind."

Richards says, "First, I need to find out what their skill level is firing from the back of a horse, which will help me figure the best way to use 'em, if and when we're attacked. Firing from the ground probably won't be a problem. It's when we're on horseback that will make the difference. If they have confidence in their riding and shooting ability to hit live targets on the run, they're more than likely to stand up under the pressure of any assault by Indians or rustlers."

Jones says, "What are you thinking?"

"This first week on the trail, I know we're all going to be busy gettin' into the flow of the drive. I know it'll be a tough time for me. As much as I can, I'll observe the men's riding skills, who sits his horse well, has it under control during critical times, the men's temperament, patience, and how they respond to orders. Then I'll get together with you and Mr. Smith on what I think is the best way to begin preparing for the inevitable."

Smith says, "Sounds like a plan to me. Plus it makes sense. I want these boys to have the best chance we can give 'em."

"Mister Smith, I'd like to eventually get 'em use to shooting from a galloping horse, hitting their target and swinging onto the next one. At first it'll be all dry firing until I feel confident they're ready for live action. I sure as hell don't want 'em shooting themselves, each other, or their horses. When I feel they're ready, I'll add real bullets, preparing them for close-quarter action without panicking, which means they're going to need to do some practicing. How much ammunition do we have on hand?"

"Each man has both a full pistol and rifle cartridge belt for this trip. That's all I'd planned on, but with what you're talking about, I can tell we don't have enough bullets. I've got an extra case of .44s in the house, which I'll have Cookie put on the chuck wagon. I've got supplies coming in tomorrow sometime, so I'd better send Jeff to town first thing and tell 'em to add some more cartridges to the order."

Richards says, "I'll make sure we use the ammunition sparingly, learning to make every shot count without blasting holes in the sky. For practicing, I'll break them into small groups, taking each group away from the cattle one at a time so as not to cause any problems. Now, it seems to me we have about a month and a half to get ourselves ready. If they're good men, that'll do."

Smith says, "Well, Jones, what's your thinking on this?"

Jones says, "Mr. Smith, I like what he says, plus he's got the look of a warrior. In the short time we've visited today, I'd trust him. I think you could tell from the talk around the supper table the men have a favorable impression of him, especially the young boys when they heard about his cavalry background. I'll let the men know when the time comes they're to follow his lead."

Smith says, "Jones, that's good enough for me. I'll see you boys in the mornin'."

Chuck Wagon Conversation

The next morning, preparations are still underway for the next day's drive to Kansas. The men gather around for their first morning's chuck wagon breakfast. Conversation is centered on the drive, plus a comment or two about the food to be served along the way.

Ben hollers out, "Hey, Cookie, what's this coffee you're fixin'? It's pretty damn good."

Cookie answers, "Ben, it's called Arbuckles."

"Is that the kind that's got a peppermint stick in it?"

"Yep, whoever grinds the beans when I need 'em gets to have that piece of candy."

"Cookie, whenever you say, I'm ready."

In unison, most of the cowboys holler out, "Me too!"

"Well, boys, I've got a crate of a hundred one-pound bags of Arbuckles loaded up, so everyone will have a turn at grinding the coffee. The only way you're goin' to miss your coffee is if we run out of water and firewood. So you boys make sure I'm well supplied. One more rule on this coffee: if any of you criticize my cookin', you'll miss your turn grindin' along with the peppermint candy."

"Cookie, what if it comes up my turn and I've gotta be on watch, am I gonna miss out?"

"Just trade it off to one of these other punchers and take their turn."

"Cookie, I'm curious; how you goin' to keep the grounds from gettin' in our cups when we pour?"

"Why, the way I'm gonna do that is to put the fresh grinds in one of my socks, tie a knot in it, throw it into a coffee pot of boilin' water. After it's boiled a bit, I'll take the sock out of the pot so you can pour your coffee, not worry about gettin' any grounds."

"Cookie, aren't you going to need a lot of clean socks then?"

With a grin, he says, "Nope, just how do you think I'm going to keep 'em washed and clean all the time?"

"You don't mean … ah, yuck!"

Jones walks up to the gathering. "Cookie, have you got 'em all fed, bedrolls and guns in the chuck wagon?'

"Done, boss. They're all yours."

"Okay, men, we've got about a hundred head left to brand, so let's get saddled up."

"Hank, I'd appreciate it if you would take Richards under your wing, start schooling him what these longhorns are about. He's got very little experience with these kind of cattle, but he knows about some other things we're probably goin' to find helpful on the trail."

"You got it, boss. Richards, come with me so I can introduce you to some of our long-horned friends. Remember this about those critters: you can't drive 'em. You got to guide, coax, and move 'em in the direction you want 'em to go."

"The more pressure put on 'em, the less likely they'll do what you want 'em to." Hank reflects a moment. "That's interesting. Kinda reminds me of my wife. But keep that in mind, and you'll be okay. The real test will come on the trail as we go along. How quick you pick this stuff up will go a long way in helping you get along with the crew, as these boys ain't slackers. They'll know real quick if someone ain't cuttin' it, just like the army when you got to depend on the other soldiers to do their part. Now, them's more words than I've said in a month. Let's get our horses from the remuda, but for the time being, we'll not use your Morgan until you've been around these critters for a while."

As they're headed for the corral, Smith joins them on the way. "Good morning, boys! Richards, I want you to watch Wrangler in action. I think Hank would agree that Wrangler is one of the best men I've seen working horses, and he prefers to be called just Wrangler. I thought I knew a lot about horses until I hired him. He's taught us all a few lessons on how to handle these animals.

"Hey, Wrangler, come over here. I want you to meet Joel Richards who, as you know, will be joining us on this drive along with his horses."

Wrangler says, "That's a mighty good-looking Morgan you got there, Richards, along with that Kentucky Mountain horse. Haven't seen those since I was last in Tennessee a number of years ago. What's their names?"

"I just call him Morgan to keep it simple, and the mare is Bluebonnet, named for the flower that grows here."

"Wrangler, tell Richards your trick to training these horses."

"Well, the main thing is to have a lot of patience, which is usually in short supply when it comes to breakin' and trainin' horses. It's best not to drag these horses down to our way of thinkin' but to raise ourselves up to their way of thinkin'. Most cowboys have trouble with that 'cause they've learned, wrongly, in order to break a horse you've got to break its spirit if you want control. You don't build trust between you and the horse this way. I know a lot of cowboys think a horse should do as it's told, either by hard reining or spurring, 'cause after all they're just animals. Well, sir, I can tell you this. They may be just an animal, but when the time comes you're depending on it to save your butt, you better have worked with that horse the right way. It's got to have confidence, faith, and trust in you that you're not putting it in danger, or you'll lose when your ass is on the line."

"Well, Richards, what do you think of that?"

"Makes sense to me. I'd like to visit with Wrangler some more when I can." He looks at Wrangler. "One of the things I'll want to know is how many of these horses had riders shoot from their backs, whether it's been at rabbits, snakes, coyotes, or even men. This is going to be important when the time comes to make our stand, and we damn sure don't want any skittish animals taking us out of our plan because of bolting or bucking at the sound of gunfire."

Wrangler says, "I only know of a couple of them for sure that can handle shooting from their backs. I've worked some with a couple Wild West Shows, so I've got an idea how to get 'em ready for that sound. I doubt if being in an arena or out on the prairie facing the real thing makes much difference to a horse. If we can get the riders to do their jobs, the horses will do theirs."

Smith says, "I didn't know you worked in Wild West Shows. Now, I know it's none of my business, but what made you decide to leave that life?"

"Well, sir, I was spending all my time back east training horses for real cowboys and people like Buffalo Bill Cody to ride in their shows and hadn't experienced any of the life these folks lived. Cody inspired me to go west and find out what the west was really about, and he said once I did, I probably wouldn't be back. So I did, and here I am livin' it.

"Richards, if you got any ideas to help prepare those horses, I'd be glad to work with you on that."

Richards says, "I got an idea or two that might help, so let's visit some more later when we figure out how and when to start working with those you think can handle gunfire."

Smith says, "Thanks, Wrangler. How are the horses lookin' for tomorrow?"

"We've got sixty-five good ones ready. I've dropped two out as one's come up lame, and another's got something goin' on with it, which I haven't figured out yet. It's best we don't take a chance on a sick horse. By the way, Richards's Morgan seems to have established dominance among the mares and geldings; looks like they've already picked him for their leader. That's a good thing; being well trained as he is, should help keep these horses calmer, making my job a little easier."

Smith says, "Now you can get back to work getting these beauties ready to go. Keep me and Jones informed on their condition and any changes."

Wrangler says, "You bet. Here comes that supply wagon we been waiting on."

"Hank, you better git Richards back to learning something about this trail business so at least he's got an idea of his part in the drive. And get him into working a rope with one of our best ropers, probably Jeff or Davy when they get a break."

"Good idea, boss. I'll check with Jones and work it out."

Head 'Em Up

Sunrise the next morning, the day breaks clear, the temperature's comfortable, and the crew of the Single Six are just finishing up breakfast. They've already loaded their bedrolls, guns, and personal items into the chuck wagon. It's been stressed to them by both Smith and Jones the importance of getting as many of the cattle to Dodge City, as the future of both Smith and Hank's ranches depends on it. If they succeed, all hands will have a decent payday along with some entertainment at End of Trail.

A normal day for on the trail starts at sunrise, beginning with a breakfast of biscuits, bacon, and plenty of strong, black coffee. Cookie fixes extra biscuits for the men to wrap up in their neckerchiefs to take along for lunch while workin' along with a full canteen of water. Jones will be the point man out in front of the herd. Immediately behind him will be the boss or dominant longhorn that's been broke to trail. This leader usually has the respect of the herd, and the others are inclined to follow the boss.

When ready, Jones will give the signal to "Head 'em up." The cowboys will be in place with the swing riders on each side of the herd and tail riders bringing up the rear behind the herd, ready to encourage stragglers to keep up as well as responding quickly to keep wanderers or bolters from trying to break away from the herd and taking others with them. Along with the herd, the chuck wagon and remuda will begin moving in unison, giving an impression of a long, loaded freight train starting up as it begins spinning its wheels until traction is gained, slowly but steadily gaining momentum until it reaches the required traveling speed usually set by the boss longhorn.

The men will be in the saddle ten or twelve hours a day, moving the herd northward and keeping a watchful eye and maintaining control over the herd, which may string out for two miles. Most will go through three or four horses a day, only takin' time to exchange tired mounts for a remount from Wrangler.

When they reach the next day's campsite along the trail, Cookie will serve up a meal of meat, beans, canned fruits, and, again, biscuits along with a gallon or two of black coffee. After the meal, the cowboy not on the first watch, or nighthawk duty, will bed down around the campfire, trying to get as much sleep as they can before it's their turn to relieve the night riders.

There'll be two to four cowboys, depending on conditions, slowly circling the herd, keeping it contained, quiet, and guarding against predators or rustlers. The sound of human voices and music tends to calm cattle, so the boys on watch, as they're circling the herd, are encouraged to sing quietly and soothingly so the cattle know where the riders are at all times.

As Smith says about the singing, "Boys, I want to hear those critters moaning like the sounds you'd hear comin' from your sweetheart when you whisper in her ear tellin' of the many pleasures you're about to bestow upon her. And, Bob, let 'em hear the 'Night Herdin' Song.' Might even be a good one for the other men to learn."

The last shift to be relieved is right before sunup. When they come back into camp, it's their job to wake the cook so he can begin preparing breakfast. About this time, the cattle are getting on their feet after a night's rest and start looking for a breakfast of their own to graze on. The night riders will keep the herd grazing slowly in the preferred direction of the drive.

Jones reminds the boys that longhorns are animals who respond to basic instincts of a prey creature concerned only with survival. They can't be crowded or they'll be looking for a way out to escape, or as a last resort trying to defend themselves by using their horns to either hook the horse or its rider. A horse once hooked or gouged will avoid at any cost close contact with a longhorn and might lose confidence and trust in its rider for putting it in that kind of situation. It's imperative the men stay alert and don't get their horses or themselves in a situation where they can get hurt.

To make the drive work smoothly, every man's got to be on the lookout at all times for any sign of trouble from the cattle or anything suspicious and then let Jones or Smith know immediately. Again the crew is reminded that any bickering or feuding has got to be handled immediately, and failing to do so is one of the quickest ways to get fired and sent packing. They were all hired as much for their temperament as well as skills in getting along with others and the cattle. The drive has enough challenges without personal grudges, so if they obey basic common sense rules, they'll get along fine.

They will probably lose a few head during the drive, so to keep the headcount up, the boys will be on the lookout for strays or mavericks, especially those looking for companionship, unmarked, or not branded, and fit enough to travel to Dodge. Those they find like this will be branded, added to the herd, and taken along.

For each one gathered and branded, the cowboy bringing it in will be paid a bonus of a dollar. If there's any doubt about any stray, Jones or Smith will decide. If there's any argument over who found it, the money will be split. Jones will keep tally on the strays and has the final word.

The men are told that when the time comes to face Indians or rustlers, they're to be ready and more than capable of defending the herd and themselves. Smith doesn't want to lose any cattle or men if it can be helped. He's very clear they are not looking for trouble, and if it can be avoided without bloodshed and loss of cattle, that's the route he will take. If there's no choice, they will be ready to protect the cattle and themselves, and that's part of what Richards was hired to do in addition to driving cattle. Along the trail, Richards will be training the crew to be ready when the time comes. Smith makes it clear that the cowboys are to listen and learn from him, and his word is law on this. They are to do what he tells them, follow his lead, and everything will work out.

Smith says, "This drive isn't going to be easy, as Jones, Hank, and Ben can tell you. A drive is long hours, little sleep, lots of dust, and maybe even a stampede along with Indians and rustlers. If we keep our heads about us, listen to the experienced men, and follow orders, we'll make it to Kansas in good shape. Jones, are we ready?"

"Yes, sir, Mister Smith. Saddle up, boys. Let's get 'em moving. We're going to Dodge City!"

The Cowboy Cavalry

A week later, the drive is well under way with good weather aiding its northward trek toward Kansas. Jones is out front with the lead steer following as the rest of the herd stretches out along the trail behind in what appears to be an orderly fashion, with constant bawling coming from different parts of the herd. An occasional longhorn wanders away looking for a patch of grass but is quickly brought back into the group by an outrider before others get the notion to do the same.

The chuck wagon and remuda are off to one side of the herd, staying out of the dust being kicked up by the cattle as well as looking for the next place to pull up so the cowboys can exchange for fresh mounts. The crew rotates riding drag with the youngest and newest cowboys, Joel, Davey, Jeff, and Red getting more than their share at the beginning. But as the drive progresses; Jones makes sure everyone takes his turn equally from riding tail, swing, and point.

The men have begun fitting into a routine, making necessary adjustments from bunk house living to chuck wagon cooking, sleeping on hard ground by the campfire, and working with the cattle day and night. The cattle are becoming more manageable, still wary but staying together even as that occasional critter tries to go looking for greener pastures.

As it crosses some of the wide open country of north central Texas, through a few low water areas, the 2,500 head of longhorns occasionally tramples down an occasional stand of mesquite in its path. The trail winding along the terrain sometimes goes across higher ground, ground blessed with early spring rains sprouting green grass and making grazing easy to add pounds on the beef, pounds that will be needed later as the drive approaches barren areas where every blade of grass will be considered a delicacy to hungry cattle.

Mr. Smith, after taking his turn on the trail, rides into camp on a late afternoon, dismounts by the remuda, stretches his back a bit, and loosens the girth on his saddle as Wrangler approaches. "Mister Smith, I'll take him from here."

"Thanks, Wrangler." He hands him the reins and walks over to the campsite. "Cookie, I need a cup of coffee before we get to eating supper."

"Coming right up, boss. Here's a hot cup of brew fresh out of a new pot."

"Thanks. We haven't visited much lately, but now that everyone is really starting to work together, maybe I can begin relaxing just a bit, as I'm getting a lot more confidence in the boys. You know, it looks like we've got the makin's of a pretty good crew. What do you think?"

"Mr. Smith, I agree, as it seems to me that new man Joel and the young boys got the potential of being pretty good cowboys. The rest of the crew has the experience and are more than willing to help 'em get a handle on working with these longhorns. Jones is doing a good job keeping things moving, dishing out the right amount of correcting to the men when it's needed. That's kinda the way I see it so far."

"I agree with you, Cookie. Hell, Jones even got on my ass a time or two, which caused me to pucker a bit. However, it's fine 'cause it's his job as trail boss to make sure everyone does their jobs, me included. I'd forgotten some things about driving cattle that are coming back now. There are times we all need a reminder. Agreed?"

Grinning, he says, "You're right about that, boss. An occasional boot in the butt helps to remember the lesson."

"Cookie, how are the men doing so far as you're concerned on the meals and complaining?"

"Well, sir, no complaints I'm aware of about my cooking. Don't know if it's got anything to do with that peppermint stick from the Arbuckles, but nobody's missed their turn grinding the beans yet. Now, when it comes to doctoring, I've heard a groan or two.

"You know, a couple three of these boys got tender butts and just now are starting to toughen up a bit. Had to apply some medicine on some raw sores, which didn't feel so good to 'em. Plus, they had to drop their drawers to get treated. I think that probably hurt their feelings more than the liniment stung those sores.

"I know they're looking forward to the time when their butts are callused and toughened up to handle all the riding. One of 'em was even thinking about putting a pillow on his saddle but was afraid what the other boys would say. Maybe one of these days some saddle maker will construct a saddle with a padded seat for tender asses."

"Not a bad idea, Cookie. Just to let you know, it's been a little tough on my old hide too. Well, the boys are bedding down the herd and will be here shortly. What's for supper?"

After the herd is bedded down for the evening, cowboys not on watch gather around the campfire for their late afternoon meal. After they finish supper and talk over the day's events, Jingles speaks up. "Hey, Bob, how about getting that old Martin guitar out and you boys play us some songs."

Ben chimes in, "Yeah, Bob. A little after-dinner music is just like Cookie giving us an extra helping of dessert."

As the boys begin playing, Smith calls Joel over. "Joel, you've begun to fit in with the crew pretty well and seem to be getting a pretty good handle on working these critters. I think it's time we start looking ahead to what might be waiting for us in the Nations and Kansas. You've had some time to look the crew over, so tell me what you've got in mind."

"Well, Mister Smith, the whole bunch has good riding skills, and Jones is probably the best. Keeps his emotions in check and will be there when it counts. What I don't know is what kind of shots they are or how they'll stand under fire. I know most of 'em have done some hunting, dispensed an injured or ailing animal when called upon, but the kind of shooting we'll have to do is much different than firing at running game or a fallen horse or cow.

"Mister Smith, you got grit and determination, so I don't have a question about you other than your shooting ability. I'd like to talk to the men tomorrow night and lay out the plan. Plus I'll visit with Jones about finding places along the way to practice without upsetting the cattle."

"Okay, Joel, makes sense to me so far. At supper tomorrow, you lay it out for us so we can start getting ready. I'm not looking forward to this, but I know it's got to be done."

The next evening sitting around the campfire, Smith stands, looks at the men, and speaks.

"Boys, the time has come to begin thinking about and preparing for trouble. Lord knows, it's not anything I'm looking forward to, but we're gonna have to deal with it, git through it if we hope to git to Dodge in one piece.

"You all know the main reason I hired Richards was to help us fight off the savages and raiders if and when they decide to try to take the herd. Well, he's got some ideas and a plan how best to do this. Joel?"

Sitting on a log with a cup of coffee in hand, Richards looks around the group, making eye contact with each one. "Mister Smith, just so you and the men are clear on what our purpose is, I'm not training gun slingers. I want men who can hit what they aim at without hesitating, as it's the hesitant ones who get killed.

"We're going to start training and practicing some simple techniques and maneuvers, as there isn't time to teach you everything because this has to fit in with our work of taking care of the cattle. We'll practice late afternoon when the longhorns are tired and less likely to be upset by galloping horses or gunfire from a distance. I've talked with Jones, and he'll be scouting out some places we can practice, which will be beyond a knoll or ridge, out of sight of the cattle.

"Now I know you boys will be tired from working cattle all day, and so will I. However, I'd rather be tired, practiced, and ready when the time comes than tired, not practiced, and dead. There's no getting around practicing, as Mr. Smith hired me for the specific purpose of helping him get these cattle to market and not letting some band of Indians or rustlers take our lives or these cattle from us. Without the cattle, there is no Dodge City, no girls, no new boots or Stetsons waiting for us.

"I want you men to get used to shooting from a galloping horse, hitting your target and swinging onto the next one. At first it'll be all dry firing with your Colts or Remington's until I feel you're ready for live action. For practicin', I'll break you into two small groups or squads, and when I figure out which final group you'll work best in, I'll assign you to Squad A or B. A Squad will be led by me, and B Squad by Jones.

"We have about a month at the outside to get ourselves ready." Richards gets a very serious, determined look on his face. "Don't fool yourselves into thinkin' we got plenty of time 'cause our plan may not be the same as theirs. If you get to thinkin' I'm pushing you to be ready ahead of time, you're right, 'cause I don't want to be caught off guard. If you'll work with me, we'll be ready. Any questions?"

Ben speaks up. "Now, Joel, we can all shoot fair, and I think we know what to do, so can't we just talk about it around the campfire rather than doing all this extra work?"

"Ben, there's shooting, and there's killing. We can do all the talking in the world, but when we go up against these raiders and killers, the whole thing changes, as this isn't their first time out of the chute, but it is ours. They know what to do, and if you're not prepared going up against experienced raiders, you don't really know how you'll react; some of you could panic and run while others might freeze up, greatly reducing our chances to survive.

"We'll be facing some very nasty people, not like chasing cattle who try to escape. If you give 'em an out, they'll run. Give these people an edge, and they'll kill you because they have no conscience. You not only got to shoot straight, but unfortunately you must shoot to kill without hesitation."

A chill begins descending over the campfire, and the hairs on the backs of the cowboys' necks begin rising as the reality of what Richards is saying begins to soak in. Up to now, this scenario and confrontation was only someplace far into the future.

Richards continues, "If you want to get to Dodge City, then you got to do as I say, and that means practicing so each of us knows what the other one will do when the fight comes. Boys, this is serious business; just talking around the campfire don't get the job done. From the practicin', when you get into a fight for your life type of situation, you're probably only going to remember 20 to 25 percent of what I taught you, and it's got to be that 25 percent that saves your lives and Mr. Smith's cattle."

Intently paying attention, Jones and Jingles nod in agreement with what Joel is saying.

"Gentlemen, practicing with determination develops confidence, making us better prepared when the attack comes. Understand clearly, we're not in a horse race, we're in a survival to win race, 'cause those Indians and rustlers are in a kill us and steal our cattle race. So get straight in your minds what needs to be done when the time comes. You're going to have to reach deep inside for that extra grit we all got hiding down there, waiting for the right time to spring forth.

"Wrangler's had experience on what it takes to get horses trained to shoot from their backs. He'll match each horse with a rider who's best able to work with that particular horse, staying in control when the shooting starts. He'll get as many of the mounts in the remuda ready as he can so we'll have more than one horse available to each of us in case we need it. Wrangler, anything to add?"

"The other horses accepted Morgan as their leader; they'll follow him, making my job a little easier. Now I might need someone to give me a hand once in a while if we can spare 'em."

Red speaks up. "I'd like to help Wrangler if it's okay with the boss."

Jones says, "It's okay with me. Wrangler, just let me know when you need him."

Joel says, "I'll begin tomorrow with Jones, Hank, Red, Davy, and John. Then the next day with Mister Smith, Ben, Jingles, Jeff, Bob, and Mike. I'll be rotating each one of you back and forth until I get a feel of who works best at what position. Then I'll assign each man to either Squad A or B, and from then on, you will train with your assigned squad, staying with 'em until we reach Dodge. So tomorrow the work begins. Mister Smith?"

"Boys, if you have any questions or doubts, now's the time."

Hank stands. "I think I speak for the other boys when I say we're with you!"

Ben and the rest say, "You can count on us."

The next day, about an hour before sunset, the cattle are bedded down, and Joel leads the first group of men over a nearby ridge where training will begin. Once over the ridge, out of sight of the cattle, Joel reins up as the others do the same, and he tells them what to expect. "When this happens, remember, there's strength in numbers; don't go out on your own or get separated 'cause if you do, your chances of surviving are slim. They'll be looking for the easy pickin's, as that's the man who gets killed and scalped. When the time comes to stand, we've got to stay together and win together. I'll be tellin' you other things as we go along, but for now I want to show you how we're going to train. Then you will follow me through the exercises at a walk."

Richards is going to teach the basics, as he wants them to have a good foundation to work from. He wants them to know about keeping weapons clean and oiled after each practice or skirmish, learning to transition between rifle and pistol or pistol and rifle while on horseback, battlefield strategy, shooting, target, and defensive preferences.

Richards says, "Before we begin today, unload your revolvers. Afterwards, I want each man to check another's gun to make sure it's empty. Beginning of every practice, we'll do this. No cheating, no accidents, no scaring the horses. Make sure!"

Richards has set up three targets, staggered, to simulate the enemy—a bit crude, but it's what he's got to work with. They'll walk through on their horses first, single file, maintaining a space of two horse lengths between each rider. As he approaches the first target on his left, he'll draw, which will be their signal to do the same, telling them with authority that after they draw to point their gun skyward until it's their turn on the target. When it's their turn, they're to lower the weapon, making sure it's pointed at the target, not their horse, leg, or the man in front.

Richards will take aim, dry fire at the first target, and continue ahead to the next one on his left, and each of them are to do exactly the same as they approach the target, but only after the man in front has passed it.

He continues with his group, following as they pass through the target area with guns pointed skyward, and begins a roll to the right. When the real situation occurs, Richards will roll right with A Squad, Jones will roll left with B Squad, and both squads will form back up after completing the turns into the wedge to reengage the Indians or raiders. He makes the point about the importance of working on making the turn as smoothly as possible, staying together.

As they come back around, it's critical to maintain spacing. When Richards lowers his gun to prepare to shoot the target on the left this time, his group sets up to follow suit. When it's their turn at the target, they each lower their gun, pointing at the target, dry fire, keeping the spacing behind the rider ahead, holstering their gun, beginning a roll to the right, and lining back up to go through the target area once more.

"After the next pass through, when we line up, I'll put my hand up to halt. Then you can ask me any questions about what we just did before we go again. Follow me!"

After the first pass through, Joel halts the men and asks if there are any questions.

Davy says, "Joel, that was pretty easy. Is that all there is to it?"

"No, this is only the beginning. First we constantly go over the rules, then the walk through, followed by a slow trot, then a fast trot, working up to a lope and finally a gallop. You'll find it much tougher as we speed up the pace and begin using real bullets. Keep in mind, when we encounter the raiders, everything happens at breakneck speed, and that's what I'm preparing you for, but we got to take it a step at a time, making sure what I'm teaching you over and over becomes instinctive, giving you an edge when we get into a battle so you'll react based on your training and not panicking or freezing because of not knowing what to do.

"Okay, follow me, and let's walk through again. This time when I make the last roll where we began, I'll go into a slow jog, and we'll do this twice, moving up to a fast jog, which we'll also do twice, then twice around in a lope, and finally at a gallop to give you an idea of what I'm talking about. Let's go!"

After each run, Joel brings them to a halt, asking, "All right, how did you do after each run?"

Jones says, "I had no idea how difficult this would be once we got into a lope followed with a gallop. I'm beginning to see why we need the practice. Tryin' to hold the reins just right, controlling the horse, tryin' to aim, and maneuver back into position after the run!"

Hank says, "The timing needed to shoot the targets surprised me once we hit the gallop. If we'd been shooting real bullets, I'd probably missed all three of 'em There's just a lot of things to consider."

Red says, "Hank's right. I'm not as good in the saddle as I thought. Tryin' to keep my mind on the target, controllin' my horse, who I think had an idea or two of where she wanted to go, which wasn't the same as mine. Now I'm beginnin' to see what Wrangler's going to be working on."

Davy says, "Damn, Joel, I got a lot to learn. It's going to take me a lot of practice to get this down. Just talking about it around the campfire is a whole lot different than doin'."

John says, "I've shot some running game from horseback but never thought I'd have anyone riding at me wanting to do harm. After doing this, I got a whole different feeling telling me I'd better git real serious with this practicing."

"Boys, this is just the beginning. Think about what I said, what we did, and what you'd do different next time. Fortunately, you're getting a sense of what to expect before it happens. I'll start working with Wrangler on gettin' the horses used to gunfire. We'd better get on back to camp. Tomorrow I'll bring out the rest of the men and go through the same thing. This group will practice the following day, and in about two weeks, we begin working with loaded guns."

As they ride into camp, Smith approaches the group. "Well, Jones, how'd it go?"

"Mister Smith, we all got a lot of work to do, as you'll find out tomorrow. It's challenging, forces you to think. Joel makes sense, and if we all put in the effort, I can see where we're going to have a better than even chance when facing either Indians or rustlers up ahead."

"That's what I want to hear. Cookie's got grub and hot coffee ready."

The next day, Joel leads the other group out, and for two weeks they alternate every other day, slowly and surely making progress. Beginning their third session, still with empty guns, Joel has them riding one way through the target area with pistols drawn, dry firing at each target and then holstering them on the roll and immediately drawing their rifles to begin going back through the area.

By the end of the second week, Joel makes the assignments. In Squad A with Joel will be Hank, Jeff, Mike, Red, and Jingles. Squad B, led by Jones, consists of Davy, John, Bob, Ben, and Smith. Wrangler and Cookie will stay with the chuck wagon and remuda during any action.

Joel calls Jones, Smith, and Jingles aside. "Mister Smith, I want you and Jingles to bring up the rear on your squads when we form up on the wedge. You two seem to have the ability to quickly read overall what's going on in the field, that plus your shooting skills along with a determined mindset. Being in this position will allow you to quickly spot trouble with any of the men behind Jones and myself. Jones, what do you think?"

"I agree. The other boys will do just fine, but putting Mister Smith and Jingles back there will give us an added edge on the field."

Smith says, "Joel, when do we begin practicing with real ammunition?"

"First, I want to do several run throughs with both squads as soon as possible so everyone knows what the wedge really looks like. Getting the spacing down pat, adjusting to the speed we're building up to, as well as how much coordination is needed when we make the roll to come back on the next target run. They'll need to have this well practiced when we start shooting real bullets.

"The wedge is not the only maneuver, but it's the best one for our small group, teaching us to fight together from horseback, bringing the most concentrated fire power to bear on a charging band of Indians or rustlers while at the same time protecting our flanks, giving us an edge. Jones, pick a spot for us up ahead. I'll set up the area and then tell me when we can do this, at which time Cookie and Wrangler will need to be in the saddle."

"Joel, I know this country. There's a good spot about five or six miles from here. You can ride up with me and begin setting it up as I go back and get the herd to a place where we can bed 'em down for the night and get about our training. I want to keep the cattle close to schedule as possible. So far we haven't lost much time, due to your tight scheduling, which I appreciate."

"I understand. I certainly don't want to lose ground either, 'cause if and when we encounter these raiders, it will probably cost us a couple of days or more, depending on how hard they hit us and how well we hold them off so the herd doesn't scatter from here to who knows where.

"One more thing. I want us to be ready before we cross the Red River, 'cause I'm fairly certain after that crossing is when the Indians will start scouting the herd. I want to keep the element of surprise on our side, so we'll not be doing any open practicing unless we're absolutely positive we're not being watched."

The training schedule along with practicing progresses to live ammunition with continual rehearsal runs for both groups. Joel's pleased with the progress, even with an occasional hitch or error now and then. That's what this is for, to strengthen areas of weakness as well as improve riding and shooting skills. The training continues throughout the drive as they make steady progress toward the Red River.

A More Harmonious Outcome

wo days' ride from the Red River, Joel notices that at certain times Cookie will play a few hands of poker with the cowboys after supper, always winning a little but never a lot. Joel's curiosity gets the best of him, so he approaches the cook when nobody's around.

"Cookie, it appears to me you know a lot more about gambling than you let on. I notice you fold more winning hands than you play, never going all in. Now why is that?"

"Joel, you're a lot more observant than most of these men, but I've yet to see you play a hand. Either you're pretty wise to this game or just naïve, thinking you don't know enough about poker to play. So what I got to say is just between you and me, You strike me as a fellow who minds his own business, can be trusted, and wants to learn what this part of life is all about.

"I've been a gambler, at one time a pretty damn good one, until the day I broke a friend of mine who was trying to run a bluff on me. He bet his farm, I called his hand, he got angry, went storming out before I could tell him I really wasn't going to take his place, just wanted to teach him a lesson about never betting the farm in any game.

"Well, before I could tell him, he shot himself out of guilt for losing everything his family worked for. So when I play poker these days, I win a little bit but at the same time try to keep these cowboys from going broke, maybe teach 'em a thing or two before they get their hard-earned money at End of Trail. However, most of them don't listen and wind up broke, looking for the next job.

"It's part of my job to help the boss keep these men satisfied on this long drive, so besides feedin' 'em, the aim is to strive for a more harmonious outcome when we play poker. Most of these men know nothing about playing the odds, when to stay, draw, fold, or walk away. I'm not about to take advantage of their ignorance. These men are my friends, and I'm not into breaking my friends."

"Now I understand. By the way, I know Cookie's just a nickname, so what's your real name?"

"It's Brad Dalton. I'd appreciate if you wouldn't let the others know 'cause somewhere out there somebody might be lookin' for that name."

"I'm not into spreading things or rumors that are none of my business, so Cookie it is."

Everything in Texas Will either Eat You, Bite You, or Stick You

After completing his late-night duty riding herd, around four in the morning, Joel is relieved by the next rider and returns to camp. One of the jobs upon returning is to wake the cook, who begins preparing breakfast so the men can be fed and in the saddle by sunup.

After putting his horse with the remuda, Joel grabs a lantern and heads to the chuck wagon where Cookie's supposedly asleep under it. When Joel approaches the cook, he senses a problem, as the faint light from the lantern reflects off of Cookie's face, showing he's not only awake, but wide eyed, and he appears to be frozen stiff and in a fearful state. Cautiously approaching, Joel slowly leans over and in a quiet voice says, "Cookie, what's wrong?"

Whispering, so as not to move, he says, "There's a rattlesnake in my bedroll under the blanket."

"Where exactly is the snake?"

"He's down by my feet."

"You just lay still. Don't move. I'm going to get 'em out." Trying to figure out the best way to do this without Cookie making a move, Joel remembers how good a poker player Cookie is. He tells him, "Now to get your mind off what I'm going to do, I want you to think about the greatest poker game you ever played, the best hand you ever held or the biggest bluff you ever ran. I had an ol' army sergeant tell me when you bluff, you got to be focused, no expression, not giving away your hand, and that's exactly what I want you to do now. Run the best bluff of your life. I'll get this snake out of here without you getting bit. Understand?"

In a whisper, he says, "Yeah, but get to doin'. I got breakfast to fix."

As Cookie begins recollecting about his best bluff, Joel sits the lantern on the ground about six feet away from Cookie's feet. He stands next to Cookie's side, leans over, raises up the bottom corner of the blanket slowly, and eases it back toward him. Joel wants that damn ol' snake to think he sees daylight from that lantern so he'll head toward it with nothing in his way to make him want to coil and strike."

Joel leans over Cookie from the side by his legs, away from his feet. He reaches over and gently grabs the opposite bottom corner of the blanket, lifting it up very slowly, pulling it back toward him, making sure if that snake strikes, it'll be at the opening in front of the blanket, not at him or Cookie. As Joel hoped for, that snake slithered out from under the blanket toward the light, heading in the direction of the rocky outcroppings by the campsite.

"Cookie, lay still a bit longer while I finish pulling this blanket off, making sure there ain't any more of 'em in there." Satisfied, he says, "Well, it's clear. You can get up now."

"Joel, I got to get me a smoke before I get breakfast started. That was a smart, calm way you handled this deal. If I can ever do anything for you, just let me know. By the way, I'd appreciate it if you wouldn't let the cowhands know what just happened, as they might want to tease me in a way I might not like 'cause I hate snakes. I'm getting a real anger in me about rattlesnakes. Plan on killin' every one of those sons a bitches I find!"

"You got it, Cookie. This little episode is between you and me. Maybe sometime you can teach me the finer points of poker, so I can at least hold my own in a game. I want to know what to look for when I run up against one of those slickers or card sharks that always seem to take these cowhands to the cleaners."

"I owe you, Joel. We got a deal, so the next break we git, your poker education begins. Now I got to get to cookin'."

Cookie's Revenge

ookie begins his vendetta against rattlesnakes, killing every snake he sees. There are a lot of creeks and rocky ridges and prairie in the path of the cattle drive, so snakes are not hard to find. At this time, Cookie's revenge is only noticeable to Joel, who smiles, not letting on to anybody else what the cook's up to. However, he begins sensing something else is going on here.

"Cookie, I've been watching you some. It seems to me you've been killing a lot of rattlers. Now what's going on, as I don't see any dead snakes laying around."

"Joel, when I kill these snakes, I'm skinning 'em, keeping their hides, putting their rattles in a jar. When we get to a large town with a hat making shop, I'm planning on sellin' those skins for hat bands and the rattles for novelty items to any merchant who's looking for a way to make some extra sales. Hell, maybe even trade 'em to some Indians for something. I figure it's one way I can git me an extra stake set aside for when I might need it."

"Well, Cookie, seems okay to me, but what are you doing with the carcass after you skin 'em? Feeding it to the vultures?"

Cookie, a bit sheepish, says, "I'm disposing of it so it won't go to waste."

Joel, with a surprised look on his face, says, "Just make sure you bury their heads so these cowboys or their horses won't be stepping on those fangs. They still got poison in 'em. We can't afford to lose any one due to snake bite from a dead snake. Besides, you probably don't want these boys figuring out what you're doing. By the way, Cookie, what's for supper?"

It Ain't Chicken

The trail drive is about halfway, and some of the provisions are getting short, as it's almost impossible to pack enough for the entire drive. The thinking is to get what's needed along the way. However, because of some shortages, the men are starting to complain about not having any meat with their beans and biscuits.

Jones, the trail boss, gathers them together. "Men, I know it's tough when you're used to eating beef with your meals to go without. However, we can't be killing any cows for meat now; we need to save all we can for the market. You're gonna have to eat an extra helping of beans and biscuits. That's what we got the most of right now. Just as soon as I can, I'll see about getting some bacon to toss in the pot with those beans."

"We understand, boss, but the sooner we can git some meat with our beans, the better us boys will like it."

The next night when the riders come in for supper, anticipating the same beans and biscuits, Davy joking calls out, "Cookie, what's for supper?"

"Boys, I've got a special treat for you tonight. I was rummaging around in the chuck wagon and found a slab of salt pork I'd stored away to use as a last resort when times got a little tough. I figure that time is now, so I've cut up some of it, put it in with those Pecos strawberries you all've been eating every day, and added a little seasoning, hoping this will help fill your bellies for the time being. Now if you'll git in line, I'm ready to dish it up."

Eagerly, the cowboys grab their tin plates and step in line. Cookie begins dishing out the beans, biscuits, and coffee to each of them. They each find a place to sit and dive in.

Jones looks up at Cookie after taking a few bites, causing Joel and Cookie to be on guard when he speaks. "Cookie, this really hits the spot, just pretty damn tasty, but I don't ever remember pork tasting like chicken. I'm going to have to have me an extra helping of this if you've got enough."

"You bet, boss."

From around the campfire, several others speak up. "Save some for me, Cookie. This is to my likin'."

"You cowboys just help yourself until she's gone. Glad you like it."

It isn't long before the pot's empty and the hands are treating Cookie like a hero. Joel, quietly with a grin on his face, sips his cup of coffee, thinking this probably isn't going to be the last meal where the skills and persuasion of a good cook miraculously make what appears to be pork taste like chicken.

Mister Smith calls out to Bob, "Hey, Bob, how about gettin' your guitar, and you boys sing us a couple of good songs celebrating this feast, maybe something like the 'Old Chisholm Trail' or 'Jake and Rome.'"

Hank chimes in. "Don't forget 'Git Along, Little Doggies.'"

Out on the prairie, under the stars, sitting around the campfire after having finished Cookie's chuck wagon special, the cowboys are at peace once again, with a full belly, joyful camaraderie, and a couple of tunes.

They begin curling up in their bedrolls, and those riding night herd are feeling a sense of contentment, not only within themselves, but in the cattle as well.

The Lessons Begin

After supper one night, Joel approaches Cookie. "Okay, Cookie, I'm ready to learn some about this game of poker without losing my wages the hard way."

Cookie looks at Joel to get a read on how serious he really is. Satisfied, he says, "Can you add, subtract, multiply, and divide?"

"A little."

"Well, that's more than most of these boys can do, which means you got a better chance of walking away with some money in your pocket so those other fellers will have a little less in theirs. Do you know what each possible winning poker hand is, its ranking? Such as a pair, two pair, three of a kind, straight, flush, full house, straight flush, four of a kind, royal flush?"

"Only because I played some small-time poker in the army, meaning I paid for those lessons."

"Good, 'cause I want you to take this deck and start learning to figure the odds of drawing the one needed card for every possible winning poker hand. Begin with two pair. Figure out what the odds are of drawing one card to hit a full house. I'll give you an example. There are fifty-two cards in a deck. There are four possible cards you can draw to make a full house, meaning you have a one in thirteen chance of drawing a card to make that hand. Not very good odds. However, your odds improve when drawing one card to a flush; one in four chances of filling the hand. You figure out how I came up with those odds.

"When you do this, forget about the cards already dealt. Just focus on the total cards in a deck, fifty-two. Do the same with each hand. When you can give me the odds of filling any of the possible winning hands without thinking or hesitating, then we'll talk about the next step. Knowing the odds is what it takes to win; without 'em you'll be just another cowboy ready to be fleeced by the slickers. Plus, this will be a good way to pass the time and exercise your mind when riding out there.

"When you got this down pat, then you'll be ready for the next lesson where we'll get into readin' the other players, bluffing, when to stay, when to fold, knowing when you're up against a card shark or a stacked deck. Then I'll teach you to spot not only the slickers, but the tricks they use that most cowboys know nothing about, including marking cards, wearing shaded glasses so you can't see their eyes, or palming certain cards to slip into their poker hands to give 'em the winning hand. It's time to turn in as morning comes pretty damn early."

Throughout the trail drive when time permits, Cookie continues with Joel's poker playing education, teaching him such things as how to become aware of when there are two players in a game working together to fleece the other players, where the sharks carry their pocket guns, as well as what body gestures indicate they might be reaching for trouble.

He wants Joel to have a better than even chance at winning and at the same time stay out of trouble. He tells him to never take a man's last dollar; leave him with some dignity. Never try to win it all, just enough so they'll keep coming back. Cookie compares this to driving cattle to market. Go slow and steady toward the payoff. This way they'll never think of you as a sharpie, just a cowboy who's had a string of good luck.

Other pointers deal with reading the other fellow's facial expressions and eyes, without giving away any telltale signs of your own. Usually when someone has a good hand, the pupils of their eyes widen, indicating they're holding something they like, or if they wrinkle their forehead, it might indicate they don't like what's in their hand. If they are getting ready to make a big bet, their noses might flare like an ol' bull whose got his eye on a young heifer or his competition.

"One last point, Joel. The life of a gambler is not one to chase 'cause the odds will eventually catch up. Learn to play to put few dollars in your pocket, not piss it away like most of these cowboys do, especially if you want your own ranch one day. When I think it's time to sit in on a hand or two with the men, I'll let you know."

"Thanks, Cookie. I'll get started tomorrow."

Throughout the drive, Joel practices the things Cookie taught him, especially concentrating on playing the odds and reading the other players. In addition, he constantly reviews the signs to look for when someone's not being totally honest when playing the game.

With the long days and short nights, there isn't much time to play in camp. Most of the time the cowboys are bone tired, ready to hit their bedrolls after supper. But with Cookie's tutoring when he can, Joel's skills and knowledge of the game show steady improvement. Joel wins a small sum at times in their campfire games and loses just a little at other times, never winning or losing big but testing Cookie's lessons, preparing him for a higher stakes game, possibly in Dodge City.

"Joel, you've just about learned all I can teach you without actually getting into some bigger games 'cause that's where your learnin' will really pay off. Just remember there are certain principles that'll help you succeed in this game, and ignoring them will bust you. So remember what I taught you and keep practicing."

PART III
Red River and Indians

The Warning
Plan of Attack
Epilogue

The Warning

Everything on the trail drive has gone reasonably smooth for the first three weeks, bringing the herd within sight of the Red River, where they'll pick up the Western Trail on the other side of what will later be known as Doan's Crossing and then head northward toward Kansas. The Red River on the northern border of Texas is well known to Jones, having learned on past drives how deceiving it can be to trail drivers if they don't keep their wits about them.

Although majestic as the river appears within its banks, the height of the red waters from previous risings left its marks high on the trees lining the banks, along with driftwood caught in the branches, a warning of what might be expected if taking the Red River for granted. Jones understands the river has no conscience, a total disregard for life, human or animal, as drowning and quicksand await the careless drover and his herd who fails to heed the obvious signs of potential danger. His job is to be aware of the risk, pick the right time and place for crossing, and then get the herd and men safely over to what's often referred to as No-Man's Land on the other side of the Red River before picking up the Western Trail through the Indian Nations to Kansas.

Jones has the men working well together at this time with very little discord, keeping everyone focused on the main objective, doing their jobs, and getting the longhorns to Dodge City. The experienced hands and the young ones have begun developing a healthy respect for one another, making Jones's job easier, not to say there isn't the usual poking fun between the young whipper snappers and ol' timers. That's the way it's always been. Occasionally, Bob will break into a guitar-strumming rendition with Mike adding a soulful sound from his harmonica of "Red River Valley" while sitting around the campfire.

As the herd approaches the Red River, three cowboys are seen crossing headed south. Jones hollers, "Where you boys headed?"

One appears to be the leader and rides toward Jones, reins up. "We're goin' back to Texas. We lost our herd to Comanches up ahead."

Jones goes on the alert. "Boys, how about coming back to camp with me? I want you to tell Mister Smith, the owner of this herd, what happened."

"Sure, but can you spare us a hot meal? We been ridin' pretty hard to get out of this godforsaken territory, praying we get through the Nations without losing our scalps. We haven't taken much time to stop and eat, only had some jerky in the saddle, hoping we could make it to some place safe. Plus, our horses need a rest."

"You bet. Follow me."

In camp, Jones takes them over to where Sam's sipping a cup of coffee. "Mister Smith, you need to give a listen to what these men got to say. They've been up north on the trail ahead of us. Lost their herd to marauders and are headin' back to Texas. They're wonderin' if they can get a hot meal, some coffee, and a little rest before they light out again."

Sam hollers out, "Cookie, fetch these boys some food. They don't look like they've eaten right for several days. Jones, get Joel. I want him in on this."

"On the way, boss."

"When Jones and Joel get back, I want you boys to tell them everything you can think of about what happened so we know what we're headed into. Eat up, and later you can throw your bedrolls by the fire, maybe get yourself a decent night's sleep."

"Thanks, Mister Smith. I'm Pete Winters, the drover on that drive."

Joel and Jones walk into the powwow, pour themselves a cup of coffee, and sit down.

"Gents, this is Joel Richards, one of my top hands who's had a little battlefield experience. I want you to tell us everything that happened."

"Mister Smith, we lost part of our herd plus four men to the Comanches in the Nations about fifty miles north of here, and the rest of the herd to a bunch of rustlers who killed three more of our crew. We started out with ten men, only the three of us left."

Joel speaks up. "Men, this is important. You got to tell me everything you remember, all you saw and heard on the ways they attacked the herd. Where did it happen? How were they able to get past your riders and scatter the herd? Exactly how were they able to ride up, surprise, and kill four of those riders? How many were there? What did you men do to stop them?"

The cowboys, after reflecting a bit, let Winters explain.

"Between the three of us, we been over this whole attack and raid a dozen times. It was the damnest thing any of us have ever been through. Those savages, there must have been twenty or twenty-five, popped up over a ridge in front of us, spread out like a cavalry charge, yelling, firing their guns, riding at us in a dead gallop. When that happened, the men panicked, took off to save their own necks, forgetting about the herd. When we scattered, some of those Indians took after the closest cowboys who must have gotten disoriented and became easy pickin's. Were shot off their horses and scalped. By that time, the rest of the Indians had ridden into the herd, driving 'em toward the arroyos and hills.

"After they were gone, I was able to get the men back together, bury the ones who lost their lives, and round up what was left of the herd, about nine hundred or a thousand of 'em. We were able to get moving again toward Kansas, but most of the men wanted to turn back. However, we were between a rock and a hard place. The trail back was just as dangerous as the one ahead, so we gambled, kept moving."

Joel says, "Tell me about the rustlers. Where did it happen? How they were able to steal the rest of the herd? Did they attack like the Comanches or ambush you?"

Pete again takes the lead. "My guess it was about fifty or sixty miles north of the Cimarron because after crossing, we'd been on the trail about five days. It happened around one or two o'clock in the morning on a moonlit night about a half-hour before the two men on night herd were to be relieved.

"Those thieving bastards must have known we were coming 'cause after we'd bedded down for the night and were asleep, part of the gang hit the camp in a surprise attack, killing two of my men in their bedrolls who didn't have a chance to defend themselves. Roped and pulled over the chuck wagon, only stayin' long enough to scatter the horses, keeping the rest of us from mounting up. Being surprised like that, those of us who hadn't been shot hid ourselves in the dark.

"They left the camp. Must have rejoined the rest of the gang, which hit the herd at the same time, surprising the night herders, gunning down one of 'em and driving off the herd. When daylight came, only the three of us were left along with four horses we were able to round up. We quickly buried our dead, grabbed what supplies we could from the turned over chuck wagon, saddled up, and got the hell out of there."

Joel says, "About how many were in that gang would you guess?"

"About fifteen as near as we can figure. I think if they'd had more or realized how shorthanded we were, they might have hit us in the daylight."

Joel says, "Anything about 'em you can remember might give me an idea of what they looked like? Their horses, anything? Were they a ragtag bunch or seemed to be highly disciplined?"

"There is one thing. When those riders rode down on us in camp, one of 'em was outlined by the campfire and moonlight. He had a mustache with a patch over one eye, barking orders to his men like an army major, wearing some kind of uniform with a plume or feather in his hat like an officer might wear. It was that son of a bitch who shot those men in their bedrolls. I've seen some mean bastards, but this one took pleasure in his work."

"You recall anything else?"

"No, boss, that's more than we remember. We were just trying to save our asses."

Sam speaks up. "I admire your courage for pressing on after the Comanche attack. It had to be impossible to ward off that gang even if they'd chosen to attack in the daytime."

Smith continues, "Since you men been through this, any of you willing to join up and help us out? I'll pay you working wages just like I do my own men."

"Mister Smith, speaking for the other men, we appreciate it. However, we've had enough. Want to get back to Texas and tell those folks what happened. We're going home broke, disgusted, feeling shame, knowing what this will mean to 'em. They put their trust and hope in us drovers to get their cattle to market 'cause they needed the money to make it through next year to rebuild their stock. We ran once but feel facing those folks is something we can't ride around."

"Well I respect that, so get some sleep. Cookie will fix you up with what he can in the morning to help you out on your ride back. Before you go, let me know where in Texas you'll be heading."

Plan of Attack

Joel's strategy for dealing with these kinds of attacks will be tested shortly. There's no doubt in anybody's mind now about the seriousness of what's up ahead, Smith, Jones, and the other cowboys are feeling a sense of urgency as the training takes on a real intensity to get them physically and mentally ready for what's waiting for them on the trail. Joel knows this is what Smith is paying him for, even though both Smith and Jones have told him he's developing into a pretty fair cow hand.

The plan is in place. Joel has the men practice a few more times before they get within range of the Indian scouts.

Joel speaks to the cow hands. "If this plan's going to work, it's got to be a total surprise. You boys have got to pull up every ounce of courage you got and follow through with what I've taught you. You ride hard with me, pick your target to shoot, we'll make it through. Every man does his best to cover the back of the man next to him while at the same time facing your enemy.

"Wrangler, make sure we all got fresh mounts available and under us, 'cause when we think we're getting close, I want the boys to rotate more often and keep Morgan in reserve. When I give a signal, you ride him up to where I'm at, switch horses with me, and head on back to the remuda.

"The Indians probably anticipate since we're outnumbered, we'll cut and run. The thing he doesn't figure on is our standing pat, attacking. That's our advantage. Remember our resolve to protect the cattle and our lives is greater than his in trying to take 'em. We all committed to delivering this herd to market. I'm sure as hell not going back to Texas and tell those folks we weren't capable of doing our jobs!"

After the meeting, Red nervously approaches Joel, telling him he's not sure he can do this because up to now it's been more of a game, the practicing, riding, and shooting. He's afraid he'll panic and run, letting everyone down. Joel tries to reassure Red that his riding and shooting skills are now on par with the other boys and how he wouldn't have chosen him for his squad if he thought Red couldn't cut it. Red lowers and shakes his head in a gesture of powerlessness, a lack of confidence and fear.

Joel looks Red sternly in the eye. "Red, you can do this, but if you don't think you can hold up your end, then stay with the remuda. I'll have Wrangler take your place even though he hasn't been training like you have. I'll tell Wrangler to be ready."

After the river crossing with the chuck wagon and supplies, Joel repositions the chuck wagon back alongside the remuda, just off to the side of the tail end of the herd.

He's planning, when the attack is imminent, that Cookie and Wrangler will stay there to guard the horses, although Wrangler will trade off with Red, covering the rear and allowing the cowboys riding drag to move forward quickly into their assigned squad positions. After driving the longhorns like this for three to four days, it'll look natural to anyone scouting the herd without raising suspicion.

The men have been fully armed since the crossing. Now four days into the drive after crossing the Red River, there are trail signs—fresh unshod horse tracks heading in the same direction as the drive, along with distant smoke signals indicating the Comanches may be no more than a day or so away. Under Joel's watchful eye, at the ready, everyone's in position, acting normal without a hint of what they've got prepared.

On the fifth day around noon, Jones alerts Joel, who's riding point off to his right side, saying, "That ridge where the attack took place is less than two hours ahead. I can see it already."

Joel gives Wrangler a hand signal, and he rides Morgan up, switching horses with Joel. Then Joel gradually moves to the front of the herd, replacing Jones in the trail boss position. Jones slowly slides back, taking over Joel's place on point. With this movement, the other cowboys know it's time to begin moving forward quietly without putting any pressure on the cattle. At the last moment, Red rides up, asking Joel if he can have his assigned place in Squad A.

Red says to Joel, "I'm not a coward, but if someone gets hurt bad or killed, I don't want it to be 'cause I wasn't there. I don't know how I'll do, but I got to try!" Wrangler looks at Joel, who nods okay.

Joel responds firmly, "Red, you'll do what you got to do, and we need you. Take your place."

As Wrangler starts to head back to the remuda, Joel tells him, "Wrangler, tell Cookie to keep that Greener handy, and you your Winchester in case some of them come your way. Keep out of sight until they're well within range. Then open up with all you got."

"You bet."

Within minutes of reaching the ridge, the Indian attack comes, straight at the herd as Pete had described and as Joel had planned for.

Joel's plan kicks in as all eleven of the cowboys, including Smith and Jones, follow his lead and form up into a single stationary line on each side of him, in front of the cattle as if preparing for a cavalry charge. The two best guns are Jones on his right and Hank on his left.

Joel quickly calculates the Comanche raiding party consists of twenty to twenty-five Indians who are spread out, riding hard, swooping down, shooting, hollering, and screaming, thinking the cowboys are going to break and run in the face of such a formidable, overwhelming enemy. This way, it'd be easier for them to scatter the cattle and pick off the fleeing cow hands one by one. It reminds Joel of a couple of charges he faced against some Confederate cavalry with their yelling, thinking they were sending fear into their enemy, which would cause them to break and run.

The men are prepared but hoping they'll be able to do their jobs, knowing everything depends on it, including their lives. A couple of the cowboys break out into a cold sweat, and some are trembling as they anxiously await the command, seeing the Comanches are almost within spittin' distance.

Joel says, "Hold your positions. Watch me until I give the order to form up into the wedge."

The cowboys are sweating profusely, as they're facing a fearful savage beyond what they had ever expected. However, what keeps them from breaking and running is the way Joel has taken command. In his calm way, he keeps them steady until he gives the command to form up into the wedge. Joel's final words to the men before the attack is what God told Gideon when he too was facing a superior, overwhelming enemy. "Men, this is what you've trained for. Now 'Go in the strength you have, o' mighty warriors, for I am with you!'"

Surprisingly, a calmness comes over the cowboys. Their eyes grow cold, their faces become taut, and their body language changes from one of fear to one of inner strength. All eyes are now on Joel, watching for his signal, which will be when he begins moving forward, putting the reins in his mouth, drawing his saber with one hand, his pistol with the other, and preparing to charge. His Morgan knows what's coming, quivering with anticipation of the upcoming battle.

At the last moment, Joel gives the signal. They move into position behind him, forming a wedge, with Jones and Hank flanking Joel on each side so they can bring the deadliest amount of gunfire quickly into the charging Indians. Jingles is in the rear position on the right side, because next to Joel, he's the best shot when swinging to his left or right. The very second they form the wedge, they charge the Indians, heading straight for the center where the chief is riding.

Diagram of the Wedge

                    Joel
               Jones   Hank
           Davy   Jeff
        John   Mike
         Bob   Red
      Ben   Jingles
    Smith

The Indians are totally surprised, but by then it's too late to take any kind of evasion action as Joel and his cowboy cavalry hit the Indians hard, with Jones and Hank shooting down the warriors on both sides of the chief. Joel's Morgan rams the chief's small pony, allowing Joel to quickly and boldly cut down the chief with his saber.

The split second the cowboy cavalry break through the ranks of the Indians, Joel rolls his group to the right and back around as Jones, at the same time, rolls his group to the left, joining back up with Joel's group in formation, pursuing the remaining Indians. What's left of the charging Indians scatters, with the cowboys in pursuit, killing a few more before Joel calls them back. Part of his strategy when the Indians break ranks to run is to pursue only a short distance, inflicting as much damage as quickly as possible and then turn back to avoid any ambushes they might be led into.

One of the Indians trying to get away heads in the direction of the chuck wagon at a full gallop, unsuspecting of what's waiting. As he's about to pass within ten feet of the wagon, Cookie, crouching behind his seat, rises up, shouldering a 12 gauge coach gun. He takes a lead on the Indian and fires. The impact knocks the Indian off his pony in a backward somersault, and he falls dead in the dust. Cookie murmurs under his breath, "Damn! The poor bastard never knew what hit him. Maybe best he didn't."

Joel tells the cowboys to stay alert and on their horses, watching the area in case any of the retreating Indians decides to return. He and Jingles check the fallen Comanche, finding four wounded and seven killed. Jingles approaches one of the wounded who's still moving, trying to grab his weapon laying just out of his reach on the ground. He shoulders his

Winchester, pointing it at the Indian's head, but before he can pull the trigger, Joel moves between him and the wounded, telling him the fight's over, there's been enough killing. The Comanches paid a heavy price, losing almost half their war party.

Jingles looks at Joel with fire in his eyes, and then they begin to soften.

"You're right, Joel. It just dawned on me how a man's emotions can feed some pretty ugly actions. This war's over. What do you want me to do?"

"First, bring over one of those Indian ponies. After I patch up his wounds, we'll send him back. Then get a couple of the boys to help you pick up any good weapons and ammunition those dead and wounded Indians were carrying. Put 'em in the chuck wagon in case we need 'em later. Leave their ponies. They can round 'em up whenever they've got a mind to."

Joel will keep Jingles's action and courage under fire in mind for possible future engagements.

Joel questions the Comanche, who seems to understand, speaking some broken English. "Why did you attack us?"

"Our tribe is starving; the buffalo and wild game are no longer on our lands."

"Hold still," Joel tells the Indian. "I'm goin' to doctor your wounds so you can go back to your tribe. Tell your new leader to come under a white flag to not only pick up their dead and wounded, but maybe I can get my chief to give your people a couple of cows to get by on. Understand?"

Breathing a sigh of relief at what this white man said, he says, "Yes, but I do not understand why you not kill me as I would you?"

"It's not always the way to kill one's respected enemy. We must show mercy in our hearts to those who survive.

"Jingles, help me put this brave on this pony so we can send him on his way."

Upon returning to the chuck wagon, a quietness hangs over the gathering until finally Sam speaks up. "Damn! Ol' Pete was right! I've never been part of such an encounter, been so scared and excited at the same time. I've seen some brave men in my day, but you boys stood tall, followed orders under intense pressure, and recovered the herd. Anybody hurt?"

Jones says, "Red got nicked in the arm. Cookie's looking at it now."

Smith says, "Joel, your training and leadership made all the difference, which I think the men will admit. We didn't lose a man or any cattle."

"Mister Smith, they performed well, as did Wrangler, who got these horses used to gunfire."

Wrangler says, "Joel, it was Morgan that made the difference with those horses. Him being their accepted leader, they'd follow him anyplace."

The men are not in a jubilant mood, but quietly in their own way, they express gratitude for being alive, able to confront their own fears of wanting to run in the face of the Indians. Most of them had never shot anyone before, even though they did what they had to during the attack to save their own lives, their fellow riders, and the herd. Jeff and Davy fall to their knees, throwing up from what they've just been through, each experiencing their first encounter with Indians intent on killing them.

Joel spends a few quiet moments with each one of them, understanding because at one time he was in their position. In this one encounter, both of these boys rode hard, shot accurately, and didn't back down, life-defining experiences for each one of them.

Joel says, "Jeff, you and Davy stood tall when it counted. Taking a life is a hard thing to do, but it was either them, us, or the herd. Mister Smith hired us to do a job, and we all agreed to do what it took, and this had to be done. Lord knows none of us asked for this or wanted to be a part of the violence that showed up. You'll get through it just as we will, and we all understand how you're feelin'. You know what you can do, and next time it won't be any easier, but now you've learned what it takes, and that's what will get us to Dodge."

Smith speaks up. "Jones, now that we've kinda regrouped ourselves, we got to get back out there, get those cattle rounded up, head toward Kansas, and get the hell out of this Indian territory!"

"Yes, sir! All right, men, get some fresh horses, mount up, and back to work."

"Mister Smith, some of those Indians are goin' to be comin' back to pick up their dead. I told the one Jingles and I sent back to his camp to have their new leader carry a white flag of peace 'cause we'd honor it if they do, possibly giving them five to ten head of stock to take back to their camp to help feed their tribe. Most of the buffalo have moved out of here. I figured this might be a gesture of peace and good will if you're agreeable."

"Okay with me if you think it's the right thing to do. I'll have some of those slow cows from back of the herd brought up to give 'em because it's looking like they might not make it anyway. Besides, we've picked up more than enough good strays to offset our 'gift' to those Comanche.

"John, you and Bob bring up ten of those slow cows and take them over to Joel, who's going to give 'em to those Indians when they come after their dead. I want you to stay with us, holding these critters together while Joel talks to the Indians. If everything goes right, they'll take over the cows. Then you boys rejoin the rest of the crew, helping get those longhorns back on trail. While you're maintaining these cows, stay alert in case things go all to hell.

"Joel, when the boys get 'em up here, I'll join you when we meet the chief."

"Mister Smith, while we're waiting on those cows, I'm going over to see Red for a minute, and I need to take a little walk after that battle to do a little thinking if it's okay with you."

"You bet. We've all got to deal with what happened in our own way. I'll give a holler when those longhorns are here."

Joel stops by the chuck wagon where Cookie is finishing bandaging Red's wound, asking Red how he's doing. Red tells Joel that was the scariest thing he's ever done, and he's still shaking some. He's glad he faced his fear, did his job, and he extends his hand to thank Joel. He takes it and says, "Red, I'm proud of you. So are the rest of the boys, as it took all us to this. Now we got to get back to getting these cows to Dodge."

Joel walks away from the chuck wagon, leading his Morgan out into the open prairie to deal with his feelings, possibly his own inner demons. He can never get used to the killing. About thirty minutes later, Smith calls out letting him know those cows are ready. Slowly he mounts up, riding back, glancing at the cattle strung out along the trail, thinking one day he, too, might have his own herd to look over.

Smith says, "Joel, it looks like we're going to have company shortly, bearing a white flag. How do you want to handle this?"

"Let's move these critters off to the side, away from the herd, so those Indians can see you and me in front of the cows facing them. That way they should come straight to us. Keep John and Bob behind us and on each side of the cattle."

"You hear the plan, boys?"

"Yes, sir. Bob and I'll do our part."

Five of the Indians are approaching Joel and Smith while the other ten are leading empty horses, heading for the dead ones on the ground. The Indians rein up in front of Joel and Smith as each side looks the other over. The one carrying the white flag speaks. "I am Isa-tai of the Quahadi Band of Comanches, now chief of my tribe. We come in peace to speak to the long knife that killed our chief in battle this day."

Looking at Joel, he says, "I see you carry the long knife, so you must be the great warrior my brave spoke of. It is to you I speak. I am told you allowed him to live as a sign of honor, because the battle was over, and the killing must end. Not only are you a great warrior in deeds, but one who speaks with great wisdom as a chief must."

"You honor me. However, my chief is Mister Smith, who has selected ten head of cattle to give your people as a sign of peace between us."

Smith says, "That's right. We have no desire to fight the proud Comanche, only to get our herd through this territory as soon as we can."

"You do not want to take our lands and buffalo as other white men have?"

"No, we have our own land further south and have no claims on the land of the Comanche or their buffalo. You would honor us by accepting our gift as a token of friendship. In return, we ask there be no more war between us."

"You, too, speak wisely as a chief should. There is wisdom in your words and strength in your promises. So be it. My braves will take these cattle to our camp now. There is a lot of unrest among my people toward the whites because of their greed in killing buffalo for the skins, leaving the body, the life blood of our people, to rot on the prairies in the hot sun. One day if the wanton killing does not end, the Nations will run red with blood.

"Let them know I, Isa-tai, have spoken. Now go in peace."

As the chief rides off with his dead, the cattle, and his braves, Joel turns to Smith. "Mister Smith, I have a feeling this new chief's going to be a force to be reckoned with in the next year or two. He's learned a lesson here, and probably the next herd coming through is going to pay a lot higher tariff than ten slow cows."

"I agree, Joel. Let's hope we can get back to Texas before anything happens."

Epilogue

I t was not the element of surprise determining the outcome but the swift and decisive actions the cowboys took in disrupting the Indians' attack plan, causing them to cut and run. The story of this battle—the bravery, honor, and respect those cowboys showed their enemies—will long be told around the campfires of the Comanche as a reminder they can no longer underestimate the courage and strategy of the drovers.

The word travels fast through the Nations to be wary of the one carrying the long knife and his cowboy cavalry. Consequently, there are no more Indian attacks during this particular cattle drive through Oklahoma. Most of the men on the trail start to feel pretty good about their chances of getting through without another hitch. They've handled the Comanche without any casualties, so what could possibly stand in their way? However, once the drive crosses the Cimarron River headed toward Kansas, Joel starts thinking long and hard about what's going to come next.

PART IV
Cimarron River and Rustlers

The Cimarron River

As they approach the Cimarron and before crossing, Smith calls the men together after supper, telling them another leg of the journey has been completed with some interesting times. Two and a half months ago, they started some two hundred plus miles deep in Texas. They came up the Chisholm Trail across the Red River, through two hundred miles of Oklahoma and up to the banks of the Cimarron.

From here, they will "bend 'em west" toward Kansas approximately a hundred miles northwest of tomorrow's crossing, going along parts of the Cimarron River to the Kansas border, with only about sixty miles remaining after that to Dodge City. If everything goes right, in two weeks they will be in Kansas, and then it's only another week to Dodge. Although everyone's beginning to think about rustlers, Smith tells them to stay focused on the cattle because without the cattle there will be no good times waiting in Dodge City.

Sam takes off his hat and wipes his brow. "Even though we are close to getting out of the Nations, I want everyone to remain vigilant. We've had some luck so far. The Indians shouldn't be a problem anymore, but you never know where some rustlers might be lurking."

Jingles lets out a laugh and says, "I sure don't think we need to worry about a few rustlers causin' trouble. Not after the way we handled them Comanche."

Smith sees a lot of satisfied nods from his men. "True indeed," he says. "You boys are certainly earning your keep. Before we start the cattle across in the morning and muddy the waters, I want everybody to take turns taking a bath, as Lord knows we all need it. This'll probably be the last one you'll get before Dodge.

"Keep in mind, once we get through the next couple of weeks, our sleeping habits will get better, especially when we hit Dodge. Then we can get lots of sleep. So be alert when you're on duty and watch out for each other. Now we've got a bath and river crossing to do first thing in the morning, so let's get some sleep."

Smith likes seeing the smiles on his men's faces, but this isn't the time for over-confidence. He knows that no word of his will change their mood right now, and part of him doesn't want to. The boys did him proud against the Comanche. He needs another way to make them see how dangerous their situation still is. He finds his solution in the form of Joel Richards.

As everybody's settling down for the night, Smith pulls Joel aside.

"What are your thoughts regarding the way these hands are starting up on this last leg of the drive?"

Joel takes a long, careful look at the herd. "They're gettin' cocky. And that's never a good thing."

"That's 'bout how I make it. Listen, soon as we cross the river, I want you to ride up ahead a ways. See if you can get the lay of the land. Even better, find some folks who know the area. They might have heard something."

"Understood."

It's barely sunup on a clear, warm morning. The cattle are beginning to stir, and the men finish breakfast and head for the river to take a quick bath before saddling up. Joel has been told to cross the river ahead of the herd so he can wait on the far bank and keep an eye on everything going across. Moving slowly, Jones brings the lead steers to the front of the herd and leads the longhorns toward the river crossing. After Jones and the lead steers enter the water without panic, the herd begins crossing, slowly and cautiously, up the banks and onto the level prairie on the other side.

Joel's assigned river duty not only to encourage the cattle to keep moving, but also to watch for any cows that might wander away from the herd or get into trouble during the crossing. There aren't many strays, so for what feels like the first time, Joel just sits and watches 2,500 head of cattle in motion. The river isn't deep, which is why this spot's a common ford, but the banks are steep. The cattle aren't in any hurry. After about twenty minutes, the sheer size of the herd becomes clear. Joel shakes his head, almost unable to believe what he's witnessing. Another twenty minutes go by, cattle steadily lumbering down the slope, through the water, and up the other side. Then another hour. And another. Joel nearly has a fit of laughter when he sees the sun almost at its highest point, and the cattle are still crossing.

His acquired roping skills learned along the trail come into play a few times. A couple of the cattle flounder. One gets stuck in the mud. He and Jingles work together to rope and drag it out of its predicament so it can rejoin the herd on the other side. He's found it's a whole lot easier to rope one of these critters when they're stuck in the mud than when they are trying to run away in wide open spaces.

By noon everything has gone reasonably well, primarily because the river's low, affording the cattle little to get excited or spooked about, and they don't feel a lot of pressure from the herdsmen. Slow and easy gets it done.

The chuck wagon and remuda cross at last. Cookie nods to Joel, who remembers that he has scouting duty this morning. He sets to it.

Just after the crew is sitting down to supper, Joel rides into camp. He's tired and thirsty, so Smith dips some water for him before asking how things went.

"I thank you for that drink," says Joel. "But I fear I haven't earned it. There's nothing to report."

Smith can't believe it. "Nothing? You must've run into somebody out there."

"Not a soul. And that worries me." Joel tucks into his supper, chewing slowly and deliberately. After a couple of mouthfuls, he goes on. "There's no reason to think it, but my guess is we're riding into trouble."

Smith must've figured Joel would say something like that, because he's got his next move ready. "I want you to talk to the boys about that. I think they'll listen better, coming from you. Especially if you let on that you've spotted some signs of trouble, without being too specific. So let's assume the worst and prepare them for it best we can."

Soon enough, Cookie and Smith have rounded up as many hands as they can get and still keep eyes on the herd. "I want to change things up," says Smith when everyone's quieted down. "Just a bit. Since we're headed into some new territory. Richards here is going to fill you in." He took a step back, and Joel came forward.

"Most of you noticed I rode on ahead this afternoon. What I found didn't agree with me. We've all heard of outlaws, so we're going to be ready for them. I'm thinking that we have to assume the leader of this band of outlaws has a military background. It's the safest bet. Meaning, he likes to pick his spot to attack, and he utilizes his men for maximum effect with minimum loss. He'll attack when least expected and probably at night. That makes these next few days as dangerous, if not more so, than the Comanche.

"We're still going to keep the wedge as an option in case of a daylight attack, although I don't think that'll happen. We've still got good numbers, which means that a night attack is all the more likely. One thing I want you to remember, all of you, is that just 'cause we're expecting trouble doesn't mean we'll be ready when it comes. We had some luck with the Comanche, but it might just have been that. Luck. Anybody can get lucky. What happens next is our chance to prove we aren't just anybody."

Joel explains how his strategy will work. They will begin by protecting the rear of the herd. Three riders will be on drag, and the chuck wagon will move up front off the point man on the left side of Jones. They want to give any raiders the impression that the cowboys are traveling unarmed, which means the Single Six boys are to keep their .45s out of sight but handy.

Smith will begin lookout duties, working both off his cow pony and the chuck wagon. He will act like he's got some saddle sores and occasionally ride in the wagon where they won't be aggravated. The wagon has the advantage since a man can be inside without being noticed. Smith cut a few peep holes in the canvas on each side of the canopy on the chuck wagon so he won't be seen looking through his binoculars, searching for any movement or riders off in the distance. He can also see out the front from inside the wagon as well as out the back. The object is to see the rustlers' scouts without them knowing anybody is looking for them.

"You boys need to be on the lookout also, as we need all eyes looking for anything unusual going on out there. You see anything, let Jones or myself know quietly so as not to bring attention to yourself. I'll take it from there.

"We'll set up night camp in the most defensible place we can find that won't give our plan away. We want to control the direction the rustlers have to come riding in to attack the camp. If we can do that, we got a chance to make 'em pay the price. Also, when you put your bedrolls down around the fire, wait until the fire dies down and then slip out of 'em and fix your bedrolls so it looks like someone's asleep in it. Then slowly, one by one with your weapons, move back into position away from the fire where you can't be seen but have a clear shot at any riders who try to attack.

"Cookie will place some blankets near where you'll position yourselves. Then he'll throw some extra logs on the fire, making a higher flame so anyone coming in will be more visible and exposed.

"Now one more thing. More than likely, the attack on our camp will be the signal for the other part of the gang to hit the herd. So as not to leave the herd with only two night riders, Hank, Jingles, and I will follow, at a safe distance, the next set of night riders who'll take over the watch when it's time to relieve those there. This will give us two men circling the herd with three of us in reserve, out of sight, close to where I think they might hit. Plus, this will leave eight of you in camp, including the returning night riders, enough to surprise the raiders when they attack.

"When they hit the herd, assuming we'll have enough moonlight to see them, Hank, Jingles and I will plan on coming up behind them quickly, not only to disrupt 'em, but to eliminate as many as we can before they realize what happened. We should be able to reduce the odds pretty fast.

"In camp, Mister Smith or Jones will fire the first shot, and the rest of you show no mercy in your shooting, as those cattle thieves surely won't. Once the shooting starts, we can only rely on our training to hope things go our way."

Joel has run out of things to say. Too many possibilities and too many variables make it hard to plan any further. But from the looks on the hands' faces, he's at least gotten through to some of them.

The Rustlers

The night is quiet. Maybe there are rustlers, still planning their raid. Maybe there's nobody between the herd and Dodge City. Either way, Joel is glad to get moving the next morning. They take their positions as Joel specified, with Jones moving further out in front of the herd to begin scouting the trail ahead, locating a place where the chuck wagon will set up for the night. Whether it's the anticipation—getting close to the end of the trail—or the dread of rustlers is hard to say, but most of the hands feel like the day just won't end. Jones returns, and Joel joins him in the chuck wagon. Once the chuck wagon is in a defensible position as planned, Cookie begins preparations for the evening meal.

Wrangler tethers the remuda, sets up the campfire for Cookie where Joel intended, and then begins locating firewood for feeding the fire late into the night. This placing of the chuck wagon in an unassuming, defensible position, building up for the evening fire, the cowboys placing their bedrolls strategically around the campfire—this will be the routine for the next couple of nights or as long as it takes to get past the danger of a late-night attack by the rustlers. Joel likes what he sees. The hands aren't as talkative as they have been. There's no laughter. The act of getting ready for an attack makes them feel like one is coming. They might feel less prepared, but they're acting more prepared.

Bright and early the next morning, the herd once again is on the move, heading toward Kansas. The chuck wagon's loaded, along with the pack horse. The team is hitched up to the wagon, which begins moving, taking its place up front to the left of the forward point rider, with Mister Smith riding alongside the chuck wagon.

"Cookie, there's a hint of a storm coming in the next day or two. God, I hope it's not a thunderstorm. That's the last thing we need right now—something to spook the herd, especially now that we're so close to Dodge. When the boys come in for supper tonight, I'll have a powwow with Jones and Joel, seeing what we need to do in case of a storm along with the threat of those rustlers. Now I'd better act like there's a saddle sore or two on my butt, climb into the wagon, and start my lookout duty."

"Boss, tie your horse on the back and climb aboard."

That evening around the campfire, Smith, Jones, and Joel discuss the pending storm, which may arrive the next night. "Joel, what do you think? Is there a chance the rustlers will attack during a storm?"

"I'd be surprised if they did. More than likely, they'll attack the night before 'cause they know there'll be more of us on alert during the storm, keeping a watchful eye on the cattle. So beginning tonight, we start figuring they'll hit us any time between now and the storm. Hank, Jingles, and I will begin backing up the night riders like we talked about. These boys are pretty good riders and shooters. Told me they have no qualms about shooting these rustlers from behind to save the cattle and our lives.

"Mister Smith, you and Jones know what to do here. Just because we haven't spotted any riders scouting us doesn't mean they're not out there somewhere. We've got to spot them tomorrow if we get through this night without the raiding party showin' up."

As the morning sun breaks over the horizon, everyone's up, fed, and saddled up, feeling in their bones the rustlers are not far away. The cattle have begun moving, and everyone's taken their position on the drive.

Mister Smith rides for about an hour, circling the herd. He keeps his head low, but the whole time he's got his eye on a rider to the northeast. There's no doubt about it—this rider's moving parallel to the herd, never too far ahead. Smith reckons it's time to get in the chuck wagon, feigning saddle sores. An hour goes by, and the rider's still there, so Smith gets back on his horse and moves up toward Joel.

"Joel," says Smith, "don't look now, but there's a man on horseback riding low on that ridge, about a quarter of a mile from here."

"I thought I'd seen movement earlier over in that direction, although

I hadn't been able to pin it down. Now we know for sure they're in the area and more than likely will hit us tonight. Go ahead, make your circle on the cattle, giving a nod to the men they've been spotted, then rejoin Cookie on the wagon and continue to look out.

"Make sure everyone carries on as usual while I drop back to that last stand of trees we just passed, using the cover to slip away and begin trailing the scout. There's probably two of 'em, one to keep an eye on us and the other who'll head back to their camp before dusk to report where our campsite is located. He's the one I'll follow."

"If they're closing in on us, more than likely their headquarters is no more than a mile or so away. In all likelihood, they'll be saddling up, waiting on the report. I should be able to scout it out and be back here before they begin moving on us."

The Setup

J oel uses the grove of trees to shield him from the ridge until he can move out unseen and begin tracking the scouts. Getting within seeing distance, he dismounts, keeping out of sight, and ties his horse up far enough away so as not to be detected by the rustlers' horses. Using the existing cover, he works his way up to within fifty yards of where they're watching the herd. He was right; there are two of them.

If they noticed Joel leaving the herd, they give no sign. That means they haven't taken the time to keep a close count on the cowboys. It's a strategic error on their part, but Joel can't hope that all of the rustlers will be so foolish. He takes a glance back down below and sees the chuck wagon has stopped. The team is being unhooked and placed near the remuda. The men have begun circling the cattle, settling them down for the night. They leave to report back, rather than one of them staying to keep a watch on the herd, the cowboys, and their backside.

Joel can't believe how easy they're making it for him. Not leaving a man on watch means either the scouts are not very bright or Joel and the men did a great job disguising their plan so nothing appears out of the ordinary. Scurrying back to his horse, Joel circles around so as not to be seen, picking up the trail of the reporting scouts.

Just at night falls, the scouts ride into their camp, past a guard, with Joel not far behind. Seeing the scouts stop at the guard's position, Joel reins up, dismounts, and tethers his horse a safe distance from the camp. Now that he knows where the guard's posted, he works his way around to within hearing distance of the rustlers. Their campfires are burning in addition to a couple of lanterns hanging on each side of a tent where Joel believes their leader is holding up since it has a military look about it.

A man emerges wearing a southern officer's uniform, pistol, saber, plumed hat, and an eye patch. Joel tightens up because he recognizes this man as the same Confederate officer who got most of his own men killed by Joel's Third Cavalry Rangers in their last battle of the Civil War in the early morning hours in 1865!

The two scouts come up to report. "Major, they've bedded down for the night and should be easy pickin's."

The major, in a very stern voice, says, "Perfect. How many were there?"

"Twelve, including the cook and wrangler."

Exactly what Joel hoped for. They'd miscounted; there are really thirteen men. Joel continues to listen as the major speaks. "Listen up. We ride in one hour."

This is Joel's cue to get back to camp quickly, alerting the boys to what's coming. He turns to get back to his horse, only to find two men pointing pistols right at his gut. Behind him, the Confederate growls, "You didn't think we were that stupid, now, did you?"

"It did cross my mind to hope," returns Joel.

The Confederate steps forward to remove Joel's guns from their holsters. As he does so, Joel lunges around behind him, cutting off any clear shot the other two might have. The Confederate is surprised, expecting any man in Joel's position to come along quietly. Before he can respond, Joel has thrown an elbow into his back. Joel kicks the Confederate into the other two, who dodge out of the way but still can't get a clear shot. They call out to the other men, but before anyone can arrive, Joel is already halfway to his horse.

The Raid

Back at the Single Six camp, Jones is getting more than a little bit worried. Richards hasn't returned, and they've lost sight of the scouts. The fire's starting to burn low, so he crouches down so he can whisper to the men. He's about to start asking for a couple of men to go scouting about when Joel rides straight up to the fire.

"We ain't got much time. They were laying a trap for me all along. I got away, but they'll be here any minute. Get straight in your mind, boys. It's either you or them! Wrangler, got my Morgan saddled up?"

"Yes, sir, he's ready, and so are Hank's and Jingles's horses. I held these four back today. They're well rested and got good night vision, along with the ones for Mister Smith and Jones. Their horses will be at the ready when it's time for 'em to meet up with you after we get our work done here with those raiders. I got 'em hobbled so they won't be running when the firing starts. They ain't getting my horses!"

Sam says, "What are we in for, Joel?"

"I counted fifteen. Their leader's an old Confederate soldier I'm familiar with from the war. My guess is, you get him, the rest will scatter. Probably half will hit camp, the other half after the herd."

Wrangler comes with the horses.

"Thanks, Wrangler," says Joel. "Okay, Mister Smith, the camp's in your hands." He mounts up. "One more thing. They're making it easy for us by wearing yellow bandanas. Aim for those, and you'll be all right. Hank, Jingles, let's go!"

Joel and his party leave for the herd. The Single Six men have already arranged their bedrolls to look like someone's sleeping in them, and nobody sees the point in undoing the ruse. They just slowly slip back to their hiding. Sam and Jones take positions about five feet apart where they'll have a clear view of the incoming raiders.

Jones has Jeff, Bob, and Mike spread out on one side of the campsite, Davy and John on the opposite side. By the time everyone's in place, they've formed a horseshoe pattern, hoping the raiders will ride into a crossfire. Cookie begins feeding the fire with logs that should be burning brightly when the raiders attack and then takes his position under the wagon. Wrangler has taken a defensible place to protect not only the remuda, but to be able to bring his Winchester into play when the action starts. It's not long before they hear the sound of hooves on the ground, coming fast.

Reaching the herd, Joel tells Red and Ben, the night riders, "When the attack comes, you boys drop back to that place I told you about so when we scatter 'em, you'll be ready if any come your way. They'll think you're running for cover, which will keep 'em focused on you just long enough to give us time to drop in behind and attack from the rear."

Joel, Hank, and Jingles take their positions far enough away from the cattle in a concealed area where they can fall in behind the raiders before they get to the herd. The men haven't long to wait. Maybe two or three minutes later, a rustling sound is heard, the moon comes out from behind the clouds, and all hell breaks loose!

The raiders ride in shouting, firing into the bedrolls spinning their horses about, continuing to shoot into empty bedding. Between the fire burning and moonlight backlighting the raiders, another kind of deadly hell erupts.

Smith and Jones simultaneously yell, "Fire!" and begin shooting. The others join in, and two of the raiders drop within the first ten seconds. The remaining two raiders, including the captain, turn tail and try to get out of the line of fire right away. Smith and Jones get a few shots off. Jones drops one of them dead out of the saddle, but Smith only wings the other. As the wounded raider vanishes, Smith notices the soldier's hat on his head.

Jones hollers out, "Don't let 'em get away!" It becomes clear that the raid on the camp was planned to be a distraction."

As they follow the rustlers, they fire a few more shots. One hits a horse, and its rider goes down with it. His guns fly out of his hands, and he doesn't even try to pick them up. The rider gets up to run, but he's limping. "Davy, Jeff, get that son of a bitch!" yells Jones.

He doesn't get far. The boys hop off their horses and tackle him high and low. They start stomping, hitting, and kicking him viciously.

"Hold on, boys," Smith yells. "We're going to save him for a hanging as soon as we get back. Tie him up good, spread eagled to the wagon wheel so there's no chance of him getting away. Check and make sure none of those other bastards are alive. If they are, tie 'em up too! Then meet us over at the remuda. We're likely to need the help."

"Damn, that was nerve racking, but we ain't through yet.

Just prior to the camp attack, three rustlers pass Joel, Hank, and Jingles, but before reaching the herd, they spread out and then rein up, waiting for the signal to attack, which will be the gunfire coming from the camp. Joel and his boys haven't quite made it to their concealed positions, but they're close—about twenty yards behind and to one side of the rustlers.

The rustlers spot them right away and start shooting at the same time gunfire erupts from the camp. Joel, Hank, and Jingles are pinned down.

"We can't stay here, Joel," says Jingles. "Sounds like they're going to need our help at the camp."

Joel judges the distance to some trees behind them. It's maybe not too far to make it. "You two keep some cover fire for me. Then wait till those three go quiet." Jingles and Hank reload and lay down as much fire as they can. Joel slinks back to the trees and circles around. In three quick shots, he takes down the rustlers. Now that they're free, Hank and Jingles head for the remuda, where they see another four riders heading toward the herd. Joel mounts his Morgan and joins them.

The rustlers start firing in the air, scattering the cattle while looking for the night riders to gun down. Joel's Morgan closes the gap on the lead rustler, riding up beside him. Joel turns in his saddle facing him. The rustler looks over with a disbelieving look on his face as Joel shoots him out of his saddle.

By this time, the remaining three rustlers figure out they're under attack and begin spurring their horses hard, trying to escape and save themselves. One of them, unsuspectingly, heads straight for the waiting night herders who, following orders, give no quarter, gunning him down. Hank and Jingles catch up with one of the two remaining rustlers who tries to gun it out, but Jingles shoots him first. The other rustler gets away with Hank in pursuit.

Joel hollers out, "Hank, pull up! We don't know if anyone else is lurking out there waiting to ambush us."

Not close enough for a shot, Hank pulls up, returning to where Joel and Jingles have met up with the night herders. After checking the downed rustlers for any live ones, it appears the Single Six boys have done their jobs. Not a rustler's alive except for the one that got away. Luckily, because of their own preparation, the boys again escaped any injury.

Smith and Jones ride up cautiously so as not to be mistaken for rustlers, hollering out, "We're coming in! Don't shoot."

"Joel, did we lose any men?"

"No, sir, these boys rode and fought in such a way that can make us all proud. Even the best cavalry units I've been with couldn't have performed any better. How about at the camp? How did that go?"

"It went better than I expected, not losing a man, gunning down six of theirs, but the one in a soldier's hat got away. I think he's wounded. Joel, you were right about this. It was the element of surprise that saved our butts and put 'em in a panic tryin' to get away. I don't think those boys had been on the receiving end before."

"Mister Smith, we've been damn fortunate things worked out the way they did, but we got one more piece of work to do. That's to get after the ones who escaped, seeing if we can catch them at their camp, eliminating these outlaws from bringing any harm to the herds behind us."

"Okay, Joel. You night riders get back to rounding up the herd. The other men will join up with you shortly. Fact is here they come now. You boys do your jobs, and we're going to finish ours."

Final Showdown

Joel, taking the lead, is followed at a short distance by Smith, Jones, Hank, and Jingles heading toward the rustlers' camp. "Mister Smith, I think the rustlers left one man behind on guard. When we get close, hopefully they won't know we're coming. We'll rein up, and I'll dismount and find the guard. When I do, the shot that gets him will be your signal to ride in, surrounding the camp and shooting any of those who try to put up a fight."

Jingles speaks up. "Joel, let me take out the guard. You don't know this 'cause I keep my personal life private, but I've had a little experience with Apaches and their ways. I've not said anything, as you and Mister Smith always seem to know what you're doing. Besides, it wasn't my place to interfere. But from my Apache experience, I learned a little something about night stalking."

Joel's not surprised by Jingles's admission because his courage and actions implied there was more to this cowboy than anyone suspected, a secret Jingles was protecting. "All right, the guard's yours."

"Joel, I may not shoot him if I can get close enough with my knife. If I can, then I'll come back here, mount up, and ride in with you boys. That way we might be able to ride in a little closer before charging the camp. Otherwise, if I do have to shoot him, I'll work my way down to the camp while you're riding in, maybe give 'em another surprise before you get there."

"Okay, Jingles, we're almost within range of being heard, so any talking from here out will have to be in a quiet whisper." With a hand signal indicating for them to stop, everyone reins up quietly as Joel whispers, "Jingles, we're close enough. Remove yours spurs and start heading in the direction of that faint glow over the ridge where their camp is. The guard should be stationed about fifty yards this side of it, near the trail into the camp. Don't assume he's the only one, so be alert. In about ten minutes, we'll begin easing our horses toward the camp to get as short a run at them as we can. On your signal, we ride."

"Jones, would you keep my spurs in your saddlebags until this night's over?"

"You bet. Until the guard's no longer a threat, let's keep the odds in our favor by not charging into what could still be an armed camp. More than likely, the remaining rustlers will be packing up what they can, wanting to get out of there, thinking those cowboys will be looking after their herd."

Ten minutes passes, and just as the moon slips behind a cloud, Joel, Hank, Jones, and Smith begin easing their horses forward.

At the same time, Jingles, who slipped off his spurs, locates the only guard who's intently watching the trail into camp, allowing Jingles to make a wide circle around the guard to get behind him. Jingles moves silently into position, approaching from the guard's backside. The moon slips behind a cloud, and in true Apache fashion, he sneaks undetected within arm's reach of the guard with knife in hand.

In one swift move, Jingles throws his left arm around the guard's neck in a strangle hold to keep him from screaming and plunges his knife deep into the guard's back with an upward movement to pierce and rupture the heart and organs, causing instant death. Dropping the guard and pulling his knife from his back, Jingles takes a quick look at the camp, seeing only two rustlers, one leaning up against a feed sack, apparently wounded, the other scurrying about, loading up a pack animal.

Jingles quickly moves up the trail to meet Joel before the rustlers realize their guard is dead. Within moments, they meet. Jingles mounts up, telling Joel in a whisper, "There's only two left in camp. One's lying down looking like he's wounded, with a patch over one eye, and the other man's packing supplies. We got a clear run at the camp. The guard is no longer on guard."

Joel nods his head to Jingles and then gives a hand signal to draw weapons and prepare to ride into and encircle the camp. At the ready, having moved as close as possible without being heard, Joel lunges his Morgan into a gallop, with the others closely following.

The one rustler packing supplies is caught off guard. He immediately throws up his hands without drawing his gun, offering no resistance. Joel and the men surround him, along with the man on the ground by the fire. Not a shot is fired.

Joel says, "Hank, disarm and tie up that rustler. Jones, cover our backside by keeping watch while Mister Smith and I check out this one on the ground. Jingles, check the camp to make sure no one else is here!"

Approaching the leader who's propped up against a sack of grain with his hands in his lap, Joel first removes the wounded man's pistol from his holster and then asks, "Who are you?"

"I'm Major Beau Clarkson of the Confederate Army of America. You will address me as sir!"

Smith says, "Wrong! The war's over, and you're no longer in the army, just a thievin', murdering bastard. You don't deserve to be addressed as sir."

Joel says, "He's a disgrace to his country and the cause he fought for. He's become a rustler, murderer, and you can bet justice will be served."

The major exclaims, "Justice? Well, whatever you men got the guts for. I see by the saber on your saddle you were in the Union cavalry, so the rumors are true. You're the long knife the Comanche sing about. I knew it couldn't have been any dumb-ass drover who planned this campaign against us; it had to be a cavalry trained man. Obviously you were the man. What was your rank?"

"I was a first sergeant."

"A sergeant! Now I know who you are. You're that Yankee bastard that ambushed my troops on that road in the Civil War. Here I thought we were up against General Sheridan himself, and instead I find out we were beaten again by a fuckin' cavalry sergeant, son of a bitch!

"Well ... what are you gonna to do with me? Haul me to Dodge and turn me over to the sheriff?"

Smith says, "No, Captain, we're not going to take you to Dodge. We're going to hang you!

Hank, get some rope, tie him up, and forget about his wound when you do. I want the pain from my bullet to be part of his punishment. The hanging will be the rest. Joel, let's check out the tent and equipment and see what else these boys been up to. Whatever of value we can use, we'll, what's the word, confiscate?

"Anything we find to identify these rustlers we need to take with us and turn it over to the law so they know the trail's going to be a little safer travelin' for a while."

Smith and Joel head toward the tent when Hank comes back with some rope and starts tying up the captain's feet. Unseen and unbeknownst to Joel and Hank, the captain has hidden a short-barreled Colt .45 with a bird's head grip under his leg by his thigh. As Hank is tying up his feet, the captain grabs the Colt and shoots Hank in the head at point-blank range.

With the shot, Joel, still with pistol in hand, whirls around, dropping to a crouched position, shooting the captain before he can take aim at anyone else. By this time, Smith brings his gun to bear, firing another bullet into the captain, who jerks, dropping his gun, and dies.

Hurrying over to Hank, who's lying motionless on his back with his eyes open, Joel, Smith, Jingles, and Jones can't believe what just happened. After all the planning, execution, and capture of the leader, they failed to search the captain for any other weapons.

Joel says, "Damn! I'm sorry, Hank. It's my fault for not looking for another gun. I should've known he'd pull something like this."

Smith says, "Joel, it's all our faults. We got careless for a moment, thinking we had 'em whipped."

Jones says, "Mister Smith's right, Joel. We all should have known better."

Jingles says, "Hank was a friend, a hard worker, and a damn good cowboy. I know he wouldn't want us to hold his death as our fault. That's just the way he was."

Smith says, "After we're finished here, we'll take him back to camp, do a proper burial. Then we're goin' to hang these bastards, including their dead leader. I'm gonna make an example to others who might follow their path, including my men, in case any of them think this is an easy way to make money."

Joel says, "Mister Smith, I'm not sure in my own mind hanging's the thing to do."

"Joel, I've made up my mind. This is one decision I ain't goin' to change, especially now. So let's get to looking over their stuff, then get the hell out of here back to our cattle."

"You're the boss," says Joel.

In the tent, along with some other items, Joel and Smith find a money box.

"Joel, there's about $7,500 here along with a receipt for the cattle they've stole and sold. The date on the receipt tells me this money was probably for the herd they stole from Pete's drive. I'm going to take it back to Texas and locate Pete so he can get this money to the folks who lost their cattle to these rustlers. Not near what the herd was worth, but at least they'll get something."

Joel nods. "It seems the right thing to do."

Jones comes in and says, "Mister Smith, Jingles and I found a couple new Winchesters along with a case of bullets these rustlers been carryin'. Wonder if we can split the guns and ammunition up with our boys? There'll be some other guns from the dead ones we can also give 'em. One more thing we found; these rustlers been eating pretty good with lots of eggs, bacon, steaks, and some pork slabs on that pack horse. How about us taking the food stock back to Cookie?"

Joel says, "Mister Smith, if it's all right with you, I'd like to keep the captain's .45 he shot Hank with as a reminder to never take anything for granted."

"I got no problem with what you boys want to do with the guns. However, we'll take their horses, tack, and anything else helping to identify these rustlers with us and turn it over to the sheriff. I know Cookie and the rest of the men will certainly appreciate this food. Bring their pack animal along. Also put that dead son of a bitch of a captain on his horse 'cause we're gonna hang him along with the other two, but don't put him close to Hank. Hank don't need to be any closer to him than he has to. I have a feeling Hank is on his way to heaven, and this bastard is goin' the other way, straight to hell! We've been here long enough. Let's load up and get movin'."

Riding back to camp, Smith says, "You men are the best I've seen in getting a dirty job done. We got Joel to thank for saving our herd and our asses, 'cause if it weren't for him, probably only a few of us might be lucky enough to make it back to Texas."

"Mister Smith, I'm not a hero just because I was professionally trained to do a job to the best of my ability. Your men, including Hank and yourself, are the heroes for not cuttin' and runnin' when things got tough. I'm just proud to work with all of you."

"Thanks, Joel. Now let's get the rest of this nasty work done and get our herd back on the trail to Dodge City."

Tribute to Hank

Arriving back at the campsite, Smith says, "Well, I see you boys been busy gathering up the herd. Looks like we're about ready to go. What do you think, Cookie?"

"Mister Smith, we're all glad to see you men back. We've been wonderin' how it turned out. Our boys been after it since you been gone. I got some hot coffee, beans, and biscuits ready to feed everyone for the work that got done. By the way, I don't see Hank. Oh no, Mister Smith! Is that him draped over the saddle?"

"Yeah, it is. We got to plan on givin' him a proper burial before we hang these thievin' sons a bitches. Get the boys fed 'cause at sunup we got some grisly work to get done. I'll explain what happened later. Wrangler, take good care of these horses of ours 'cause they did their part. These extras are from the rustlers. We'll take 'em along with us to Dodge."

"You got it, Mister Smith. I rounded up the other raiders' horses, put 'em with the remuda."

Jones says, "Mister Smith, I'm gonna make a quick check on the herd. When I get back, let's get this thing done and get movin'. These boys can try to catch some sleep in the saddle once we get those longhorns headed toward Dodge peacefully and orderly."

"Cookie, we brought you back some pretty good fixin's from the rustlers' camp. Make the best of it for the boys."

Smith finds a good spot on a slope overlooking the trail to bury Hank.

"Wrangler, get Jeff and Davy to help you dig Hank's grave up there on that knoll where I marked. I'm goin' to pick up three ropes from your equipment, ride back to that grove a few yards off the trail, and find me a tree."

"Mister Smith, we should be ready in about an hour for Hank."

"Thanks, Wrangler. I'll be back shortly."

In the tree grove, Sam finds a tall walnut tree with a thick limb jutting out about fifteen feet above the ground, a perfect hanging tree. He begins preparing the three ropes for the execution.

When the grave's ready, Smith gathers his men around it just as the sun rises above the horizon, casting sunbeams upon the gravesite where they're about to put Hank's body. After laying Hank in the grave, Mr. Smith gives a brief eulogy.

"Boys, take off your hats.

"Lord, Hank was one of our best hands. I know he leaves many a friend and family behind, so we'd appreciate it if you'd look after him.

"Hank, you're in good hands now. It won't be long before you'll become a top hand with the Lord. That's about the best any of us can hope for. Don't worry about your family 'cause I'll make sure they're takin' care of. Now don't go worryin' about nobody being able to find you either. I'm going to have a gravestone made up in Dodge. On our way back to Texas, we're gonna stop here and place it on your grave. Bless you, son. We'll miss you. Amen.

"Okay, boys, cover him up, put a marker on his grave, say any last words you're called to, and then let's get about takin' care of some unfinished business."

Bob speaks up; "Mister Smith, John, Mike, and I would like to sing one of Hank's favorite songs, 'The Red River Valley,' before we leave. I know it ain't much, but it had some special meanin' for him and his family, especially Mike's soulful version on the harmonica."

Smith says, "Bob, we'll just take the time, as I think that's appropriate, and any of you boys want to sing along, I know ol' Hank would appreciate it."

Trail Justice, the Hanging

"Jones, you, Jingles, and Wrangler get those rustlers mounted like we discussed. Lead 'em back to that tree where I've got the ropes dangling, waiting to go around their fuckin' necks. I want to make this quick and get out of here. Any questions?"

"No, sir, we're ready to get ridin', as we got another kind of storm coming."

Joel walks up and says, "Mister Jones, I'd like to volunteer to stand watch over the herd while you boys do this, if you don't mind. I know you're doing the right thing because in this part of the country lawmen and judges are few and far between."

"No, son, I don't mind. I think I understand. Go relieve Ben and any of the boys wanting to see justice done. We won't be long."

Joel relieves Ben and keeps close to the cattle. There's a distant, pensive look in his eyes. He's thinking of his sister.

The remaining rustlers have their hands tied behind their backs and are placed on horses along with the dead captain and led to where the neck tie party will take place. Smith says, "Get those ropes around their necks, including the captain's. You boys want blindfolds or got any last words?"

"Keep your damn blindfolds. Get this over."

"Then, boys, go to hell! Slap those horses out from under 'em and let 'em swing!"

It's not a pretty sight watching the rustlers hanging from that tree, twisting in convulsions as they slowly strangle to death. The captain's hat with its plume falls off, and Smith picks it up. It'll help the sheriff verify the rustlers' deaths.

"All right, men. We're done here."

At night fall, the herd is bedded down close to the Cimarron, and the boys begin readying themselves for the night watch. Prior to the shifts beginning, Jones gathers everyone around the chuck wagon.

"Men, we've got a storm coming in, but I've got a feeling it may not be as bad as expected. If it does come in strong, be ready to ride. Make sure you get with Wrangler and have fresh mounts picked out and saddled up ahead of time. Keep your slickers handy just in case.

"We'll be riding in shifts of four tonight. As you circle the herd, be sure and let those cattle hear your voices with your harmonious singin' so any sudden noises will be less likely to set them off. If we can keep a bunch of 'em stirred up, on their feet and awake so they don't get rested from the day's drive, less chance we'll have of a stampede. Tired cattle don't run very far.

"Those of you who've been with cattle during a thunderstorm know what can happen in a split second from a lightning strike or the rattle of thunder, so everyone be careful.

"Make sure your bedrolls are under some kind of cover; a wet bedroll ain't my idea of how to get a good night's sleep. If we catch a break tonight, just maybe we can sleep in a bit to help from the past sleepless nights 'cause of those damn rustlers."

There's not much sleep to be had. Joel keeps an eye on the sky, and even without a moon, he can see that the clouds are racing along. He's not the only one who can't sleep. Jones joins him at the edge of the remuda. Behind them, a couple of the nightshift riders pass by. The horses nicker. They're nervous.

A few flashes of sheet lightning set some of the cattle to shuddering.

"No rain yet," says Joel.

"Might not be any," says Jones. "Sometimes these storm clouds pass over before any rain falls." He looks at the herd. "Doesn't mean there won't be trouble, though."

They almost make it through. There aren't any lightning strikes, but Jones can sense the herd ready to explode. He and Joel start circling, eyes on the herd the whole time. "What do you see?" says Jones. "Where's the trouble going to come?"

Joel doesn't know what he means at first. He looks harder, not at any one head, but keeping his eyes on whole patches at a time. He sees the cattle as currents running in the ocean, each with a different direction. Most are relatively calm, just shifting back and forth a few feet at a time. But there's one, on the northwest side, that's got more activity. "There," he says.

"That's what I'm thinkin', too." Jones hails the next rider by, Davey. "I need a horse."

"You out of your mind, Jonesy?"

"It's too far back to get mine." A streak of lightning flashes across the sky. "Now!"

Davey dismounts, and Jones is up in the saddle. He canters over to the northwest side. Joel watches him work, noticing how Jones is singing, though it's so soft Joel can't make out the words. He doesn't follow—doesn't want to disrupt anything Jones is doing.

Now Jones has a lasso in his hand. Another flash of lightning, and Joel is sure there's going to be a stampede. But before the sky darkens, the lasso flies. It circles the horns of one of the cows, and Jones leaps from the saddle, singing all the while. Slowly, the energy from the cows slows and then dissipates. The currents in the herd are all calm again. Joel shakes his head. That's why Jones is top hand.

Morning arrives with the skies clearing. Cookies got breakfast ready, including eggs and bacon, compliments of the rustlers, along with his famous biscuits and hot coffee. Smith fills a cup, looks up at the partly cloudy sky just as the sun's peeking up over the horizon, and says, "Cookie, this breakfast is more to my liking. It sure beats hell out of those Pecos strawberries."

"Thanks, Mister Smith. We'll be having steaks tonight, if the boys are agreeable?"

"Cookie, you got no concerns on our part. We'll be ready."

"Men, it looks like we weathered the storm. It's gone north of here, raining just enough to cool things off. I'd say the good Lord must've been looking after us, thinkin' we've had enough chasing of these cattle around between the Indians and rustlers. He's probably savin' all that rolling thunder and lightning for another time when he thinks things have been goin' too smooth. I don't know about you boys, but those extra hours of sleep makes me feel a whole lot better, plus knowing Dodge City isn't far away. We should have a calm drive the rest of the way. Jones, take 'em to Dodge City!"

"Saddle up!"

PART V
End of Trail

Dodge City

Arriving on the outskirts of Dodge City, a man rides up to meet Smith and Jones. He sits tall in the saddle, with shoulders as broad as Kansas. He says, "Howdy, I'm Jack Shelton, cattle pen controller. Glad to see you boys; we've got buyers here in need of cattle to be shipped to Kansas City and Chicago. It looks like you got here in pretty good shape."

Smith says, "Two questions. The first is where do you want these cattle, and the second is where's the sheriff's office?"

"Tell your trail boss he can hold your herd over in the area where you see that cowboy on his horse. Don't worry about those buyers; they'll find you before you get to town. It won't be long before you'll get down to the deal makin'. When you're ready, I'll lead you into town and introduce you to Rich Turner, our sheriff."

"Jones, you heard the man. While you're gettin' those critters holed up over there, I'm going to take Joel along with the rustlers' horses and belongings to the sheriff. Maybe then we'll be rid of the smell of their rustling, murderin' ways.

"Keep the men busy until I get back, but let 'em know just as soon as we can, I'll start letting 'em take turns goin' into Dodge. Wrangler! Get those rustlers' horses up here with their gear so we can turn 'em over to the law."

Meet the Sheriff

With Jack in the lead, Smith and Joel follow, leading a string of twelve of the rustlers' horses with each one packing empty saddles and what gear Smith thought was necessary to help identify the raiders. On the way to the sheriff's office, several town's people and cowboys have taken notice of this unusual procession. Out of curiosity, they fall in behind the horses, tagging along, wondering what these twelve empty saddles are about. By the time Smith and Joel rein up in front of the sheriff's office, quite a crowd has gathered, surprising the sheriff and two deputies coming out of the office.

The sheriff, not recognizing these cattlemen, looks at the controller. "What's going on here, Jack?"

"Rich, this is Sam Smith and Joel Richards of the Single Six Ranch who just brought a herd in from Texas. These men got quite a story to tell about some rustlers they ran into. It's theirs to tell, so I'd better get back to work. Mister Smith, I'm glad you're here."

"Thanks, Jack. We'll be seeing you later. Now, Sheriff, can we go inside, get this done? I've got some trail hands in need of a good washing up and a drink or two."

"You bet. I have a feeling this is one story I'm going to like." Looking at one of his deputies, he says, "Fred, I want you to write down for our report what these boys are about to tell us."

Sitting down in some chairs next to the sheriff's desk, Fred begins taking notes as Smith outlines the run in with the rustlers, with Joel filling in some of the details. However, they leave out one small detail, the $7,500 found in the captain's tent. The sheriff and his deputies look at each other in amazement, listening, mesmerized, but having trouble believing what they're hearing, how a bunch of cowboys defeated a gang of organized rustlers. After Smith finishes the story, the sheriff speaks up.

"Mr. Smith, we've been trying to run that gang out of the area for months. You boys did something no one else, including ourselves, has been able to do. Forgive us if we find it hard to believe your story. If it weren't for their horses and gear you brought with you, we'd laughed you all the way back to Texas. The gear fits the descriptions given to us by some of the survivors who had a run in with 'em, especially the yellow bandanas and this feathered officer's hat and saber. Plus, you've got enough witnesses from your crew to back it up.

"I'll send a couple of deputies out there to have a look. When we get this report written up in a couple of hours, I want you and Richards to read it over. If it's correct, then sign it so we can formally close this case."

"Well, Sheriff, I appreciate your help. You can deal with the horses and gear in whatever way you think best. We sure don't want to see it anymore."

"Mister Smith, far as I'm concerned, you can sell those horses and use the money for whatever you boys want. Might even be a good idea to take that money, give it to the family of the man who was killed. We'll keep the equipment."

"That's a good idea."

"I'll have my deputies unsaddle 'em and bring them out to your remuda shortly."

"Sheriff, if you don't mind, I'll leave the explainin' to the town folk up to you on what happened, but try not to make us out as heroes 'cause we were just doing what we had to do to protect our property and save our lives."

The Reward

"**M**r. Smith, I'll take care of it. By the way, I didn't see any guns or ammunition with the raiders gear. Know what happened to them?"

"I told the Single Six boys they could have 'em to replenish their own as well as a reward for their courage. I hope that's not a problem."

"No, Mister Smith, it's not, they've earned em. Speaking of rewards, you probably don't know this, but there's a $10,000 reward, Dead or Alive, for this gang. Many tried to claim it and died trying. The money's been put up by the buyers, railroad, and some of our merchants. I'd say you boys earned it. Just as soon as I file this report, the money will be available at the bank."

Without hesitation, Smith says, "Thanks, Sheriff. Joel and I'll be back in a couple of hours. Then I'd like for you to take us over to the bank as inconspicuously as possible so we can claim the reward."

"Mister Smith, I'm not sure how quietly I can do that. Once the word gets out, there's going to be a bit of celebrating of this gang being wiped out, and folks are going to want to know who you are. My deputies and I will do the best we can, but understand you've lifted a load of fear off this town, allowing folks to sleep better because of it."

Joel and Smith leave the office with the sheriff close behind. He stops at the edge of the wooden sidewalk while Joel and Smith move through the waiting crowd, not saying a word. They mount their horses and ride back toward the herd.

Bath and a Gift

On the way back to the herd, passing the Barber and Bath Parlor, Smith glances over at Joel. In unison, they pull up their horses, dismount, tie them to the hitching rail, and head inside. Smith sets up a tab for the boys.

After a shave and a haircut, they're led to the bathing area where they shed their clothing and boots. Sam calls the attendant over. "Would you mind runnin' down to the mercantile and buy us each a pair of pants, shirts, socks, and underwear?"

"No, sir. What size do you gentlemen need?"

The attendant writes down the sizes.

"Here's some money. If it's not enough, come back. I'll give you some more. If it's more than enough, I'd appreciate gettin' some change. And ask 'em if they got any of those 'Boss of the Plains' Stetsons as I'm going to be needin' a couple."

"Yes, sir, I'm on my way."

Soaking away in the tubs, side by side, Sam says, "Joel, I'd forgotten how good it feels to get a civilized haircut, shave, and a bath all at the same time, which makes me feel human again. Damn, I'm enjoying this!"

"I know what you mean. It's almost enough reward in itself. Mister Smith, that was a bit of a surprise about the reward, wasn't it?"

"Yeah, it was, Joel, although it shouldn't have been. You know anytime there are robbers, crooks, and murderers about, the law or someone usually posts a reward. But we were so damn busy saving our hides and watching the cattle, I don't think any of us gave a thought to it, do you?"

"No, the only kind of a reward any of us might've had in mind was just hoping we'd get out alive."

"Joel, I've got to figure out what might be the best use for that money before the men are told. Any ideas?"

"Not off hand, but I know you'll do the right thing. It might be a good idea to talk with Jonesy about it; he's got a good head on his shoulders."

The attendant returns with some store-bought clothes, handing Sam back his money. "Son, these look pretty good. How much did they cost? From the money you just gave me back, it doesn't look like any of it was spent."

"Well, sir, it was a surprise to me. When I walked into the store, tellin' the owner what I was there for, he asked me who these clothes were for. I told him they were for those two men who just brought that big herd in from Texas, the ones who delivered those twelve horses to the sheriff.

"The storekeeper looked at me, called his wife over, told her to pick out some good clothes in the sizes you told me. Then he looks at me. 'Boy, you tell those men these are on me 'cause we appreciate what they've done. Give their money back. If they need anything else, come see me.'"

Joel and Sam look at each other, not knowing what to say. Finally, Sam looks at the bath attendant. "Son, we're grateful, but we can't accept something like this without paying, so you tell that storekeeper we'll be over in a bit to pay him."

"But, mister, he told me not to take no money from you. If I go back over there, he's goin' to think I've been disrespectful in some way 'cause you wouldn't accept his gift."

"Mister Smith, let's just accept his generosity so this boy can keep his honor. We both know he'll be repaid many times by the time the Single Six boys get their shoppin' done."

"You're right. Son, let that storekeeper know we're thankful for his gifts. Our boys will be in later to do some buying. Ask him to set up an account in my name, Sam Smith of the Single Six, and to take care of any of my men who might need something before they get paid. Plus, Joel and me need some new boots and hats. We'll be over later. Oh yeah, tell him he needs to find some forty-dollar saddles. I have a feeling the boys will want to be riding something new back home. Will you do that for me?"

"Yes, sir, and he does have some of those Stetsons on hand and they're about $4.00 each."

Smith looks at Richards smiling; "Well, Joel, I think we can afford to splurge a bit now. " Looking up at the attendant, "Boy, here's a couple of dollars for helping us out, plus I want you to get rid of our old clothes."

"But, mister, two dollars is more than I've ever gotten before. It's usually fifty cents or less. You're payin' too much!"

"No, son, I'm not. You take our money just as we took these clothes. Use it wisely. Now there's going to be some of my crew coming in. I'd appreciate it if you would take good care of them like you have us. Now, if any my boys treat you unfairly, let me know, okay?"

"Yes, sir, I will. Thanks."

Splitting the Reward

Sam and Joel ride into camp. Cookie sees them, acts flabbergasted, and then turns around to where the cowboys are. He throws his arms up in the air, thrashing about, hollering, "Mister Smith, Mister Smith! Oh Lordy, Lordy, heaven help us! Won't somebody get Mister Smith and tell him a couple of slickers just rode up lookin' like they're wantin' to take all our money!"

Sam begins chuckling. "Okay, Cookie, I know you haven't seen us cleaned up for quite a spell, but your time's comin'. Arrangements been made at the Barber and Bath Parlor in town for all the boys. Now that Joel and me are cleaned up, smelling different, it's your turn. So when you can, get to the bath house and take advantage of what they got to offer."

Jones rides up to see what's got Cookie raving on about. Seeing Sam and Joel, he says, "Well, don't you two look like a couple of dudes ready to go out on the town. What's the word from the sheriff's office?"

"Jones, I need to talk with you about that, so let's get a cup of Cookie's coffee, step over by that tree, and have a visit."

Sam tells him what went on at the sheriff's office, the deal with the rustlers' horses, and how both he and Joel were taken by surprise about the reward money.

"Jones, we got to figure out how best to use it."

"Mister Smith, it seems to me everyone who was a part of this should see something from the reward money, including Hank's family."

"I was thinking about that as well as adding some of it to help Pete repay some of those ranchers for what they lost. Okay, Jones, here's what I think I'm going to do. Each man, including myself, who was on this drive will get an extra $300.00 for their part in helping get rid of those rustlers. That's going to leave $6,100 to split between Hank's family and Pete's ranchers. How does that sound?"

"It seems fair. When you and Joel go into town, can I tell the boys 'cause they need to know what's going on?"

"You bet! They're going to have more money in their pockets than they've ever seen at one time. Let's try to keep 'em roped in a bit so they'll have something to take with 'em wherever they might go after this trip. Well, it's about time for me and Joel to go sign the report and pick up the reward money. Would you tell him to meet me over by the remuda?"

"Will do. Keep a good lookout. I'm sure the word is getting out about who's getting the reward money."

Joel and Sam once again rein up in front of the sheriff's office, dismount, and walk inside. They're greeted by Sheriff Turner and his deputy, Fred.

"Howdy, gents, been expectin' you boys. Wanted to let you know everything checks out. The report's on my desk. All it needs are your signatures. Take a read on it. If it's as you recall, date it, sign it, and we'll head for the bank."

After reading and signing the report, Sam says, "Sheriff, we've been out at the camp most of the time. I been wonderin' if the town folks are aware yet and what kind of reception we might expect at the bank."

"Mister Smith, there won't be a lot of shouting and celebrating, just a bunch of congratulations from folks showing their appreciation. Now I have a feeling the town is pretty much yours. Just keep it lawful so me and my deputies don't have to step in and be the bad guys. Understood?"

"Yes, sir. If any trouble flares up, let us know."

"Deal. Now one more thing, Tell your boys there are quite a few drifters, gun hands, and a card shark or two hanging around. That said, let's head over to the bank."

Entering the bank, a certain quiet descends among the customers and tellers as if they're intimidated by these Single Six boys who brought down and eliminated the most notorious gang in these parts. Sheriff Turner introduces them to the bank president, Todd Martin.

"Mister Smith, Mister Richards, it's a pleasure to do business with you under these most pleasant of circumstances. That gang hit us hard a couple of times, and it's taken a while to rebuild. Since Sheriff Turner took over, we've enjoyed a certain amount of safety, and folks, including the cattle buyers, are willing to put their money in our bank. I know you're not here for a lecture about the merits of our bank, so tell me how you'd like the money. All at once or part now and the rest when you leave?"

"We'll take $4,000 now, but I'll wait till morning before picking it up. Then I can begin payin' the boys something until I sell those cattle. We'll probably get the rest when we're ready to leave. I'd like to figure out a way to send the balance to my bank back home so we won't be a tempting target for any bandits when we head back to Texas."

"Mister Smith, we can certainly do a transfer. Just let me know what bank you want it sent to and when. We can confirm the transfer by telegraph. I'll have your $4,000 ready first thing in the morning."

"Sounds good. Joel will be picking up the money. I'll be in to see you later in the day after the tally's been done."

"Mister Smith, you have the town's gratitude and I'm sure as well the drivers of the next trail herd coming in."

Sam shakes hands with the banker and then turns to the sheriff, extending his hand.

"Sheriff, thanks for your help. We'll be talking later."

After shaking Sam's and then Joel's hand, Sheriff Turner says, "Richards, if you ever want to consider law work, I got a position for you here."

"Thanks, Sheriff, but you boys got a tough job; it's not to my liking. Maybe one day, when I finally figure out where I'm going."

Sam and Joel return from the bank, reining up at the chuck wagon where they see Jones having a cup of coffee. "Mister Smith, I need to do a little grooming work on my horses, so I'll be over by the remuda."

Fairness

s Joel leaves, Jones calls Smith aside. "Mister Smith, the boys and me been talkin'. We're of the agreement Joel should get a little more than just a share like we're getting, I know you want to be fair to Pete and Hank, but if it hadn't been for Joel, there might not have been anything to share nor any of us to spend it. You're the boss, so it's your decision. We just wanted you to know how we felt."

"Jonesy, that's one of the reasons I hired you is to keep me from takin' the wrong trail, especially where fairness is concerned. I agree with you and the men on this, so have Joel come see me."

"Thanks, Mister Smith. I'll send him right over."

Heading for the remuda, Jones says, "Joel, Mister Smith wants to see you over at the chuck wagon when you're done currying your horses."

Finishing up his work, Joel heads over to the chuck wagon and pours himself a cup of coffee, waiting on Sam, who's talking with Cookie. Sam walks over to Joel. "Joel let's take a little walk. Jones's been talkin' with the boys about the reward money, and they're one voice on this, thinking you should be entitled to more than $300.00."

"Wait a minute, Mister Smith. They all did their part. Not one of 'em backed down when it counted. That says a lot to me about their courage and character. I know it does to you too. I just want you to be fair with everyone."

"I know you do, Joel, but don't argue with me on this. You're getting $500.00 for savin' our tail's, helpin' us be bigger men than most of us ever thought possible. Accept it, son. One day maybe you can put it to good

163

use." He tells Joel about his intentions for the rest of the money: $3,000 of it along with the $7,500 to help Pete pay off his obligations to the ranchers he represented, and the other $2,900 will go to Hank's family.

Thinking of having his own ranch someday, Joel says, "Mister Smith, thank you."

The Cattle Buyers

Jack comes riding up and says, "Sam, there's a couple of cattle buyers ready to talk with you. They'd like to meet over at the Longhorn Hotel at your convenience. They've got the money, and as far as I know, they're honest men who've been doing business around here for quite a spell. They're a little short on fillin' their quotas of beef, so you should get top prices. They do appear to be in a buying mood."

"Thanks, Jack. Can you give me an idea what cattle like ours are going for before I deal with these buyers?"

"Right now you can expect in the neighborhood of nine to ten dollars a head. Sam, I'm goin' to suggest something to you, and how you use it is your business. These ol' boys have already heard the rumors about what your Single Six riders did to those rustlers. Because of that, I think they're willing to pay a little bit more than the going price just to get their hands on your herd. The reason being is the story those cattle represent will be told all the way to Chicago.

"Sam, this is business, anything you can do to get the best price, I think you got to consider, as an extra dollar or two might make all the difference in your building up the Single Six. Plus I want to see you boys back here again in the next year or two. But like I said, it's yours to do in whatever way you think best. Just remember you're in the driver's seat on this one."

"Jack, you're a good man. I appreciate the information. I'll get Jonesy and Joel. Then we'll be comin' in to do some business."

"Good luck, Sam. We'll talk later."

With a final word to remind the men that tomorrow should be payday, Smith takes Jones into town to look for buyers. The buyers are the ones who'll finalize the count before taking possession and putting the cattle in pens for shipping. Joel rides along with them but Jones decides to go for a bath and shave before the meeting. Smith says, "We'll see you in an hour."

An hour later, Sam and Joel rein up in front of the Barber and Bath Parlor just as Jones comes walking out of the parlor, barely recognizable.

"Jonesy, now that's what I call getting slicked up. It looks like that storekeeper's wife knew exactly what'd look best on you."

"Thanks, Mister Smith. I still got to get some new boots and a hat, but I'll do that when the herd's sold and the money's in the bank."

"Well, boys, let's go get this selling business done so we can be rid of the responsibility of those cattle and start enjoying ourselves for a day or two before we start thinking about heading back to Texas."

Walking confidently into the lobby of the Longhorn Hotel, the Single Six boys have shed their trail riding, dusty, scraggly herdsmen look, giving the appearance of determined cattlemen ready to do business, be it buying or selling.

They're met by two men who introduce themselves. "I take it you boys are from the Single Six bunch."

"Yeah, I'm Sam Smith, owner of the Single Six. This is Jones, my trail boss, and Richards, one of my top hands."

"Good to meet you fellows. I'm Joe Peterson representing the Chicago Beef Company. This is Harry Ferguson of the Wyoming Cattle Company. We're glad you made it to Dodge, knowing you faced some challenging situations. However, we know you're not here to tell stories until our business is completed."

Sam says, "Okay, Mister Peterson, let's get to dealin'. What is it you boys have in mind?"

"Mister Smith, we've taken a look at your herd, estimate you've got about 2,400 head. Only a final tally will tell us for sure. If a deal's made today, we can begin that first thing in the morning. Your herd's in pretty fair shape considering the trip, so here's our offer. Harry, you go first."

"Mister Smith, my company wants to buy five hundred of your healthiest heifers and young cows to take to Wyoming to use as breeding stock for some short horns we've got coming in from Oregon. I don't want to dicker with you, so here's my best offer. The Wyoming Cattle Company will pay you $15.00 a head for those five hundred heifers and young cows. Joe will make you an offer on the rest. Joe!"

"Mister Smith, my company will buy the rest of your cattle for $12.50 a head. How does that sound?"

"Well, sir, I'll take Harry's deal. However, because of the shortage of cattle at this time, I've got to have $13.00 a head for the rest."

"Mister Smith, I'm not going to haggle or waste any more of your time. I need to get some cattle to Chicago. It's a deal. Harry?"

"It's a deal. Mister Smith, if you got any horses to sell, I'd like to talk with you about that as well as whether any of your men might be interested in trailing these five hundred to Wyoming. I've got a couple of men with me. I figure if I can hire two or three more, we can get them to Wyoming before winter."

"I'll have about fifty horses plus those rustlers' to sell, so we can visit about that later. As far as the men are concerned, let me talk to 'em 'cause I know there might be some interest. Gentlemen, do you have some papers to sign so we can get back to the herd and begin preparing for tomorrow's counting?"

"Yes, sir. Give us a minute to fill in some numbers, including an estimate of the cattle to be bought, and then you can get on your way. Mister Smith, after the counting and finalizing the deal tomorrow, we'd like to buy you boys dinner here at the hotel and a few drinks afterwards over at the Long Branch Saloon."

"That's a deal. We'll do it soon as our boys get some of their hard-earned money."

The Wild West Show

On the way out of the hotel, having finished with the buyers, Sam, Joel, and Jones meet a man coming through the front doors who might be a cowboy. However, he's got long, flowing hair, a goatee, and a handlebar mustache and is wearing fancy buckskins, high-top boots, and a tall, ten-gallon hat. He's carrying a pair of pearl-handled, silver-finish Colt .45 Peacemakers in his holsters. He stops them.

"Excuse me, gentlemen. I'm Montana Jack—Indian fighter, outlaw catcher, former frontier marshal, and showman."

A bit taken back at first by this man's appearance, Sam recovers and says, "I'm Sam Smith. This is Jones and Richards. Well, you look and sound interesting, but what does that have anything to do with us?"

"Well, sir, I just stepped off the train from Kansas City, and the first person I met started telling me what you boys did with those Indians and rustlers on the trail drive up here from Texas. I had to meet you and let you know what's on my mind."

"Mister Montana, it'd be a good idea if you could get to the point. We got work to do."

"I have a Wild West Show traveling the east, bringing the skills of the cowboy, real-life experiences, and the beauty of the west to people in Kansas City, Chicago, St. Louis, and points east who've never known what it's like out here. I want to see if we can make some sort of arrangements for the horses and equipment you captured 'cause I think these would be a good addition to my show, using them to do a reenactment of those exploits for folks to see. What do you think?"

"Montana, those twelve horses of the rustlers are for sale, but you'll need to see the sheriff about the equipment, although I'm sure he'd make a deal if the price is right. Make me an offer on the horses, 'cause they're going on the auction block shortly."

"Mister Smith, are those horses strong and healthy?"

"Son, you won't be disappointed."

"All right, I'm taking your word for it. So, right here and now, I'll give you $50.00 a head for all twelve of them."

After pondering a bit and looking at Jones and Richards, who nod their heads in agreement, Sam, knowing he's already cast the line, thinks it's time to reel it in. "Montana, these horses have quite a history, which should help tell a great story in your reenactment of their exploits, especially the three that the rustlers swung from."

"Which ones were those, Mister Smith?"

"It was the bay, sorrel, and the captain's Blue Roan those sons-a-bitches were swung off of. Considering all of this, the price will have to be $60.00 a piece if you want 'em."

Not wanting to miss an opportunity by hesitating, he says, "Mister Smith, you got a deal with one condition. You've got to tell me the whole story of what you boys did on that trail to defeat those rustlers. When I tell the story in my show, I want to make sure it's authentic and the way it was. Now that don't mean I won't enhance and embellish it a bit to put on a good show, but I want to keep it straight and true."

"Okay, Montana, it's a deal. I'll have a bill of sale prepared, verifying where these horses come from. I'm sure the sheriff will witness the transaction. That way you'll have reliable proof if anyone raises a question. Now the sooner you can get over and take possession, the quicker I can get the rest of my work done. Jones was the trail boss on this drive. He can tell you the story of this adventure so you got it straight. You can make arrangements with him when you're ready for the story tellin'."

"Mister Smith, I'll be over first thing in the morning with the money."

"I'll see you then and will have the bill of sale ready. Jones, you and Joel ride on back to camp. I'm going to stop by the sheriff's office, let him know what we're doing with the horses. I'm sure he's looking for a deal on the gear, so it should work out for all of us. Let Wrangler know to have those horses ready for Montana first thing tomorrow."

"Boys, we got a big day, a big payoff coming, so let's make sure everyone stays alert, on their toes till our work's done. Then we can think about enjoyin' the pleasures of Dodge City."

Completing a Deal

Bright and early the next morning, Montana shows up at the chuck wagon just as the boys are finishing breakfast,

"Good morning, Mister Smith. I'm here to get those horses."

"Cookie, get Montana a cup of coffee while he meets some of the boys and we take care of business."

"You got it, Mister Smith. Montana, enjoy some of my best coffee. If you got time, help yourself to some bacon, beans, and biscuits."

"I appreciate the coffee but will pass on breakfast. I had a bite before I came out. Mister Smith, I could hardly sleep last night thinkin' how much the addition of these horses and your story is going to make to my show. I stopped by, talked to the sheriff about the rustlers' equipment last night. We made a deal, including the captain's hat, saber, Confederate saddle, and his holster rig. He did say the captain's personal revolver was lost during the hostilities, which I was sorry to hear."

"Montana, that revolver won't be hard for you to replace. I remember seeing him shoot it in the attack on our camp. It was just a Colt Peacemaker, nothing fancy but deadly. Folks will never know the difference unless you tell 'em."

"I guess that's part of show business. I'm sure I can make a replacement work."

"Montana, I have a bill of sale for these horses signed and witnessed by the sheriff. Do you have something for me?"

Montana reaches in his pocket and pulls out his money, "Yes, sir, I do. Here's $720.00, which was our agreement."

Sam takes the money and puts it in his pocket, "Thanks, the horses are yours."

"Aren't you going to count it?"

"Montana, you and I been in this business long enough to know the importance of our word. We wouldn't be talkin' if I didn't trust you."

"Now that's a compliment, which means a lot to me. If I can take a quick look at those horses, then I'll be on my way. I know you boys got a lot of work to do today. I've made arrangements at the livery barn to keep them until it's time to ship out to Kansas City."

"Wrangler, get Montana his horses so he can be on his way and we can get to work."

Wrangler brings the horses up, and Montana shakes hands with Sam.

"Thanks again, Mister Smith. By the way, there's one more thing I forgot. If any of your boys are looking to get into show business, I could have a couple of spots available, especially for someone who can make sure we get it right when we do the reenactment of the raid."

"Look, Montana, I'd like to have as many of these boys return to Texas with me, but I know we each got to follow our dreams or what we think is our callin'. I'll let 'em know when we're finished here. If any of them are, they can find you. Okay?"

"Fair enough. I'll talk with you later."

Smith says, "Joel, I forgot to tell you, when I stopped by the sheriff's office, he said some army officers from Fort Dodge had stopped by to get the information on the raiders for their records. One of them, a general, remembered your name from the war and planned to look you up. I hope they're not going to get you to reenlist, as we kinda got used to having you around."

"Don't worry about that, Mister Smith. The army's not for me, but I'm curious who this general is. I'm sure we'll run into one another shortly. Thanks for letting me know."

The Tallying Begins

T he Single Six boys, all saddled up, slowly herd the cattle to the
holding pens, where the buyers' representatives begin counting them
as they pass through the chutes.

Joe Peterson of the Chicago Beef Company and Harry Ferguson
of the Wyoming Cattle Company are on hand to witness the count.
Ferguson's boys are culling out the heifers and young cows, moving them
over to another pen for their journey to Wyoming. By the middle of the
afternoon, the tallying is completed, at which time Sam, Joe, Harry, and
their representatives confer on the numbers. After some discussion, they
agree the numbers are accurate and sign off on the count.

Sam expected the count to be a little less, figuring they might've lost a few more head on the trail, plus the ten given the Comanche, temporarily forgetting the 160 strays the boys added along the way. The way it turned out, Sam's Single Six count totaled 2,382, a few more head than the 2,350 they'd started out with in Texas. Hank's count was 142, only losing eight of his on the trail drive, but Sam took eight of his extras and added them to Hank's share. Sam's glad those 160 strays that were looking for company decided to join his herd and follow along. All in all, a good drive with a better survival and arrival rate than most herds' experience.

The Wyoming Cattle Company select 455 of Sam's and forty-five of Hank's heifers and young cows at $15.00 a head. The balance of Sam's 1,919 cattle and Hank's 105 are bought by the Chicago Beef Company for $13.00 a head. Joe Peterson addresses Sam. "Well, Sam, it looks like you had a pretty good drive. I'm satisfied. Hope you are too."

"Yes, sir, I know you boys were as glad to see us as we were to see you. It's good to get this herd sold."

"Sam, Harry and I'll take these final numbers over to the bank so they can finish up the paperwork for both our companies. Your money will be available in either cash or draft, whichever way you prefer, just as soon as you sign the papers transferring title to us."

Harry says, "Sam, just one more piece of business. That's the horses. How many do you have to sell? I'd like to buy fifty or so of those from your remuda."

"Harry, there should be at least fifty, maybe more, for sale. Joel's Morgan and that Kentucky Mountain Horse are his. I know they're not for sale, but his Morgan was the only stud in our remuda. Some of those mares got a visit on the way up from him, so I'm sure there's at least a half dozen, maybe more, that'll be dropping colts in six or seven months. I've got to check. I promised Joel his pick of two of the mares, and I'm going to keep one for myself."

"Sam, I've seen his Morgan. From the looks of him, he comes from outstanding stock. I'll buy the rest of those pregnant mares you and Joel don't lay claim to and take them to Wyoming with me. I'm thinking they'll improve some of our blood lines. Of course I'm willing to pay a bit more for those."

"Fair enough, Harry. One more thing about those horses. After you've picked out those pregnant mares, each of the men who are going to Texas with me gets a horse to ride back to the ranch. After that, the rest are yours, except for a couple of pack animals, which will give you about fifty good horses, including the pregnant mares … providin' we agree on a price."

"Sam, I'll give you $50.00 apiece for every pregnant mare and $20.00 for each one of those other horses you don't keep."

"It's a deal. I'll get a hold of Joel so he and I can get our mares selected and set aside. I'll talk to the boys to find out how many of them are goin' to be leaving with me, and then I'll have a final count. In the meantime, see Wrangler. He can help you determine which ones are pregnant."

"Sam, I think Joe and I are finished here with the cattle, so we'll head on over to the bank. Afterwards we can have that dinner at the Longhorn Hotel."

"Gentlemen, I want to thank you for the way this has gone, better than I hoped for. We'll see you in about an hour after I've visited with the boys. I know they're ready for some bright lights and entertainment now that the work is done."

Payday

The final longhorn's been counted and put into the railroad's holding pens, ready for shipment in the next day or two. The Single Six cowboys ride up to the pens, stopping side by side, taking a long look at the cattle they herded all the way from Texas, showing reverence for those longhorns. They pause in a moment of silence. The moment is brief as the cowboys, as if on cue, roll their horses to the right and spur them into a gallop, heading toward the chuck wagon whooping and hollering.

The boys rein up, dismount, and put their horses in with the remuda. They are met by Sam, who's standing in front of the chuck wagon with his hands on his hips, grinning from ear to ear. The celebration's beginning as they slap each other on the back, shake hands, and congratulate one another for being here for this End of Trail success. Sam steps into the middle of them, sharing in their victory, thanking each one for working with him to make this most difficult of jobs possible.

At this point, Jingles hollers out, "Mister Smith, when's payday?"

Jingles is joined by a chorus of his sidekicks, who are full of anticipation of what's to come. "We're ready to go to Dodge!"

Sam says, "Okay, boys, gather around 'cause here's what's on tap. First, you're all to go down to the Barber and Bath Parlor with Cookie to get a shave, haircut, and a warm bath."

"Now? But, Mister Smith, we're ready to celebrate. I've got an itch that needs scratchin'!"

"I know, boys, but first do this. Now as you're getting a shave, haircut, and a bath, give the attendant your clothes sizes. He'll run over to the

General Store, pick up some new ones for you, and throw away your old ones. You can pick out your new boots and hats on your own. It's all arranged, so when you get cleaned up, got those new clothes on, follow Cookie over to the bank. I'll meet you boys there, and you can line up to get your wages.

"One more thing. When the sale's completed, which will be tomorrow, I'll have the rest of your money along with your part of the reward. In the meantime, enjoy yourselves tonight. Don't get crazy. The sheriff and his deputies are on alert. They're tough but fair. Also Jones and Joel will be around to keep an eye out, but don't get so carried away you'll keep them from having a good time too.

"If you want me to hold some of your wages back until later, I'll do it. Okay, boys, don't spend all that money tonight. Save some of it to take home with you along with those new boots, hats, and saddles most of you have talked about ever since this drive began. Give that some thought while you're bathing. See you at the bank!"

PART VI
Night Lights and Interesting Times in Dodge City

Getting Ready for the Festivities

The Single Six boys line up at the Barber and Bath Parlor, giving their clothing sizes and names to the attendant, who then hurries off to the General Store to place their orders. The storekeeper tells him, "You leave that list with us. I know you're going to be busy keeping those cowboys supplied with hot water. As soon as we get the clothes picked out, I'll bring them over and disburse them to the boys as they get out of the tubs and dry off.

"Thank you, sir," says the attendant. "I'll get on back there."

It's not long before the floor of the barber parlor is covered with shavings and hair from the nine cowboys, keeping the attendant busy sweeping up the floor as well as leading the boys to the bathing area. The barber tells Cookie, "It's a good thing we got that fifty-gallon tank of water heated up ahead of time or the boys at the tail end might be in for a cold bath. Our attendant will do his best to keep up with reasonably clean, hot water."

Cookie says, "Yeah, I know, but I have a feeling those boys aren't going to be spending much time soaking, knowing what's waiting for them on the streets of Dodge. I can hear them talkin' about what they're heading for first."

The storekeeper arrives with a load of clothes and goes to the bathing area. "Boys, I've got your clothes. Just shout out your names, and I'll hand over the ones we picked for you."

It doesn't take those cowboys long to dry off, jump into their new duds, put their boots and hats on, and line up outside, waiting on Cookie.

"Hurry up, Cookie," says Jingles. "Mister Smith's waiting, and so are those gals over at the Long Branch."

"I'm comin', boys," says Cookie. "Just as soon as I dry off, admire these new clothes, and thank that General Store owner. Don't they look nice?"

Wrangler leans down to get a closer look. "Sure they do, but get a move on. We're in a powerful hurry to do a little drinking, dancing, and get to know those gals over there a whole lot better. It's been a long time!"

"Boys, here I come. Okay, follow me, mind your manners, and try to act like you've been in a big town before, at least until you get paid."

Like chicks following a mother hen, they march over to the bank where they're met by Mister Smith, Joel, and Jones.

"Line up, boys. Step up to the table one at a time, tell me how you want your wages, and then either sign for it or make your mark. Cookie, Jingles, I want to talk with you a minute before you leave."

Four of them take all their wages, $100.00. Four, including Cookie and Jingles, ask Mister Smith to keep $50.00 of their pay until they ask for it. After being paid, the boys are out the door ready to take in the sights and pleasures of Dodge City.

"Cookie, you and Jingles are probably pretty savvy about towns similar to Dodge. Some of our boys are in for the experience of their lives, especially the young ones when they're taken for a ride by some of those upstairs princesses.

"The sheriff tells me there are a few unsavory characters here—drifters, gun hands, and a card shark or two. I'd like to keep the boys out of trouble as much as we can, but I know we can't be every place. It's just I don't want anyone getting shot for having a good time. I'm gonna ask you to be on the lookout for any trouble that might be headed their way. I know it's asking a lot during celebration time, but I'd appreciate it."

Cookie looks at Jingles, who nods his head in agreement, "Mister Smith, Jingles and me will do it. I've kinda gotten attached to some of these men. I'd like to think they got a few more cattle drives in 'em."

"Okay, Mister Smith, we'll do our best."

"I know you boys will. Soon as we finish dinner with the buyers, we'll be over to the Long Branch for a few drinks ourselves. That way we can keep a watchful eye, too."

Cookie and Jingles head out the door.

"Okay, Jonesy and Richards, how do you want your wages?"

"Mister Smith, I only need $50.00 now 'cause I know how careless a person can get with too much money in his pocket at one time. I'll get the rest later."

"Joel, how about you?"

"I'm like Jonesy. Fifty dollars will be enough for now, as money's pretty hard to come by. If I'm not careful, it can be gone real quick."

"You're right. I hope these boys can save something, but I remember how it was. More often than not, they'll have to learn the hard way.

"Mister Martin, I'm gonna close it up here. Thanks for all your help. I'll be back in tomorrow to work out the details on the rest of the money."

"Mister Smith, everything will be ready. I appreciate your business."

"Thank you. Now, boys, lets head over to the Long Horn, get us a sit-down meal from those buyers. I don't know about you all, but it's time for a break from Cookie's cookin'."

"Jonesy and I been looking forward to this meal for quite a while. We're ready for a good steak without those beans, special pork fixin's, and biscuits."

Dinner's on Us

Sam, Joel, and Jones enter the Longhorn Hotel. Joe Peterson and Harry Ferguson have gotten up from their chairs and are walking across the lobby to greet them. They extend their hands. "Gentlemen, good to see you boys. Everything taken care of at the bank?"

"Yes, sir, it's all in order."

"Gentlemen, they've got a table reserved for us in the dining room. Shall we?"

"I thought you'd never get to it. After you, men."

As they enter the dining room, Joel notices three army officers seated having dinner. One of them looks up, sees Joel, smiles, and stands up from his table and begins heading toward Joel.

"Mister Smith, I'll join you in a few moments if you don't mind?"

"Not at all, Joel. We'll see you shortly."

Meeting in the middle of the dining room, the army officer and Joel grasp hands and shake firmly. "General Jarvis, I had a feeling it might be you, although the last time we talked, you were a colonel. It's good to see you, sir."

"I can't believe this. Sergeant Richards. Here in the middle of nowhere, we meet after six—or is it seven years?" He looks over at the table where Sam, Jones, and the cattle buyers are. "I see you have another party to join, but would you mind taking a few moments to visit with me and my officers? Then you can get back to your business?"

"No, sir, not at all. Let me tell Mister Smith I'll rejoin him shortly."

He walks over to the table and says, "Sam, I'm going to spend a few moments with these officers. Then I'll rejoin you for dinner. Oh, if you order drinks, please have the waiter bring one over, 'cause I'm ready."

"You bet, Joel. See you in a bit."

As Joel approaches the general's table, Jarvis stands and introduces Joel to the other officers. "Gentlemen, this is former First Sergeant Joel Richards of the Third Cavalry Rangers who General Grant personally decorated for his outstanding service to the war effort. This is Colonel Stratford, commander of Fort Dodge, and my aid, Captain Lawin."

"Mister Richards, it's a pleasure to finally meet you. Your reputation and war exploits are frequently talked about, especially by the general."

"Gentlemen, nice to meet you."

"Joel, have a seat and let's visit. First of all, I'm here at Fort Dodge on a fact finding and evaluation mission of the army's effectiveness in dealing with Indians and troublemakers, such as rustlers that might be outside the sheriff's jurisdiction when it comes to crossing the borders between Kansas and Oklahoma.

"Apparently an organized band of thieves has been very active just across the border in Oklahoma, stealing herds, killing drivers, and selling the cattle in Kansas. In seeking a solution, Colonel Stratford and I stopped by the sheriff's office to find out what he had done and determine if some kind of joint effort could be incorporated to put a stop to these raiders.

"Now imagine our surprise when the sheriff informed us the problem had been resolved by a bunch of cowboys. I couldn't believe it … until I saw your name on the report."

"I was hired for that cattle drive primarily because of my cavalry training. I became a cowboy later. Mister Smith, over there at that table, was concerned we would be meeting Indians and rustlers on the way. He wanted to make sure when that time came, his men would be able to keep anyone from stealing or taking the cattle. His grit and determination helped me prepare these cowboys to face the fear from these kinds of people, and they did their jobs."

A waiter approaches and sets down Joel's drink.

"Thank you," says Joel.

"Mister Richards, just how were you able to take a bunch of unskilled cowboys and turn them into an organized bunch of effective horse soldiers?"

Taking a sip from his glass, he says, "Colonel, this was an exceptional bunch of men. They were experienced cowhands and young men not yet out of their teens. The biggest factor was they were trainable and motivated to succeed."

"Well, General, I could certainly use a few men like that in our cavalry."

"Colonel, a couple of the young men talked to me about the army, and they'd make good cavalrymen. Good riders, quick learners, handle guns well, and know a little bit about cavalry tactics now. I'll head 'em your way, but I would appreciate it if you and the general would personally talk with them first before they're turned over to your training command."

General Jarvis says, "Joel, we certainly owe you that. You have mine and Colonel Stratford's word on it. We need some good men. By the way, would you consider joining us? I still have that officer's commission available."

Smiling, he says, "Thank you, sir, for the offer once again. However, I'll be moving on from Dodge. Now I'd better be rejoining my boss, as payday's waiting over there. It was great to see you, General, Colonel Stratford, Captain Lawin, a pleasure to meet you."

"Joel, send those young men out. I'll inform the officer of the day to be on the lookout for them and have them personally escorted to my office. By the way, what are their names?"

"It'll be Davy Snodgrass and Jeff Erin. Thank you, and, gentlemen, please excuse me."

In a sign of honor, all three officers stand and salute former First Sergeant Joel Richards of the Third Cavalry Rangers, United States Army. Joel returns the salute, and then turns away, walking over to join Sam, Jones, and the buyers.

Upon arriving at the table, Sam looks at Joel. "Joel, that was damned impressive. You must have been some soldier for a general to salute you. Of course, they ain't telling me anything I don't know. Did they get you to join up?"

"No, Sam, they didn't. I was offered a commission, but my military career is over. Gentlemen, I'm ready to eat."

As Joel sits down, the waiter approaches their table. "Good evening, gentlemen. Would you like to have another drink before ordering your meal?"

Harry says, "If it's okay with you boys, I'd like to order a bottle of champagne to celebrate this occasion."

"Harry, I don't think I've ever had champagne before. Jonesy, how about you and Joel?"

"Same here, Mister Smith, but I'm not afraid to try something new."

"That's it then. Waiter, bring us a bottle of your finest along with five glasses. When we run short, bring another bottle."

"Yes, sir, I'll be right back."

"Sam," says Harry, "before we get too far along here, I have a favor to ask."

"Sure. What is it?"

"You know I'm planning on driving those heifers and cows to Wyoming in a couple of days so we can be there and settled in before winter. Now, I brought a couple of men with me. One of them will be our wrangler, and the other will be riding herd. They're going to help on the trail drive, but they've got no experience with longhorns, so I'm looking to hire two or three experienced men who know how to work these cattle who can work together."

"Excuse me, sir," says the waiter with a bottle in hand, "may I go ahead and pour drinks while you're visiting?"

"Certainly, thank you."

During this conversation, Joel and Jones are listening closely, forgetting for the time being about partying later. They cautiously glance at each other and then back to Harry as he continues.

"Sam, you've got a good, experienced bunch. Do you think any of them might be interested, and if so, who would you recommend? I'll pay top wages."

Smith rubs his chin for a moment. "I'd hate to lose any of these boys. However, I'm a realist, knowing not all of 'em will be going back to Texas. Other places might be callin'. Let me think about it. Jones, does anyone come to mind you feel would make Harry a good hand?"

"Mister Smith, I hope this doesn't upset you," says Jones. He turns to Ferguson. "Do you need a trail boss?"

Harry hesitates, looking at Sam, who's somewhat surprised with Jones's question. Sam pauses. "Jones, you're a good trail boss, so if this is something you want to do, I'm not going to stand in your way."

"Yes, I do need an experienced trail boss of your caliber. If you're interested, as I think you are, you're hired."

"Thank you, Mister Ferguson. I've got a man or two in mind, providin' it's okay with Mister Smith."

"Jonesy, now that you're going to be working for the Wyoming Cattle Company, I think it's time you called me Sam. It's okay to tell Harry who you have in mind. Fact is I have a feelin' he's sitting at this same table. Right, Joel?"

Joel says, "You're right. I don't think Texas is what I'm looking for. Maybe Wyoming might be. I'm available if you want me."

Ferguson has a smile on his face. "I was kinda hoping it would be you and Jones. Glad to have you both working for me. Who else did you have in mind?"

"I might suggest Ben," says Jones. "He's pretty good with cattle and can do some doctorin' when it's needed. Good worker and loyal." He looks at Sam and says, "What do you think?"

"Ben's a good man if he's willin'. You've put together a pretty good crew, Harry, one of the best. I'll ask Ben later, makin' sure he knows it's his choice."

"Well then, that just about completes it, except maybe for a cook," says Harry.

"Damn, Harry, you've got most of my good men. Now you're thinking about Cookie, too. That could mean on my trip back to Texas, I might have to do my own cookin'. Looks like I better be packing a lot of jerky. I'll let him know. If he's interested, he'll come by, probably along with Ben."

Harry does some mental figuring before saying, "Jonesy, you and Joel get together with me tomorrow so we can get this drive laid out and under way in the next day or two. Sam, I know this puts a dent in your crew. I hope it's not going to interfere with our friendship."

"No, it won't," says Sam with a laugh. "A man's got to cut his own trail. These boys will serve you well. Plus, you and I might do some more business down the road. I'm not one to close the gate on friendship."

"Thanks, Sam. A toast to the best cattle businesses in the west—the Single Six Ranch, the Chicago Beef Company, and the Wyoming Cattle Company."

Jones stands. "I'd like to propose another toast, to the best owner and drover that I've ever known, Sam Smith."

A resounding "Here, here!" is echoed by Joel, Harry, and Joe.

The men talk and eat, far too much—living it up now that the job is done. But as can happen with any such gathering, the merriment eventually lulls. The men know that something has ended, and there's always a little sadness to that. It's at that moment that Joel says to Sam, "I've not told anyone this before, I owe it to you, as it might help you understand why I'm heading to Wyoming. When the war was over, I went home to find my family's farm devastated, with only my father still alive. He was in bad shape, tryin' to hold on until I got home. He lived for a few more months afterward and then passed on, but his final words to me, which I've never forgotten, were …" Joel's eyes become tear filled, and his voice is trembling with emotion as he says, "'*Son, you need to get away from here. Take only the good memories with you. Leave the rest behind. When you're ready, git some good soil under your feet, a piece of ground you can call your own. Plant something, grow something, get some animals. When you do, your wandering days will be over. You'll leave a legacy we'll both be proud of. If you do this, no matter where it's at, your mother, Elizabeth, and I will feel we at least served a purpose for being here.'* That's what I'm lookin' for, and I ain't found it yet."

There's a solemn pause in the conversation with a bit of reflection going on about what Joel said. Sam looks at him. "Joel, we all appreciate that and understand. You'll find it, son. Perhaps it is in Wyoming."

Not wanting to dwell on Joel's issues, Joe says, "Sam, I'm also looking forward to us doing some more business in the next year or two."

"Joe, so am I. Well, gents, looks like the food's here. Let's eat."

After dinner's finished, Sam says, "Boys, that was damn tasty and fillin'. I can't eat another bite, nor can I remember another meal that tasted so good … except the ones my wife fixes."

"You'd better say that, Sam. Word has a way of traveling fast in this country. We sure don't want it beating you home or she might be looking for another pony."

Now that dinner's over, cigars are passed around and lit up. Harry orders brandy for the final after-dinner drink before adjourning to the Long Branch Saloon.

Raising his glass for a toast one last time, he says, "Gentlemen, to your health, prosperity, and safe journey home, wherever that might be."

Sam says, "I'll drink to that."

The Long Branch Saloon

Sam and company head for the Long Branch. The sound of music and a crowd are echoing out into the night air. Lanterns burning brightly on each side of the swinging doors give a beckoning glow to those entering.

Passing through the saloon doors, the boys pause and look around, taking note of the many overhead chandeliers lighting up the place. A roulette wheel and poker tables are busy working the house odds, and music comes from a piano, accompanied by a lone, attractive singer who catches Joel's eye. In that brief moment their eyes meet, she nods her head, smiles, and continues singing her song, occasionally glancing his way. Joel cautiously raises two fingers of his right hand, touching the front brim of his hat and nodding his head toward her as a sign of acknowledgment, hoping it was really him she was giving the nod to.

Joel's thinking she's probably one of the soiled doves working the place who's earning a few extra dollars by singing. However, his focus shifts to the other parts of the saloon where bar girls are working the crowd, enticing the men to buy drinks and partake of their favors. A couple of cowboys are ascending the stairs with the upstairs princesses, passing others on the way down to do some more partying. It's a good night for the Long Branch.

Sam says, "This reminds me of some other places I've been, but they weren't as rowdy."

Ferguson speaks up. "That was Harry's and my reaction the first time we came here. I suppose this isn't anything new to Jones and Joel."

"All these places are different but similar in some respects. Same kind of people, but there's a hell of lot more of 'em here," says Sam.

As they're standing just inside the swinging doors, Sheriff Turner and one of his deputies greet them from a vantage point where they're watching over the festivities.

"Sam, your boys are enjoying themselves, with a couple of 'em—I think they called them Davy and Jeff—trying to drink the bar dry. A couple more just headed upstairs to spend a little time with the ladies. Long as those boys been on the trail, they probably won't take time to remove their boots. Barely get their pants down before these ladies will have 'em rode, finished, and down here in a few minutes. Jingles and another one …"

"That's John," says Sam.

"John. They're trying to dance with the gals out on the dance floor. See any of the others?"

"Well, Sheriff, it looks like Ben's trying his luck at the roulette table. I see Cookie over there playing a little poker."

"Fred, where's the other two?"

"Sheriff, one of them is over in that far corner crying in his beer, trying to have some kind of meaningful conversation with one of the ladies. She'll be listening as long as he's buyin'. The other one, I think they call Wrangler, said he had to check on the horses."

"That sounds like Wrangler," says Sam. "I sometimes think he prefers horses to people."

The sheriff chuckles. "So far, everything's gone okay. My only concern is a pair of hard cases sitting in that poker game over there. They've been drinking sparingly, watching the crowd pretty closely, especially your boys. I've got to go make my rounds on the street, but I'll leave Fred here in case anything happens. I'll see you later."

"Harry, I see an empty table over there in the corner. Let's sit down there, have a drink, and watch the goings on."

"Sam, you, Joe, and Harry go on over to the table. Joel and me will do a little standing at the bar. That way we've all got a good look at the floor, along with Fred by the door."

Joel can't help glancing at the singer as he and Jones walk toward the bar, noticing she's following him with her eyes. He almost bumps into

Jones. "What's the matter, Joel? All this excitement of being in the big time got you distracted?"

"Sorry, Jonesy. Guess I wasn't watching where I was going. You know, some of the things here we just don't see out on the trail."

Not saying anything to Jonesy, Joel's starting to feel a little warm under the collar, figuring a cold beer will cool him down a bit.

As Sam, Joe, and Harry walk to their table, Joel and Jonesy move up to the ornate bar with its brass railing for propping one's foot on while drinking. The bar runs half the length of the saloon, requiring two bartenders to man it in order to keep beer and whiskey steadily flowing to the customers.

They pause, looking upward at what's hanging above the bar. They stare in awe for a moment at a four-foot-high, eight-foot-long painting of a beautiful, nude lady lying on her side on a red velvet rug with one hand perched behind her head and the other lying on her thighs. Although covering a vital area, it stills leaves enough exposed for the imagination.

Her long, light brown tresses lying over one shoulder, flowing across her bare chest, barely cover the nipples on her breast. Her face is looking skyward with a seductive, angelic smile, as if inviting one to go to heaven with her.

A bartender steps up. "She looks pretty good, doesn't she, boys?"

Jonesy says, "I'd sure like to meet that lady sometime."

"If you're lucky, it might happen. What'll you boys have?"

"A couple of cold beers if you got 'em"

"Coming right up."

Something about the lady's face intrigues Joel so he slightly and casually turns to take a quick look at the singer who's looking at him … and smiling. Joel grin's back, thinking to himself, *I knew who that face reminded me of … it's her! Maybe I'll be the one who gets lucky enough to meet her.*

Quickly wanting to change the subject, he turns back to the bar and Jonesy. "Movin' into position at the bar is a good idea, Jonesy. It appears you might've done this before."

"I've learned the hard way to take care of myself and kinda developed an instinct for trouble, whether it's from animals or men, just like you have."

"Here's your beers, fellows. That'll be a dollar."

"Joel, I got the first one. By the way, what your father told you is beginning to make some sense to me. It seems I've been drifting from one place to another, in and out of jobs and situations all these years. Maybe this drive to Wyoming will also help me get straight on what I really should be doing from here out with my life. Maybe it's time to be giving some thought about settling down. Just wanted you to know that.

"Anyway, Joel, are you going to partake of any of the activities available tonight?"

"I don't think so. It's tempting, but I believe I'm going to stay on the sidelines tonight. Maybe tomorrow if we got some time before we head out to Wyoming. I'd like to feel a little more comfortable with the surroundings first, then maybe later do a little partakin'." Joel keeps sneaking a look at the singer, and she also seems to be looking his way at times.

"Yeah, I'm kinda thinkin' the same way, although if I find one of those gals that strikes my fancy, I'd be willin' to give her some of my time. Of course I'm such a good lookin' fellow I just know she wouldn't want any of my money."

"Jonesy, right now the ones I've seen, except for that singer, look like they been up and down the stairs more times than I can count."

"I know, but you got to realize those gals are just tryin' to make a livin'. It's our duty to help 'em out when we can. Don't you think?"

"It sounds to me like you might be an angel of mercy comin' to bring prosperity into their lives by doin' 'em a good deed."

"I sometimes feel that way, Joel, but I always walk away from 'em feelin' a whole lot better for what I done!" He laughs.

"You boys ready for another beer?"

"You bet. This time, Jones, I'm buyin'."

When Jonesy isn't looking his way, Joel turns his head toward her, getting a better look at her shoulder-length, wavy, brunette hair and low-cut but classy gown cinched at the waist, causing her breast to gently rise with her breathing. Along with her trim figure and sparkling eyes, she's not at all what he expected for a dance hall queen, but rather someone he might've envisioned as the lady of his dreams.

Confrontation and Justice

The time is closing in on midnight, and everyone's having a good time, with the cowboys still whooping, hollering, dancing, visiting with the princesses, and drinking their fill of beer and whiskey. So far, there have been no fights, just cowboys enjoying themselves.

Sam turns to Joe and Harry. "Boys, I'm about ready to call it a night. I still got some things to do in the morning that require a clear head."

"I know what you mean," says Joe. "Harry and I are feeling the same. Surely it can't be an age thing?"

Harry says, "I know you two remember those days before we sobered up to our responsibilities. Those times when the morning sun would nearly blind us when we woke up with our heads throbbing and sometimes hanging over a rail puking our guts out, swearing that was the last time we'd ever do that again."

"Yeah," says Sam. "I sorta remember making one or two of those promises. Then a funny thing would happen; the next month when I'd go to town, for some reason I forgot what I'd promised, wind up doing the same thing all over again. Some of us are just slow learners, as many of these boys are, but one day they'll come to realize it's a lot easier tending cattle and takin' care of business when you got a fair night's sleep. Plus, you might wind up with a couple of dollars in your pocket instead of loose change."

"Fellows, it looks like Richards and Jonesy are going to be hangin' around a while longer, so I'm going to finish this drink and turn in. The way those other boys have been going at it all night, I have a feelin' most of them are getting close to callin' it."

"We're with you, Sam."

"Jonesy, ol' Jingles has sure been doing a lot of dancin' tonight. I can hear those spurs of his jingling clear over here. One thing I've noticed, he don't seem to be drinking much, just dancing with the ladies. Of course that ain't a bad thing to be doin'."

On the way out, Sam leans over to Joel. "When you can, look over at those two hard cases the sheriff told us about; they seem to be stalking our two drunken cowboys, Davy and Jeff, like a mountain lion."

"You're right. It's the same thing I been seein'," says Joel. "We'll need to keep an eye on those boys. I don't think they've noticed or realize you and I are anything more than just a couple of older cowboys takin' it easy on the drinkin' and partying."

Davy and Jeff, who've been trying to drink the place dry, finally realize they've had enough. They begin staggering and stumbling toward the door, arm in arm, holding each other up. When they reach the swinging doors, the two hard cases excuse themselves from their poker table one at a time. One heads out the back door as if going to the outhouse. The other slowly meanders toward the front door, keeping an eye on the direction his quarry is headed.

Before Joel and Jonesy make a move, Jingles pardons himself away from the ladies, also heading for the front door. Now it's obvious he was doing more than just dancing; he was keeping an eye on his fellow cowboys as Mister Smith had asked him to.

Sensing imminent trouble, Joel tells Jonesy, "Follow Jingles. I'm goin' out the back door after that other hard case. More than likely, we're all going to meet in the alley. Be careful."

"You too."

Fred knows something's up when Jones goes out the doors. Quickly glancing around to make sure nothing else is going on, he hesitates to leave as his orders from Sheriff Turner are to stay inside the saloon at all times.

Outside, the two drunken Single Six boys stagger around the corner of the saloon, zigzagging arm in arm down the alley toward camp, unsuspecting of the hard case behind and the one coming toward them. All at once, the following hard case closes quickly and hits them from behind, knocking both to the ground just as his partner comes up to join him. They quickly begin rummaging through their pockets to get any money they've got left.

Jingles comes around the corner, sees what's going on, and hollers at them, "Get away from those boys!"

The first hard case turns around with cold eyes and pistol drawn. Jingles, in a flash, draws his Colt and fires, dropping the first one just as Joel comes up from behind the second one who's trying to turn around and run. Joel surprises him when he turns, giving the hard case a Peacemaker barrel over the head, dropping him like a ton of bricks to the ground.

By this time, the sheriff is close enough from across the street to see what happened. He dashes toward the confrontation, arriving just as it's over. At the same time, Jones gets there. He's followed by Montana Jack, who was on his way over for a late-night drink.

The shot fired was muffled by the noise from the saloon, so none of the customers realize anything went on except Fred. At the sound, Sam came out of his room to see what was going on, arriving just as Sheriff Turner says, "All right, Jingles, you and Joel holster your guns while I sort this out. What happened here?"

Each one tells their story, how they saw it and their part in the confrontation.

The sheriff takes a few moments going over the details presented and then says, "Jingles, this looks like a clear case of self-defense 'cause you gave that hard case the chance to give up or get away, but he chose to draw down on you first, so you had no choice but to do what you did. Joel, did you see it any differently?"

"No, Sheriff, it happened just as we said."

His other deputy shows up. "Pete, get the undertaker and get this mess cleaned up. I'm going to haul the one Joel pistol whipped off to jail. This boy's going to have a hell of a headache when he wakes, wishing he stayed in the saloon rather than making the choice he did. Sam, take Jingles along with those two drunks back to camp, and should they remember anything in the morning, have 'em see me. I'll see you other boys later."

"Okay, Sheriff. Jingles, let's see if we can walk 'em back or if we need to go get a wagon to haul 'em."

Joel comes up to Jingles. "Are you all right?'

"Just a little shaken. It's not something I relish, takin' a man's life. Between rustlers, Indians, and thieves, I've got to find a better way."

"You had no choice. We can talk later if you want."

As Joel and Jones go back into the saloon, Montana Jack, who's been watching and listening, approaches Sam and Jingles.

"Mister Smith, I saw and heard what went on here tonight. I'm wondering if I might have a word with Jingles in the morning. I could have an opportunity for him in my show."

"That's up to him. I think things will look a little clearer by then. Stop by if it's okay with you, Jingles."

"It's okay with me. I got some thinkin' to do between now and then."

Joel and Jones are back at their bar location, looking the room over. "Joel, it looks like things are winding down some here. Sure don't want any more situations like we just been in. I had a feeling Jingles knew his way around a gun fight, although it's a hell of a lot different goin' against a bunch of Indians and rustlers opposed to goin' one on one, face to face with a hard case."

"No doubt. Maybe that's another reason we got to get busy finding our own place to settle down, away from these kinds of establishments."

"Amen to that."

Cookie gets up from where he's been playing poker and comes over to visit with Joel. "How did it go, Cookie? I notice you're still sober. Win any money?"

"Won a little bit but was more interested in who the real players were. Playing poker and drinking don't mix if you want to keep your wits about, especially if you're playin' to win. It didn't take long to know who was goin' to be holdin' the winning hand and who was going to be suckin' hind teat. A few lessons were dealt out tonight along with a few dollars, so when you get a chance, take a good look at the dealer and the man directly across the table from him 'cause you're probably goin' to run into 'em sooner or later.

"They're pretty good at working together, taking these boys' monies. A couple cowboys shouldn't even been in this game 'cause they didn't stand a chance against these slickers."

"Cookie, are you sayin' they're crooked?"

"Well, let me put it this way. Some of these drifters can take your money with a gun or knife in the alley, but these guys here get it done over a card table. Same principle, but a crook is still a crook even though they might use different methods.

"Say, it appears things been busy for you boys. I can only guess what happened when those two characters left that other table with you not far behind, especially when you boys came back, and they didn't.

"Joel, I think your education needs to climb another rail, so how about you and me set in on a game with those gamblers tomorrow night and see if you can pick up some more lessons without losing your shirt?"

"Okay, Cookie, tomorrow night it is. I don't know about you all, but it's time for me to pack it in for the night. Most of the boys have left. Let's make sure we don't leave any stragglers between here and camp on our way back."

"I'm ready, Joel. How about you, Cookie?"

"Lead the way. Our boys are goin' to be needin' a few pots of Arbuckles in the mornin' when they get up. It's a good thing we can sleep in, but I'd be surprised if any of them are going to want any of my famous beans churnin' and bubblin' in their stomachs, but I'll have some biscuits handy. Plus, I got a little tradin' to do with a fellow in town first thing in the morning."

Wrapping up Business

ookie starts off the day with the breakfast bell ringing amid grunts and groans coming from the bedrolls because a bright morning sun is no cure for a whisky headache. Slowly, the boys begin stirring, some heading for the coffee pot, others heading for the woods. Davy and Jeff fall to their hands and knees, bringing up what's left of last night's drinking.

Cookie says, "Damn, boys, couldn't you have made it at least past the remuda?"

Jeff says, "Ah, we was lucky to get out of our bedrolls and make it this far. I'll get me a shovel and cover it up in a minute soon as I find my clothes. Man, I feel like I been whacked in the back of the head."

"Now that everyone's up, come on over here, as Mister Smith has something to say to you boys."

"Men, I'm going to be heading into the bank shortly. In about an hour, I want you to come on down so we can get settled up. I know some of you got shopping to do before you even think about any more celebrating.

"Cookie, Ben. Harry Ferguson of the Wyoming Cattle Company is going to be moving out tomorrow, headed for Wyoming with those five hundred heifers and cows he bought from us. He's signed on Jones for trail boss, Joel as top hand, and wants to talk with you two about joining his crew. I told him that decision was entirely yours. It's okay with me whichever way you decide. If you want to talk with him about it, he's down at the hotel expecting you. Fact is you can see him first, then come on over to the bank."

"Mister Smith, Ben and I been with you for quite a while. We ain't never had a better man to work for. I can't speak for Ben, but I'd like to talk with Mister Ferguson. I've always had a hankering to see Wyoming and Montana. This might be my way to do it and get paid at the same time."

"Mister Smith, I know this is the end of one trail drive with a long ride home without any wages. That's just the way it is. Now, I'd like to keep right on workin' without losin' any pay if I can. Maybe once in my life this might give me a chance to save a few dollars, not wind up a broken, old cowboy. So what I'm sayin' is I'd like to talk to Mister Ferguson, if he's of a mind to hire me. I'll do it especially since Jonesy and Joel are part of the crew."

"You boys gave me everything I asked for on this drive and then some. I thank you for that. Now get on down to the hotel and get yourselves some new jobs, 'cause if you take 'em, you got a lot of work to get done today. I'll see you over at the bank."

Montana Jack comes riding up and reins to a stop. "Good morning, Mister Smith. Is Jingles about?"

"Damn, Montana, I just lost two more men to the Wyoming Cattle Company, and you're here shoppin' for a couple more. The way my day's goin', I'm going to be riding home by myself, eatin' my own cookin'. Lite down, I'll find him."

Sam doesn't have to go far. Jingles saw Montana ride into camp and is edging his way to the coffee pot. "Jingles, you and Montana can visit. I've got to get into town. When you come by the bank, let me know what you've decided."

"Will do. I'll see you after a while."

"Howdy, Mister Montana. Join me for a cup of coffee?"

"Jingles, you can drop the mister, just call me Montana like everyone else. The reason I'm here is to see if you might be interested in a show business career riding in my Wild West Show. After what you did last night, what I heard you say to Joel led me to believe you might consider an opportunity to get away from trail drives and cattle towns. Am I right?"

"Yeah, I want to hear what you got in mind."

"I've talked to Jonesy and Smith; they gave me a pretty good idea of what your background is. I know you're a good rider, pretty fair gun hand, fought rustlers, Indians, and whether you realize it or not, you do have a bit of showman about you from those Spanish spurs to your Mexican saddle rig. I know a little bit about these things. I believe there's a place in my show for you."

"What'll I have to do?"

"One of our new acts will be the reenactments of both the Single Six's attack and defeat of the Indians and rustlers. You'll help me set up the act so we can be authentic as possible in a Wild West Show. Then you'll be the one who leads the cowboys to victory. The folks back east love this stuff, paying handsomely to see it. That's a brief overview of what I've got in mind. Of course I have other acts you'll also be a part of, plus helping to set up and take down the sets when we're ready to move on to the next city."

"What's something like that pay?"

"Jingles, $25.00 a week to start. You'll live in a trailer when we travel or a hotel in town during our stay for our shows. Many times we'll be traveling by train. It just depends on where our next show is. I can tell you this, our season begins in about four weeks, and our bookings are solid for a year. So if this appeals to you, I need to know now 'cause we've got to get a move on, set up our act, rehearse, and be ready for opening day."

"Montana, did I understand you to say $25.00 a *week* to begin, you pay for everything, and you're booked for a whole year? I've been getting by on $30.00 a month and found!"

"That's right. Your first week's pay begins the moment you hire on. That's today, if you're ready. Can I have your hand on it?"

"Montana, it's a deal. When do we leave?"

"We leave on the five o'clock train today, so whatever you need to get taken care of, do it. Then gather your gear and meet me at the hotel by four o'clock."

Unbeknownst to either Montana or Jingles, Wrangler is over by the remuda within earshot of the conversation. "Jingles, there's one more man I've got to find yet before I leave. That's someone who knows horses, how to work, train, and take excellent care of them 'cause they're an important key in the shows."

"Might talk with Wrangler. He's about the best I've ever seen. Let me holler at him."

Wrangler is already making his way toward Montana and Jingles. "You don't have to holler, Jingles. I apologize, fellows, but I been eavesdroppin' and heard everything you boys said. Mister Montana, I'd sure like to have a shot takin' care of your horses. I know quite a bit about them, including some arena practices."

"Well, Wrangler, you got the Single Six bunch here on some of the finest conditioned trail stock I've ever seen. I'll pay you $75.00 a month plus expenses if you're interested—and call me Montana."

"Yes, sir, Montana. You hired yourself a wrangler."

"Good, get done what you need to do. Then you boys meet me at the hotel at four o'clock today. Wrangler, your job also starts today. The first thing after you get your business taken care of with Mister Smith is to get those rustlers' horses and gear from the livery barn over to the holding pens, ready to be loaded on the train when it comes in. Jingles, would you give him a hand? Our time is short."

"You bet. We'll have 'em ready."

"I'll see you then. I can tell you this: I've never been so excited as I am now. We are going to put on one hell of a show!"

Revelation

Cookie puts out the camp fire so he and Ben can head into town to see Mr. Ferguson about jobs herding cattle in Wyoming.

"Cookie, you ready to go now?"

"Be right with you, Ben. I've got to get something to take with me."

"Cookie, what's in the gunny sack?"

"Nothing really, just some things I need to get rid of. I'm meetin' a man in town who might want to do a little tradin'."

"Okay, but let's get goin'."

Walking into the hotel lobby, Ben and Cookie see Harry Ferguson in the dining room having breakfast. "Ben, you go ahead. I need to leave this sack at the desk and pick it up when I leave. Be right there."

Walking up to the desk clerk, he says, "Pardon me. I need to leave this someplace while we're visiting with Mister Ferguson. I'll pick it up in a few minutes when we leave."

"Sure, just set it behind the counter here out of the way. I'll make sure no one takes it."

Cookie sets it down and heads to the dining room, thinking if someone does take it, they might be in for a bit of surprise. "Good morning, Mister Ferguson."

"Good morning, Cookie. Glad to see you boys are in pretty good shape after last night."

"Well, I think Cookie and me have finally acquired some wisdom. Don't hit it as hard as we once did. We leave that to the young yahoos. Mister Ferguson, Smith said you might have jobs for us herding to Wyoming. Is that right?"

"Yes, it is. We leave in the morning. I'm sure you already know Jonesy and Richards are part of the crew. If you boys are willing, you can be, too.

"Ben, I can use a good man handling cattle. You've come highly recommended by Sam and Jonesy, and that's good enough for me. The job's yours if you want it. I pay top wages for the drive with these cattle. Plus, if it works out, I'll have a job waiting for you there with our cattle company. Well, what do you say?"

"Yes, sir, sounds good to me. Here's my hand."

After shaking Ben's hand, Ferguson turns to Cookie. "I need a trail cook. Sam says you're the best. I also pay top wages for a cook, and like I just told Ben, there could be a job with us in Wyoming. What do you say about signing on with the Wyoming Cattle Company?"

"Mister Ferguson, I've always wanted to see Wyoming. I'm lookin' forward to working with you. I accept. You got my hand on it."

"Boys, you're hired. When you can, see Jones to get lined out on the supplies so we can have everything ready and be on the trail first thing in the morning. I know this isn't your first time out. Do you have any questions?"

"No, sir! If they do come up, we'll get ahold of Jones."

"Good. Now I've got to see Sam and finish our deal for the horses. I'll see you men later."

As Ben and Cookie leave the dining room, Cookie tells him, "Ben I've got to take care of some business before I head over to the bank. I'll see you there when I get through."

Cookie picks up his sack from behind the desk clerk's counter and heads out the door and down the street. Ben's curiosity is getting the best of him, so he decides to follow Cookie and see what kind of trade's in the wind. Well, it doesn't take long before Ben watches Cookie go into a hat shop and peeks in the window to see what he's up to.

Ben sees Cookie selling a sack full of rattlesnake skins and rattles to the hatter. His mouth drops open in surprise as he puts two and two together. In a fit of rage, he heads back down the street toward the bank, looking for Mister Smith.

He finds Sam getting ready to make the final pay off to the crew, calls him outside, and starts shouting, "That crazy old cook's been feeding us rattlesnake, not pork. I just saw him selling some skins and rattles to a hat company."

"Really?"

"I'm gonna get me a rope and drag his sorry ass outa town."

"Now you calm down, Ben. Ol' Cookie got us through some rough areas with his cooking. I don't think there's another cook who can do a better job feeding his crew off the land. Now none of us starved or complained when we were eating his grub, so that goes to show if a man knows his job, he'll do what it takes to get it done. You got to remember, ol' Cookie was a pretty good card player, so he just played the hand he was dealt.

"Besides, there wasn't any harm or sickness came to any man on this drive because of eating what we thought was pork. It seems kinda strange none of us really wanted to know where he got all that pork. Just remember, Cookie gave us something that might help us survive if we're ever in a spot where there's nothing to eat but snake. Just because it don't cackle, ain't no reason we can't think of it as chicken!"

"Mister Smith, what you said, looking back on it, does make it kinda funny how we let Cookie pull one over on us. I guess it was because we were more interested in fillin' our bellies with some meat, rather than bein' concerned about where he got it. Now that I think about it, it was pretty good eatin'."

"Well, Ben, are you and Cookie going northwest with the Wyoming Cattle Company?"

"I was about to change my mind about goin' when I saw Cookie sellin' those skins, but you know … he's a pretty good ol' boy, so I'm goin' to see it through. Yes, we agreed to go with Mister Ferguson, but I'm gonna keep a little closer look on what Cookie's fixin' after this."

Traveling Money

"**B**en, come on in the bank. Let's get settled up so you'll have some travelin' money."

Before the other Single Six boys arrive, Sam finishes up the sale of the cattle with Martin's help. He separates Hank's share from his own, figuring out what each man will receive from the bonus money, the balance of their wages, and their share of the reward money.

Each man will receive an additional $99.00 from the bonus money ($.50 per head split twelve ways), which Sam rounds off to an even $100.00. They get $300.00 for their share of the reward money and whatever portion of their wages they asked him to hold back. The total is $500.00 apiece, representing more than a year's wages, an amount most of these boys will probably never see again at one time during their days of cowboying. Nine of the Single Six crew will split the $150.00 bonus Sam paid for the hundred and fifty strays the boys picked up along the way that made it to Dodge City, giving them a few extra dollars to take home.

Jonesy, as trail boss, will get an additional $350.00, making his payday $850.00. Cookie receives an extra $150.00 as the cook for a total of $650.00. Joel will receive $500.00, same as the other boys, $400.00 ($200.00 in extra reward money for the rustlers and $200.00 for saving the cattle from the Indians), plus $.50 a day for use of his horses on the drive, which comes to $60.00, giving him a final total of $960.00.

The final sale figures for the cattle come from a drive that started out with a herd of 2,500 longhorns. Out of the 2,500, Hank had a hundred and fifty to begin with, and thanks to Sam, all hundred and fifty will represent

Hank's share. Forty-five of his heifers and cows were sold to the Wyoming Cattle Company at $15.00 apiece for a total of $675.00. The balance of his herd, 105, was sold to the Chicago Cattle Company at $13.00 apiece for a total of $1,365.00, bringing the amount due to Hank's family from the sale of their cattle to $2,040.00. Hank's family will also receive his wages, bonus, and reward money of $500.00, plus the $720.00 from the sale of the rustlers' horses to Montana Jack. Sam will take them a total of $3,260.00 for Hank's part, a small price to pay for an honest and brave man's life.

Sam started out with 2,350 longhorns, lost 118, gained 142 strays on the way, and got 2,374 to market. Of those 2,374, he sold 455 young cows and heifers to the Wyoming Cattle Company at $15.00 apiece for a total of $6,825.00 and the remainder of 1,919 longhorns to the Chicago Cattle Company at $13.00 for a total of $24,947.00, or a grand total of $31,772.00. After paying off the boys, he figures he'll have around $25,500.00 plus the horses Harry Ferguson buys.

Harry arrives at the bank, greeting Martin and Sam. "Sam, I've taken a good look at your horses with Wrangler. I've picked out the fifty I want to buy and take to Wyoming."

"Harry, how many pregnant mares did you find?"

"As near as Wrangler and I could tell, there are twelve due in six or seven months, but I understand you want to keep one and Joel gets his pick of two others, leaving nine to be bought at our agreed upon price of $50.00 apiece. Plus I'll go ahead and buy the other twenty-six mares and fifteen geldings at $20.00 apiece. Sam, my calculations figure out to be $1,270.00. Is that how you add it up?"

"The same, Harry."

"Mr. Martin, would you draw that amount out of my account and pay Sam as he's making out the bill of sale?"

"Sure thing, Mister Ferguson. It'll be just a minute."

"Harry, you're getting some fine horses, and just maybe on your trail to Wyoming, Joel's Morgan might pay a few visits to those others mares, making this a hell of a buy for you. Of course I know you didn't give any thought to that possibility."

Smiling, he says, "Now, Sam, whatever would give you that idea?"

"Because that's the way I'd think."

"Sam, here's your money."

"Thanks, Harry. These horses will give you good service and some fine colts."

"Sam, as soon as you and Joel get your mares, I'll have my boys come over and get the horses separated and moved to our remuda near the pens with the heifers."

The rest of the Single Six boys show up, receive their pay, and exclaim, "Mister Smith, I ain't never seen this much money at one time before in my life!"

"I know, boys. Be careful with it. Don't blow it. Get yourselves some new clothes and saddles and take some of that money home to help out any folks you got left.

"Those of you goin' back to Texas with me, meet me over at the hotel at noon because I'm going to buy you all a good dinner along with supper later, now that Cookie's headed for Montana and won't have time to feed us. Plus, you all get to sleep in the hotel tonight if you can stand some soft mattresses and clean sheets.

"I'll let you know at supper when we're heading to Texas for sure. I'm thinking it'll be in a couple of days from now, after I get the rest of those horses sold. In the meantime, when I finish up here, I've got to pay off the Barber and Bath Parlor and the General Store and pick up that grave marker for Hank."

Jingles and Wrangler stop by to collect their pay.

"Mister Smith, Wrangler and I are going to be joining Montana Jack's Wild West Show. We'll be leaving late this afternoon."

"Boys, I've already heard. News travels fast. Here's your money. I got to tell you what a fine job you did for me. I wish you luck."

The last to come in to collect their wages, bonuses, and rewards are Joel and Jonesy.

"Well, boys, are you about ready to hit the trail again?"

"Sam, we'll be headin' out in the morning, soon as Ben and Cookie get restocked with supplies for this next leg of the journey. Joel and I are both excited about goin' to Wyoming. At the same time I'm goin' to miss your friendship along with the other men. It was a hell of a drive up here. We're hoping this one to Wyoming is a bit more peaceful."

"Sam, I feel the same way. I pray you and the boys goin' back to Texas have a safe journey home."

"You men are the best. Here's your money. Use it wisely."

As they put their money in their pockets, Sam looks at them and says, "Aren't you goin' to count it?"

"No, Sam, if we felt we needed to count it, we wouldn't have been working for you."

"Thanks, boys. Joel, you need to get your two mares picked out and marked for your Wyoming trip. I'm headed down to the remuda now to get my mare separated, as Harry's sending Ben and another man to get those horses you're takin' to Wyoming and move 'em over by the cattle. Then I got to get busy findin' a buyer for those we ain't takin' back to Texas. See you boys around and good luck."

"Thanks again, Sam."

Sam realizes he has fifteen horses left. He'll keep seven to ride plus two as pack animals for the trip back to Texas, leaving six to sell in Dodge at $20.00 apiece for another $120.00. Adding this to the $1,270.00 he received from Harry, along with the $25,500.00 for the cattle, it's a grand total of about $26,890.00 to take back to Texas before picking up supplies, presents for his wife and kids, along with a pair of new boots, hat, and saddle for himself, plus a gravestone for Hank.

As Jonesy and Joel leave the bank, Joel says, "Jonesy, I got to get over to the Mercantile and do some buying. I need a good pair of boots, hat, shirts, underwear, long handles, maybe some warm clothing. I understand Wyoming isn't like Texas in the fall. I kinda like that Stetson Mr. Smith got and think I'll get one of those."

"Yeah, me too. Now I don't know about you, but I need a good saddle outfit, new bedroll, and some ammunition for a couple of those guns I got from the rustlers. Plus whatever I find I might need on this trip."

"Good idea. That old saddle you loaned me back in Texas I'll gladly give back to you when I buy a new one."

"Joel, as far as I'm concerned, if someone wants yours and my old saddles, I'd gladly give 'em to 'em. Maybe they can put them in a museum someday to give folks a look at what us cowboys rode in during the cattle drive days."

Joel sees Davy and Jeff across the street. "Excuse me, Jonesy. I need to talk to those boys."

He walks across the street, meeting Davy and Jeff.

"Joel, Cookie said you wanted to talk to us."

"Boys, are you still thinking seriously about joining the cavalry? I got a reason for asking."

"Yep, we been talkin' about it some, and we're thinking about riding out to Fort Dodge and visiting with someone who can tell us what's involved."

"You boys know I was in the cavalry, and apparently I still have some contacts. My former commanding officer is now a general, General Jarvis, and he's on tour at Fort Dodge. I told him about you both, how well you stood up to the Indians and raiders, learned, and helped us succeed. Well, he wants to visit with you personally, so when you go out there, ask to see the officer of the day, who's expecting you, and you'll get to meet with both General Jarvis and the commanding officer of the fort, Colonel Stratford."

"Joel, we don't know what to say, as we never expected that kind of treatment."

"Boys, it can be a good life with opportunities for both of you. Take a look, listen to what these men got to say, and make your own decision about joining."

Jeff looks at Davy. "Let's ride out there now before Mister Smith leaves for Texas."

"I'm with you, Jeff. Thanks, Joel."

"Best of luck and let me know how it goes."

"You bet."

PART VII
The Mission

The Songbird

"Joel, we better get to it if we're going to be ready by morning. Maybe when we get things done, we can spend a little time over at the Long Branch tonight before leaving. I'd kinda like to see one of those 'religious' gals over there, see if I can convince her I'm an angel of mercy come to bring prosperity for her good deeds."

"Knowing you, Jonesy, you'll get it done with a smile. If I got time before meeting Cookie at the poker table, I might even see if I can talk to that songbird by the piano."

"I knew it, Joel! You were lookin' at her in more than just a friendly way. If I were you, I'd get an early start to the talkin' before things get busy tonight. Before you go over there, you might want to stack things in your favor by getting a bath and shave. Put on some new duds so you'll be smellin' pretty and lookin' good. If you play your cards right, she'll probably require some 'quality' time with you before you start gambling. Knowing Cookie, he'll have all his stuff loaded up, ready to go, and be itching to play by then. So, soon as you can, get on over there."

"I appreciate the advice, but don't hesitate to take some of it yourself before you go on your mission of mercy. I've got to go pick out my mares now, which won't take long. I can meet you over at the Mercantile and spend some of my money before we finish lining this drive out for in the morning. Let me know when you can free me up. Then I'll head on over to the Long Branch."

"You bet, Joel."

Joel heads for the remuda, arriving there about the same time as Sam. "Mister Smith, have you had time to look 'em over yet?"

"No, I was waiting on you; you got first choice. Wrangler has all the pregnant mares over there separate from the rest, so take your pick."

"Wrangler, I like that buckskin with the black mane, plus the sorrel with the white stockings on her hocks and diamond on her forehead. Would you mark them for me?"

"You bet, Joel. Those are great choices. Mister Smith, which one do you like?"

"Well, I'll take the dark bay; she's got an admirable combination of conformation, color, and disposition. I liked the way she worked on the drive, especially the times I rode her, including when we were chasing that rustling bunch. I have a feeling after being bred by Joel's Morgan, she'll produce a good, solid-working colt for my son."

"Mister Smith, I think that's a good, safe bet. Now you know I'm going to be leaving with Montana Jack late today. You'll need to have one of your boys look after the remaining horses after the Wyoming Cattle bunch take theirs to the pens. I'll send Joel's along with 'em so he can be ready to go in the morning."

"Wrangler, I'll make sure one of the Single Six boys going back to Texas with me gets over here and takes care of the horses. Who would you recommend?"

"I'd suggest you get Red to tend the horses. He's spent some time with me on the trail learning a few things about these animals. What I like about him, he's got patience and a willingness to work quietly. I'm thinkin' if you give him a chance, he'll make a pretty fair wrangler."

"I believe you're right. I'll get Red over here shortly. You can give him any last-minute lessons if he needs 'em. Wrangler, you've done a great job for the Single Six. I appreciate it. Thanks for helping me out and taking such good care of all the horses. You're going to do great with Montana Jack. He's lucky to get you."

"Mister Smith, Joel, you got your jobs done on this drive. I got a lot to thank you for. The best to you both."

Hearing horses coming, everyone turns around as Davy and Jeff come riding up.

Jeff says, "Mister Smith, we've joined the cavalry out at Fort Dodge and won't be going back to Texas with you. Joel, that general and colonel were nice to us. They laid out the facts and told us we would be slated for noncommissioned officer's training once we got through basic training. It seems Davy and me got more experience and skills than most of the other men who've signed up."

Davy says, "So, Mister Smith, we want to thank you for giving us a chance to be part of this drive. If it wasn't for you and Joel, we don't know where we might be now."

"We report first thing in the morning to the fort and may not see you all again."

"Boys, actually I should call you men, you've both grown and matured on this drive. You've gone from being full of piss and vinegar to top hands. I'm proud to have known you."

"Same for me. Good luck to you both."

"Thanks, Joel. Now we got some letters to write and let folks back in Texas know where we'll be. The general said there's even a chance our unit might be transferred to Texas in a year or two, and if we do, Mister Smith, we'll try to look you up."

"Davy, Jeff, if you like to join those of us who'll be going back to Texas—Bob, John, Mike, Red, and I—for supper tonight at the hotel, I know the men would like to see you before you take off for the army."

"Yes, sir. We'll be there."

"Gentlemen, if you'll excuse me. Maybe I'll see you all later."

"So long, Joel."

As Joel enters the General Store, Jonesy shows up. "Joel, ready to do some shoppin'?"

"You bet. I spotted some saddles back there we can look at while we're making up our minds on what we want. First thing I got to get me is a new hat and boots. How about you, Jonesy?"

"Let's start with those, then get what clothes we think we'll need, plus anything else that strikes our fancy. Maybe even a piece of jewelry for that someone special, huh, Joel?"

The store owner comes up before Joel can respond. "Boys, we have some very nice choices here, so take your time trying on some until you get the right fit and look you want. If you want to wear your new boots and hats, I'll gladly get rid of the old ones. Shirts, pants, long handles, socks, and jackets are over on the other side of the store. If you need any help, give a holler!"

"Thanks, we will."

Finally they've got what they feel are the necessities and then some, and now it's time to pick out saddles, bridles, pads, saddlebags, and rifle boots.

Having done that, they lay everything on the counter, taking up all the space. The store owner says, "Well, men, looks like you got about everything except for some saddle soap to make sure those saddles are good and conditioned for the drive. Anything else, such as rain slickers or bedrolls?"

"Damn, Joel, we got so excited over those new saddles we forgot those things. Now that would've been a bit embarrassin'. We'll be right back with those bedrolls and slickers. Would you throw in some saddle soap and maybe a few sticks of that peppermint candy for each of us?"

"Sure, no charge for those."

After paying the bill, Joel and Jonesy haul their new gear over to the chuck wagon where it'll be stored during the drive. Cookie's finishing up packing and storing the provisions. "Hi, boys. Don't you all look suave and duded up in your new hats and boots. Must be going out on the town tonight. From the looks of things, you must've bought out the store. Sure hope I got room for all that, otherwise we're going to need to get another pack animal. Just kidding, there's plenty of room."

"Cookie, we'll just keep out a new shirt and pants to go along with these boots and hats in case we want to do a little last-minute celebrating to impress the girls. Right, Joel?"

"We'll see how it works out. Cookie, will I see you later over at the Long Branch for that poker game?"

"Yep, I'll be there early evening. I'm not planning on a late night with the drive beginning in the morning."

"See you then."

"Okay, Jonesy, if you need me, you'll know where I'll be." They head off to bathe and shave.

Walking into the Long Branch, Joel pauses, looks around, and sees the song bird sitting by herself over by the piano, working on what looks like music. She's got her hair pulled back in a ponytail with a blue ribbon holding it in place. She's wearing another low-cut dress, but this time a light blue color, revealing her shoulders and again accentuating her pleasing figure. Her legs are crossed, and her gown is split in front, just above her knees, revealing longer and shapelier legs than he's ever seen.

For a brief moment, Joel's thinking about backing out the door, unsure whether or not he's deserving of talking to such a lovely looking lady. Then he's reminded of Gideon in the Bible when he was asked by the Lord to step up and serve him. "Who am I to think I'm good enough to do this?"

Joel quickly realizes if he doesn't step up now, this moment might be lost forever. After all, he's come face to face with Rebels, Indians, rustlers, and longhorns. Why should he be afraid of approaching this lady? Taking a deep breath, he begins crossing the floor, heading toward her table. She looks up and smiles. Stopping in front of her, he takes off his new hat.

"Excuse me, ma'am. I'm Joel Richards. I just wanted to tell you how much I admired your singing last night. Unfortunately I had some other business to look after so didn't get a chance to tell you then."

"Thank you. I'm Sherry Wells. Yes, I noticed you and the other fellow seemed to be keeping an eye on your men. From what I heard this morning, you did a pretty good job of it. I admire that quality when someone's willing to look out for another without regard for themselves, which seems to be in short supply around here. Would you like to sit down and have a drink with me?"

"Yes, ma'am, I'd like that. A beer would be nice."

"Joel, please don't call me ma'am or Miss Sherry like the help does. I don't get very familiar with most of these boys, but I'd like for you to call me Sherry. Mack, bring us a couple of beers and put it on my tab!"

"Right away, Miss Sherry."

"See what I mean?"

"Well then, Sherry it is. Thanks for the beer."

Not one who's comfortable in engaging in a lot of social small talk, Joel speaks frankly without seeming to be noisy. "I noticed last night you spent most of your time either singing or talking to the ladies working here, but I didn't see you spending any time with the men in the place."

"You're pretty observant, Joel. I didn't think you were paying much attention to me."

Joel feels his face getting warm as he quietly responds, "That's not exactly so."

"No, I don't spend time with any of the men anymore. Not since they let me start singing. The good, special ones are few and far between. I do look after the girls, making sure they do their jobs, don't get into any trouble. When they do, Sheriff Turner's pretty good at backing us up when we need help. I also noticed you didn't spend any time chasing the girls here. Why is that?"

Joel, feeling a bit flush, decides to answer as honestly as he can. "Well, Sherry, I've never been one to rush into anything. Perhaps it's shyness really, especially when it comes to the ladies. I always remember my mother and sister with the greatest respect. I guess Mother always told me there'll be a lot of girls out there, but I'd know when I find that someone special 'cause she'll not only catch my eye, but my breath as well. She's the one to look for. So I reckon I'm more into lookin' than samplin'."

"You're going to have to tell me about your mother and sister sometime. Now, to answer your next question before I find out some more about you, no, I don't own the saloon. However, the owners pay me to sing, plus a percentage of what the girls make for looking after them. Okay, Joel, tell me about yourself. I'm guessing your mother taught you manners and, probably, your father the values you live by."

Joel's beginning to feel comfortable talking with Sherry, like he would a friend—something he didn't expect, although he's still a bit enamored by her beauty and grace.

"Sherry, speakin' of being observant, nobody's ever honored me before by mentioning my folks. I thank you for that. I come from the farm hills of West Virginia, fought in the Civil War, been doin' some wandering since then, and signed on for this cattle drive out of Texas, and that's how I wound up in Dodge City. In the morning, I'm leaving for Wyoming with Mister Ferguson and a herd of longhorns he bought."

"I hope I'm not getting personal. Where are you going, Joel? Are you wanting to be a cowboy all your life?"

"You know … I'm not sure yet. My father wanted me to find a better life, settle down, make something of myself. I guess what I'm really looking for is a place where I can do that."

"Joel, you're not going to find it around here, but I like the sincerity of what you say because most cowboys who come in here are only longing for the next cattle drive and cow town, not some place to call their own."

By now, Sherry has gotten a pretty good sense of what Joel's about, and she likes what she sees. "Joel, how about another beer?"

"Thank you, I would, but let me buy."

"Mack, two more beers please. Joel, I consider you my guest, so let's make a deal. I buy these beers, you buy me dinner over at the Longhorn Hotel when we finish. Deal?"

"It'd be my pleasure."

Joel didn't figure on this turn of events, but time is still in his favor before meeting Cookie. Finishing their beers, he says, "Sherry, are you ready to eat?"

"Yes, let me tell Mack where I'm going and when I expect to be back. Mack, Joel and I are going over to the Longhorn for dinner. I'll be back in time for the first song."

"Enjoy, Miss Sherry." He winks and adds, "Take your time. I'll keep things under control here."

"Thanks, Mack. Joel, shall be go?"

Walking across the street, Sherry senses Joel's a bit nervous. "You're not uncomfortable being seen walking over to the hotel with me, are you?"

"I do feel a little funny. I've never had the pleasure of taking a lady to dinner before. I'm not sure how to act."

"Just be yourself. Think of it right now as two friends sharing one another's company over dinner."

Walking into the hotel, Joel's surprised to see Jonesy coming his way. They stop, facing each other, and Joel is blushing.

"Sherry, this is Jonesy, the trail boss. This is Sherry Wells.

"Nice to meet you, Miss Wells."

"Joel, I've been visitin' with Mister Ferguson. It looks like everything's ready to go in the mornin', so we've got the rest of the night off." He smiles. "Perhaps I'll see you all later over at the Long Branch."

"You probably will."

"Well, you two enjoy your dinner."

After being seated in the dining room, Sherry says, "Joel, you acted kind of funny with Jonesy. Is there anything I need to know about?"

"Jonesy and I'd been talkin' earlier today about last night and how neither one of us really spent much time celebrating as we were keepin' a watch on the men. He wanted to know what I was goin' to be doin' this afternoon. I just mentioned how I'd like to go over to the Long Branch and see you, never dreamin' we'd wind up havin' dinner together."

"Well, Joel, I'm glad you did. I'm enjoying myself. Now tell me, not a lot of cowboys who come to town bother to clean up and put on nice clothes. Since you're leaving for Wyoming in the morning, is there a reason you've done that? By the way, you do clean up pretty good."

"Now I'm embarrassed. I guess I wanted to impress you, not wanting you to think I was just another short-term cowboy lookin' for a good time."

"Would you folks like to order now?"

"Yes, we would."

After ordering, the conversation continues.

"Don't worry about that. It's a joy for me when I meet someone who treats me with respect, enjoys my company, and I'm not having to fight off a drunk all the time."

Dinner and coffee arrive with Joel and Sherry continuing their conversation.

"Tell me, Sherry, how did you wind up in Dodge City?"

"I'd aspired to a stage and singing career, was making a modest living at it, traveling all over the east, but never really going beyond doing small theaters. I guess my talent wasn't good enough for the big time. Well, our show was booked in Kansas City where we were enticed to come to Dodge City for a few days. The day after we arrived, our manager skipped with the money along with the leading lady, leaving several of us stranded here without any money or income."

"I guess there are crooks and thieves in every profession, even the theatre."

"You're right about that. Now we got no money, no job, and no train tickets to get back home. The Long Branch was the one who booked us, so I approached the management about singing for them. It seemed their last singer had run off with some cowboy, so they hired me. However, we had an understanding I wasn't to be working the upstairs. They attached another condition to my employment, as you obviously noticed. I had to pose for the painting above the bar. It was a bit embarrassing, but I needed the money, and the artist treated me with respect, saying he would only paint me if we could be alone without interference from the owners. I thank him for that."

Joel smiles. "Sherry, so do I."

With a mild laugh, she says, "Thank you. I'll take that as a compliment. I had a job, but the other two in the group were dancers. They couldn't get a job, except they were offered work in the saloon serving drinks, strongly encouraged to sell their services upstairs if they wanted to work and eat. So they did, but one of them left after she'd earned enough money to get out of town, and the other one stayed."

"Why did you stay?"

"That's a story for another time. Joel, one of these days if you ever head back this way, we can talk about it."

"Fair enough. I'll look forward to that day."

"I've got to get back to work after a bit, but I'm wondering, since I live in the hotel, would you like to come up for an after-dinner drink?"

"I would 'cause I'm not lookin' forward to this time ending so soon."

"Then while you're taking care of the bill, I'll go on up to room 207. When you've got the bill settled, just come on up and walk in. I'll be pouring the drinks."

Shortly Joel ascends the stairs and walks down the hall to room 207. He enters, removing his hat.

"Hi, Joel, have a seat over there on the sofa while I bring a glass of brandy for each of us to sip on."

Joel sits down with his eyes focused on Sherry as she slowly walks toward him. His eyes follow her alluring gait while bringing the brandy, a glass in each hand, to the table. She stops and leans over the table seductively in front of him, exposing a little more breast for this cowboy's pleasure. She puts the glasses down, smiles at Joel, and then walks around the table, sitting down next to him on the sofa, with her leg touching his.

He can't remember a time when a lady ever got his attention the way Sherry has, making him somewhat uncomfortable with the feelings arising from within his body. This is beyond anything he's ever dreamed of or thought would come out of a conversation with the song bird.

"Joel, I want you to know I usually don't allow anybody in my room. I need at least one private place where I can be undisturbed."

"I understand the need for a little solitude once in a while."

She hands Joel his glass and then picks up hers. Holding it with one hand, Sherry moves a finger from her other hand around the rim of the glass before dipping it in the brandy. She then places it in her mouth, slowly, erotically sucking the brandy from her finger while looking at Joel as she does so.

Needless to say, this cowboy's just been taken on a visual, sensual journey to a place where a special event is about to happen. Joel's feeling he's entering some new territory, not necessarily virgin territory, but certainly beyond anyplace he's ever been before.

"Sherry, I like what you're doing, but it's bringing up some deep feelings I've not known or experienced, coming from such a beautiful woman."

"Thank you for the compliment. Joel, you, too, are bringing up some of those same pleasurable feelings in me I haven't felt in a long time, surprisingly from someone I barely know. I know you're going to be gone in the morning, so I don't want you to leave without having been very close to you."

Sherry stands, extends her hand, and in a very soothing voice says, "Joel, take my hand and come with me."

Joel reaches for her hand and stands, and she begins leading him to her bed.

"Sherry, I've not done this in a long time."

"Don't worry, Joel. I don't want this to be a quickie, but some gentle holding and loving first, which I have a feeling we both need. So let's take our time, making it special."

In Sherry's bed, Joel learns a real lesson in how to be totally and completely involved, sharing the feelings of intimacy with someone deeply throughout the whole event of making love. Afterwards\, lying silently in her bed, Sherry, radiant from a beautiful, touching experience, leans over and looks at Joel looking at her. Then with softness in her voice, in almost a whisper, she says, "Howdy, cowboy."

Joel, smiling, returning from a heartfelt journey, looks deeply into her eyes and says, "Sherry, you're the sweetest song bird I've ever known."

"Oh, Joel, I've never had anyone be so tender and gentle with me like you were. Now don't say anything more. This is a moment I want to remember and cherish."

Several minutes pass with Joel and Sherry holding each other, not saying a word, knowing something special happened between them. Precious moments such as these are rare and need to be savored. Finally, time is passing. Sherry releases Joel.

"It's time for me to go to work, but you can stay here if you like."

"Sherry, I'd prefer walking you over to the Long Branch if I may, unless you'd rather say good-bye here."

"Joel, don't be silly. After this, any moment I can spend with you I consider a gift."

They begin dressing. Joel watches Sherry carefully with wonder-filled eyes, thinking about whether or not he should be going on the drive to Wyoming. She looks at him, sensing he's giving some thought to staying. "Joel, I want you to stay, or I want to go with you. But at this time, it's probably not possible for either one of us. Let's just leave it the way it is. Send me a letter whenever you can, letting me know where you're at and how you're doing. Then maybe we can think about the future. Fair enough?"

"Sherry, I know you're right, but damn I hate to leave so soon before I really get to know you."

"Joel, I'll be working till midnight. Then I'm finished. If you like, you can come by and spend the rest of the night with me until you have to leave."

"I'd like that. In the meantime, Jonesy and I'll be over at the Long Branch. He's lookin' to spend some time with one of the ladies, and I promised Cookie I'd sit in on a poker game with him."

"I know just the lady that'd be perfect for him. It's the dancer I told you about. I'll let her know so she can keep an eye out for him before anyone else tries to lay claim. She's a good girl, and they should hit it off."

"I'll hold him at bay when we get there until she finds him."

"Joel, be careful which game you sit in on. A couple of players have some questionable strategies. There's one who goes by the name of Bart Fingers. Has a mustache and small goatee with a silver-plated Remington Derringer up his sleeve. You want to watch out for him. Don't lose your money, Joel. Just be careful. I want to see you later."

"I'll be careful of both who I'm in the game with and how I play. I've put aside most of my trail money to use for my own place someday. I'm not about to lose it to some slick gambler."

Wrapping Sherry in his arms, their lips meet, their bodies touch, and for a moment the world stands still. Leaving her room, they walk together over to the Long Branch. Joel leaves her to go check his horses and supplies, making sure everything's ready to go in the morning. Sherry pauses, turns, and looks longingly at Joel as he waves. "I'll see you later tonight."

The Mission

Joel returns to the Long Branch after tending his horses. He walks through the swinging doors and immediately spots Sherry sitting with another lady. She sees Joel and waves him over. Joel removes his hat.

"Joel, this is Ellen, the young lady I thought would be a good match for Jonesy. I told her what I know about him, and she remembered him from last night. Obviously you two boys made quite an impression on a couple of us."

"Pleased to meet you, Ellen. Sherry told me a little bit about you. From what I've seen, you and Jonesy should get along great."

"Ellen," says Sherry, "I can tell right now, you're going to like Jonesy."

Jonesy walks through the doors and pauses to look around. Sherry sees him. "There he is now."

Joel turns just as he starts across the floor in their direction.

"Jonesy, come on over. There's someone here you need to meet."

With a surprised look on his face, Jonesy approaches the table and takes off his new Stetson.

"Miss Sherry, nice to see you again. Kinda looks like you and Joel have become very good friends. I'm happy for the both of you."

Smiling, Sherry says, "Jonesy, I'd like you to meet Ellen, another 'good friend.'"

"Howdy, Miss Ellen. Any friend of Joel and Sherry is a friend of mine. May I buy you a drink?"

"Certainly. Would you like to sit over there so we can talk and have that drink?"

"Yes, ma'am, lead the way." Jonesy looks at Joel and Sherry, giving them a wink and a smile that silently says, "Thank you."

Joel says, "By the way, Ellen, Jonesy's a good friend, although he's a man on a mission."

Ellen smiles knowingly at Jonesy. "Joel, I'll make sure he doesn't leave here until he's completed his mission to my satisfaction."

They all laugh because the innuendos didn't get past anyone. Ellen and Jonesy sit down at their table, order their drinks, and seem to hit it off, with both of them having similar types of humor.

The crowd has started arriving, causing Joel to realize his time with Sherry is rapidly coming to a close. The piano player walks in, taking his position at the piano, and begins playing a song. Sherry reaches over and touches Joel's hand. "I've got to go to work now, but don't forget what we talked about after I get off work ... if you still want to?"

Joel gently squeezes her hand. "If I still want to? Sherry, I'll be looking forward to that time for the rest of the night. Sing a nice song for us when you can, okay?"

"It'll be my pleasure."

"Well, I guess I'd better let you get to work. Plus I just saw Cookie come in."

"Be careful, Joel. Remember what I told you because I don't want to sleep alone on your last night here."

"Sherry, that's the best reason in the world for me not to forget."

The Game

oel crosses the floor to where Cookie's standing.

"Well, I see you boys been busy since I seen you last."

"I know, Cookie. It's the first time since we been here Jonesy's starting to enjoy himself. Since we're leaving in the morning, we all should be getting a little special attention to help us while away during some of those lonely times on the trail."

"Have you gotten some of that special attention to keep you goin' until we reach Wyoming?"

Glancing at Sherry, he says, "Let's just say I've got some fond memories of Dodge."

"Good for you. Now let's see about finding a poker game. Are you ready for this?"

"I am. Sherry told me a little bit about the card sharp you played with last night. Seems he's got a derringer up his sleeve and not afraid to use it."

Cookie looks around the room. "What's his name?"

"That fella over there, with the mustache." Joel nods toward a game in the far corner of the room. "Bart Fingers." He points to another table with a couple of open chairs. "Let's try that one. No sense in looking for trouble."

"Agreed," says Cookie. They walk up to a table where one of the men from the Chicago Beef Company and a local rancher are. With Joel and Cookie, that makes five at the table, including the dealer.

"Pardon us, gents. Mind if we join you?" says Cookie.

Joel casts a glance over to the other table. The gambler known as Bart Fingers raises his head, looking over Cookie and Joel, sizing them up.

229

"Not at all, have a seat," says the dealer. Looking at Cookie, he adds, "Didn't you sit in for a few hands last night?"

"Yes I did. Won a couple of dollars too."

"Put your money on the table. Let's get to the game!"

The game progresses throughout the evening with Cookie and Joel winning some little pots but the other two losing more than their fair share because of choosing to stay in the game, betting and calling when they should have been folding. Of course the dealer keeps ordering drinks to loosen up their inhibitions, contributing to their carelessness, making them less likely to realize they're being set up by thinking they've got the winning hands when in reality they've been dealt the losing ones.

Joel's learning that even when playing legitimate odds, he doesn't stand a chance when the gambler and dealer slant them in their favor when the big cash pots are in the center of the table. Quite a bit of money from the other two players has found its way to the stack of chips in front of the dealer. The rancher, with a frustrated shake of his head, calls it a night, gets up from his chair, and departs. Before anybody can make a move, Bart quickly takes the rancher's place at the table. Joel stands up to leave, but Cookie grabs his hand.

"Stick around. It'll be all right. Besides, it looks bad to leave right when somebody else sits down." Joel nods and returns to his seat.

Bart smiles like a wolf and says, "You boys been playing pretty safe here. I notice you're not drinking much even when the drinks are on the house. Now why is that?"

Cookie responds, "One of the reasons is we got a trail drive to start first thing in the morning. I'd rather have a clear and sober head when we do get going. I just can't handle the whiskey like I used to. We been in the game long enough. Let's get our feet wet!"

Reaching into his shirt pocket, Joel pulls out a hundred dollars and puts in on the table.

"You bet. I'm ready."

The other two men at the table are caught up in the excitement of a big payday or chance to get even. They reach into their pockets, each putting at least another hundred on the table by their chips. "Let's play cards. Deal 'em up!"

With a subtle nod noticed by Cookie and Joel, Bart has given the dealer a signal, a signal that will set the players up for a fall once the big money has been bet and in play. "Gentlemen, it's a five-dollar ante, and the game is five-card draw, jacks to open, trips to win. Everyone ante up your five dollars."

"Boys, the pot's right, cards in flight."

The cattleman setting next to the dealer's left says, "I'll open for $10.00."

Bart says, "I call." Cookie and Joel both call.

The Chicago beef man says, "I call and raise you $20.00."

The dealer says, "I'm in for the $30.00 to me."

The cattleman says, "I'll see your $20.00 and raise you $10.00."

Bart, Cookie, and Joel each call by putting $30.00 in the pot. The Chicago Beef man looks over his cards and says, "I'll see that $10.00 and raise another $20.00."

The dealer backs out, saying, "That's too rich for my blood. The raise is $20.00 to you, sir." The cattleman hesitates and then says, "I call."

"Bart, it's $20.00 to you."

Contemplating the possibilities, Bart appears to look carefully at his cards by picking up the bottom edge, revealing only to his own eyes what he's holding, thus giving the appearance of feeling he's got a chance. "I call the $20.00 to me." He throws his chips into the pot.

By this time, Joel and Cookie realize that the way Bart looked at his cards was a signal to the dealer to get ready to spring the trap. Although they both smelled the setup, they call the twenty-dollar raise.

"All right, gentlemen, the raise has been called. It's time for cards. How many?"

The cattleman takes two. Bart says, "I'll take two."

Cookie says, "I'll take one."

Joel says, "I'll take two."

The Chicago man draws one the dealer had previously folded.

"Gentlemen, the bet is to my left. Sir, you're the opener."

"I bet $20.00."

Bart says, "I see that $20.00 and raise you $20.00 more."

Cookie says, "I call."

Joel says, "I fold."

Bart looks at Joel, not believing he folded when he knew a possible winning hand had been dealt to him. "Fellow, did you lose your nerve or is the game getting too rich for your blood? You can't win if you don't stay."

"No, sir, I'm just trying to get along, have some fun, and maybe win a dollar or two."

Bart lets it go, but Cookie and Joel keep seeing the same thing happen. After a few more folded hands, Cookie can't take it anymore. When he sees it again, he throws down his hand and gets up to leave.

"Hang on," says Bart. "See the hand through."

"I think I already saw it through as much as I need," says Cookie.

"What are you saying?"

"I'm saying it looks like to me maybe the dealer isn't so good at counting cards when he deals. It seems you might be getting an extra card at times, especially now there's a lot of money in the pot."

The other players, including the dealer, sense an imminent confrontation with tensions rising as Bart's reputation is coming into question, a confrontation that won't go unchallenged.

Bart says, "Well, fellow, how you figure that?"

That's when Joel stands up. He puts himself between Bart and Cookie and says, "Now, Mister Fingers, I know it's probably just a slipup, but what little I know about poker, this kinda puts the odds in your favor. Now if Cookie's wrong, he'll gladly apologize, pick up his money, and walk away.

"If he's not, these other boys at the table may want to have a word or two with you and the dealer. I'm sure the sheriff will too. Would you mind showing us where that extra card is you were just dealt?"

"Are you calling me a cheat?"

"No, sir. You're handling that all by yourself. Now you can either place those palms face up so we can get a look or pick up your money in front of you and walk away."

Joel, anticipating his next move, lays it on the line in no uncertain terms.

"If you make a move for that derringer, I'll kill you where you sit! Now it's your choice. Walk away or turn those palms up off of the table, showing us how you been cheating everyone here."

"Fuck you." In one swift movement, Bart jerks the corner of the table up from his side, spilling all the chips, at the same time leaping to his feet, going for his gun. The derringer springs into his hand, but before he can take aim to shoot, Joel in one fluid movement draws his recently acquired Colt .45 and fires, hitting Bart in the chest.

Bart shoots his derringer off into the air as he's hit, falling backward to the floor, shooting a split second too late, a split-second difference between living or dying. The dealer makes a play for his gun, but Cookie quickly covers him with his. Then the dealer backs off with a stunned look on his face while putting his hands in the air.

By now, Jonesy has finished his business upstairs, arriving to back Joel up just as the shot was fired killing Bart. Sheriff Taylor and his deputy bust through the swinging doors with guns drawn, heading to the table where Bart's lying dead, surrounded by the players who are engulfed in a state of disbelief at what just happened.

Joel, with gun in hand, is standing beside Cookie, who's holding the dealer with his hands up in the air at bay. On the outside fringe of the crowd beginning to gather is Sherry.

Sheriff Taylor looks down at Bart, who's still holding his derringer. He picks it up from his hand and smells it, noting it's still warm from being fired. "Fingers, I knew it was just a matter of time. Now, let's find out what happened here and whether or not I need to make any arrest."

Before the sheriff can begin questioning, the cattleman and Chicago Beef man, still shaking from the ordeal, chime in with excited voices, trying to tell the sheriff how the dealer and Bart were cheating them and this man, Joel, called Bart on it.

"Slow down, boys," says the sheriff. "I got to do this properly. Joel, step over here with me for a minute."

They get some distance, and the sheriff says, "Joel, let me see your gun. I can tell it's been recently fired, so tell me what happened."

Joel doesn't hesitate. "These men were in the game when it happened. Bart and the dealer were cheating us just like they've been doing to all these other cowboys who sat in on any of their games. Cookie called them on it, and Bart started to draw down. I stepped in, shot him first."

"That sounds about what I figured." He turns back to the others. "What did you fellas see?"

They start in so loud the sheriff has to quiet them. "Let's try that one at a time."

"Sheriff," says the cattleman, "everything happened so damn fast when Bart tried to distract him by upsetting the table, going for his gun. This fellow here," he says, pointing to Cookie, "had the dealer covered so he couldn't draw or it might have gone the other way real quick. Now, Sheriff, this man gave Bart every chance to back off and leave the game without trouble, but Bart chose to shoot it out. We're just damn lucky none of us got killed."

The sheriff turns to Cookie. "Is that how it played out?"

"Sheriff, I've been watching the dealer and this Bart fellow the past two nights. They've been slippin' or palming marked cards, using a few sleight of hand tricks to get the ones they needed to win the big pots, losing the little ones in order to keep the suckers in the game."

"Anyone else here see it any different than this man protecting himself from these two-bit, thieving card sharps?"

"No, sir, Sheriff," says the Chicago Beef man. "He did what he had to do. Some of those other fellows who called Bart a cheater in the past sure didn't fare as well. Most of us knew they must have been cheating these cowboys, but Bart and his brothers put the fear in us, keeping anybody from questioning them for what they might do to our families."

The sheriff says, "Okay, Joel, it looks like enough witnesses will testify it's self-defense. Here's your gun back, but I need to talk to you after we get this dealer over to jail, along with Bart's body to the undertakers. Mack, can you get a bucket of water and a mop to clean this blood off the floor?"

"Sure can, Sheriff."

"A couple of you boys, pick up Bart's body and get him outside for the undertaker so we can clean up this place. You boys need to pick up your money while you can before Mack gets back with the bucket and mop or some of these other fellows around here might try to get some extra drinking money they figure is just laying around."

Jones steps up to Joel. "Are you all right?"

"Yeah. I just wish Sherry hadn't seen that. Jonesy, you're right, we got to get away from these places and hang around some better people."

"I know. We'll have plenty of time on the trail to talk about it, but right now, if it's important to you, you'd better find Sherry and try to explain what went on. She knows this was bound to be, but I don't think she planned on it being someone she wanted to know."

The cattleman says, "Boys, let's get our winnings off the floor before someone else picks them up."

Joel looks at him. "There are no winners here tonight, just losers. We were part of somethin' that should never have been allowed to happen. I'm starting to regret having been a part of it already. Cookie, would you pick up my share of the money and give it to me later? I need a drink!"

As if on cue, Joel feels a delicate touch on his arm, and a soothing voice greets him as he turns. "Joel, come with me. I have a brandy waiting."

The crowd parts, allowing Sherry and Joel to pass without interference while they walk over to Sherry's table by the piano.

Calming Down

"**S**herry ... I ..."

Before Joel can finish, Sherry puts her finger over his lips. "Joel, sip your brandy slowly. First, of all this had to happen sooner or later, but I'd hoped it wasn't going to be you. You don't owe me any explanation for what you did; I saw it all from my vantage point by the piano. I was more concerned for your safety and our time together than anything else. We all have a sense of right and wrong. However, in you, it runs stronger than in any man I know. Was it your father who imparted this value into your soul?"

Taking another sip of brandy, Joel looks at her, pausing before he speaks.

"Sherry, it must have come from my father. He was a religious man, a believer in his biblical hero, Gideon, who never sought trouble or riches but stood when God called. Sometimes I think I've been called to stand when I think I'm looking for something else. Lord knows, I don't go around preachin' or intentionally looking for trouble, but it always seems to get in my way even when I'm trying to avoid it. I don't know if this all makes sense to you. At times it doesn't make sense to me. Maybe that's why I've got this wanderlust about me. I hope this doesn't change things between us. You've been the one bright spot in my life."

"I'm beginning to understand you a whole lot better, and no, it doesn't change a thing between us. I see Sheriff Taylor over there wanting to get your attention, plus the piano player keeps motioning to me it's time to sing. Joel, I'm going to sing a song for us I hope you like. Although you

236

fought for the North, this song came out of the South during that time. "It's called 'Ballad to Lorena.'"

"Sherry, what a beautiful song. You might even bring a tear to my eye along with some of the boys here. Thank you, but can you wait until I'm finished with the sheriff so you'll have my ear and full attention?"

"Yes, I'll wait, and, Joel, will I see you later?"

"I'll be here at midnight to see you home."

The Threat

"**W**here you headed, Joel?"

"Jonesy, the sheriff wants to talk some more. Why don't you walk over with me? Maybe what he's got to say might be of interest to both of us. Cookie, would you order us beers? I've got a song to listen to in a moment."

"You got it, Joel. I'll be over at that table in the corner."

"Sheriff Taylor."

"Joel, what I've got to say, you both need to hear. Jones, I'm glad you're with him, as somewhere down the line, he may be needing some backup. These brothers of Fingers went to Kansas City two days ago before you boys got to town and aren't expected back until next week. I'm sure if word gets to 'em about what happened to Bart, they'll probably come a runnin' back looking for you. Even if the word travels fast, it could be three or four days before they get here."

"Sheriff, we'll be long gone by then. We're leaving first thing in the morning and should be about fifty or sixty miles from here."

"That's what I'm hoping for, I'll do what I can to keep them reined in and occupied for three or four more days when they do get here to give you some extra distance. After that, hopefully they'll have calmed down some. Keep one eye lookin' behind you because someday, somewhere, I have a feelin' these boys will still be lookin' for you."

"Thanks for the warning. Jonesy and I will definitely be looking over our shoulders, watching each other's backs."

"One more thing, which isn't to be publicized. I want to thank you for catching these double-dealing card sharks at cheating. Neither my deputies nor I knew what to look for, but we will now. I'm gonna post a notice to other gamblers, warning them to play it straight and honest if they want to play poker here."

"Sheriff Taylor, Jonesy, Cookie, and I, along with all the Single Six boys, appreciate your work here, how you've helped us out. You know we didn't come to town looking for trouble, just to sell some beef, celebrate a little, and move on to the next job. I hope we haven't been too much of a bother?"

"You boys have done pretty well here considering everything that's gone on. Overall, you've been a better behaved bunch than most of the herders that come to town. I wish you luck and a safe journey. I'll see you off in the morning."

"Thanks, Sheriff. Jonesy, let's go join Cookie, have that beer, and give a listen to the song bird singing this beautiful ballad before we turn in for the night."

On the way over to the table, he says, "Jonesy, I may need a little reminder in the mornin', so if I'm not up and about, just give a knock on room 207."

The Last Night

Midnight arrives with Joel standing outside the swinging doors of the Long Branch waiting for Sherry to wrap up. Because the saloon won't be closing until much later, the remaining patrons are still partying inside. However, Sherry's work day is over, and with much anticipation, she's longing to see Joel.

Stepping through the doors, she sees him. She reaches out, placing her hand in his, and says, "Howdy, cowboy."

Joel gently squeezes her hand, responding softly, "Howdy, songbird."

They both laugh. Sherry takes Joel's arm as they begin walking across the street into the lobby of the Longhorn Hotel, up the stairs to room 207. Inside, Sherry removes her shawl, Joel his hat, and they look at each other for a moment. Then Sherry reaches out to Joel, placing her arms around his neck. He in turn does the same, but around her waist, pulling her tightly to him.

"Joel, hold me tightly in your arms for a few moments." He does, and then longing to taste her sweet breath, he gently kisses her, once again feeling the warm emotions rise within his body.

Wyoming Calling

arlier than he wants, there's a knock on the door of room 207, and a familiar voice rings out, "Joel, rise and shine. Wyoming's callin'. We've got to answer the call. Get to the pens as soon as you can and grab a bite on the way. Tell that lovely lady, when she paired me up with Ellen, my mission was accomplished to her satisfaction, and my heart was singin.' So let's go, cowboy!"

Joel looks at Sherry as the early morning sun peeks through the window, casting sunbeams upon their bed. Then wiping a tear from her cheek, he says, "Sherry, you were right; our time has ended too quickly. But before I go …" Joel reaches into his shirt pocket, removing a small, wrapped box. "Before going over to the Long Branch last night, I stopped in the Mercantile and asked the storekeeper if you ever came into his store, and he said all the time. Then I asked if there was anything special you admired but didn't have."

"Oh, Joel, you didn't."

"He showed me this beautiful pendant on a silver chain you look at every time you come in, so I got it for you. He had a jeweler engrave it for me."

Joel hands the gift to Sherry. Upon opening, tears begin flowing down her cheeks as she turns it over and reads the inscription, *Sherry, my lovely songbird. Always, Joel.*

She grabs and hugs him. "You shouldn't have, but I love you for doing it. You weren't the only one who did a little shopping today. I have something for you to remember me by also."

Removing a chain from around her neck, she places it around Joel's neck. He notices the inscription on the small medallion. *To Joel, the brandy of my life. Sherry.*

"Sherry, I don't know what to say. It seems all the best gifts anyone's ever given me have come from you. I'll wear it, remembering you forever."

"Joel, morning's coming awfully fast. Take my hand, and let's spend what little time we have left in each other's arms."

It doesn't last long. Joel says, "I've got to get dressed and goin'. Will you walk me to the door?"

"Not only will I do that, but if it's okay with you, I'm going to get dressed, go down to the edge of town, and wave good-bye."

Final Good-Byes

Joel rushes to the dining room and orders an egg sandwich and some coffee. He's not surprised when the waiter says it's on the house, but he is surprised when the boy tells him to have a good trip to Wyoming. News does travel fast. Walking swiftly, Joel's taking a bite of the sandwich in between sips of coffee, heading to the pens. He sees Harry Ferguson and Jonesy talking. He walks up. "Sorry I'm late. I'll get saddled up."

"Don't worry. Ben's got your Morgan and the pack horse ready to go. We kinda figured you might be running a little late."

"Thanks, Jonesy. By the way, did you tell Mister Ferguson what happened last night along with what we might expect in a week or so on the trail from the Fingers' brothers?"

"He did, Joel. I don't expect we'll see them on this drive, but I've told the other boys who don't have a problem 'cause they've been around their kind before."

"Well, I just want you to know if you prefer someone else to take my place, it's okay. I'll understand."

"Joel, enough of that. I've got my crew. It's time we move 'em out."

"Thanks, Mister Ferguson. I promise to stay away from the poker tables after this."

"Joel, Bart skinned a few of us, too. It looks like we all better stick to cattle rather than poker, although on second thought, they're both a gamble. Mister Jones, let's go to Wyoming!"

"Mount up, boys, and take your positions. We're headin' for Wyoming by way of Nebraska."

Driving the herd past Dodge City, Sheriff Taylor and his deputies give a wave good-bye, followed by Sam Smith and the Single Six boys. "Joel, you and Jonesy get these cattle to Wyoming. If you ever get down our way, come and see me. We're heading out for Texas first thing in the morning. It's been one hell of a ride, son. We all wish you the best."

"Thanks, Sam. It was different. Now, you boys be careful heading back. Sam, give our best to your family."

Joel and Jonesy continue to ride on, reaching the edge of town. There sitting in a horse-drawn buggy are Sherry and Ellen.

Jones is out front in the trail boss position, leading the herd, with Joel riding point on the girls' side. Jones sees them first. He breaks away from the lead for a brief moment and rides up to the buggy. Ellen stands.

"Come here, my angel of mercy, so I can wish you a safe trip and give you something to remember me by!"

She leans over, giving Jonesy a full view of her lovely breasts, taking him by surprise, but only briefly. He grabs her with his left arm around her waist, pulling her up to him, giving her a deep kiss, and then releasing her. Smiling, he says, "I'll miss you." He tips his hat, and as he's riding back to his lead position, he exclaims, "Mission accomplished!"

Suddenly, Jonesy reins up, skidding his horse to an abrupt halt. He rolls it around, looking at Sherry with a total look of astonishment on his face. "I know who you are now! You're the lady in the painting. I'll be damned. It took me long enough, but it seems Joel was on top of it in a hurry. I'll remember you." He waves his hat, saying, "The best to you, ladies!" He then spins his horse around and rides on up ahead of the cattle.

Joel rides up. Sherry passes the reins to Ellen and then stands up in the buggy to greet him. Standing with her back to the sun, he immediately sees she's wearing a thin, brandy-colored dress with her hair draped around her shoulders. The sunlight filters through the material outlining her shapely body and long legs as her dress gently sways from side to side in the early morning breeze. Her face has an angelic quality, taking his breath away, leaving him almost speechless and wondering if this vision standing in the buggy is as close to a goddess as he's likely to get. "Sherry, I wish I was an artist so I could paint your beauty in this moment on canvas to take with me. You continue to gift me in so many ways. I feel honored to have spent some time with you."

"Cowboy, it's been special beyond my dreams. Be sure and write. I'll be living for your letters. Remember what we said; if it's to be, we'll meet again."

They embrace for what seems only a moment, and Jonesy hollers, "Joel, time to go!"

Riding away, he looks back at Sherry, who's watching him with tears streaming down her cheeks. She raises her right hand, placing it over her heart where his gift, the silver-chained pendant, rests.

In gratitude and love, he turns toward her in his saddle, putting his right hand over his heart where her gift, the medallion, lays upon his chest. He faintly hears her say, "So long, cowboy" as the haunting melody of "Lorena" plays softly in the background.

A shadow slowly moves across the ground in front of Joel, bringing him back to reality from his thoughts of the past. While he's been absorbed in looking back at the circumstances and events bringing him to this point in time, Morgan's been leading him westward, either toward the plains or the mountains, and at this moment, Joel doesn't care which.

It's now late morning. Linwood is many miles behind, and the sun's almost overhead. Occasionally, Joel looks to the rear with regret of what's been left behind and to see if anything is following him. Looking skyward, trying to figure out where that shadow came from, he spots a bald eagle soaring high in the sky just over his head, flying directly west toward the mountains as if providing a beacon to lock onto in his journey. He ponders for a moment, looks down, and pats Morgan on the neck.

"Morgan, what the hell. It might be a sign, so what do you say we just follow that eagle for a while and see where it leads us?"

Meet Charley Green

Charley's travels have taken him from the eastern farm hills of Kansas to military service, college administration along with forays into the real estate and transportation industries. He's appeared in local television commercials and movies as well as performing at the Cheyenne Frontier Days. His love of the cowboy way was ingrained at an early age fostering a deep-seated respect for our western heritage and *Code of the West*.

Charley's career as a professional author, speaker, and entertainer began later in life and what he shares is a direct reflection of his life experiences. His stories tell of people he's met along the way; those who inspired him, some who opened doors, a few who tried to discourage him plus various life situations challenging the depth of his faith as well as those events giving him hope, inspiration and courage to follow his dream. Charley currently resides in Gardner, Kansas and has one son and three grandchildren.

Books written include *The Reluctant Warrior, The Journey Begins, Will Rogers & Charley, Will Rogers for President, Charley's Thoughts, Quotes & Anecdotes, Our Thinking & Doing Determines the Outcomes & Results in Our Lives and 77 Ways to Achieve a Debt-Free College Education.*

Special prints of this novel's cover painting (18x24) will be available on a limited basis autographed by the artist, Jerry Yarnell.

For information about his books, speaking schedule and upcoming events go to www.CharleyGreen.com or his Facebook page.

He often quotes an old Cherokee saying:
The world is filled with stories which, from time to time, permit themselves to be told.
Charley's honored to be one who is permitted to do so.

CPSIA information can be obtained
at www.ICGtesting.com
Printed in the USA
BVHW080803231121
622259BV00003B/151